Wildwood Healer

A Novel

Linda Broday

EPITAPH PRESS

Wildwood Healer

A Novel

Linda Broday

EPITAPH PRESS

This is for anyone suffering at the hands of an abuser. There is hope and there's help and you'll find not everyone turns a blind eye. Reach out to someone. You don't have to go through this alone. There's a Miss Sicily somewhere for you. Just don't wait too long. God bless and keep you safe.

Chapter One

East Texas Piney Woods, October 1930

THE PINEY WOODS SURROUNDING Sicily Rossi's small dwelling whispered stories to her as she milked her cow and fed the chickens. She was luckier than most; she knew that. Everyone seemed to be starving these days unless they had a garden. Before she went inside, she studied the dark shadows of the forest that spoke of secrets and mysteries—some as old as time. She was a part of this land and knew she always would be. Here she was born and here she'd die.

There was comfort in that.

Christmas wasn't far off but it made no difference to her. It would call for nothing special.

The sun was just making an appearance when a soft whine outside drew her attention. Sicily often had sick folks appear at her home asking for her help, but they always knocked.

Curious, she opened the door to see the cutest brown dog tied to her porch railing.

What on earth? Who would've tied it there? But this was the Depression, and no one had much so it wasn't that unusual.

The chimes she'd made of old bent eating utensils and odds and ends around her place tinkled softly from a hook on the porch, creating sweet music to her ears. Sicily threw a shawl around her shoulders and stepped out, kneeling down. The small dog lifted a front paw as though to shake hands. Accepting the act of friendship, the animal licked her hand with its velvety tongue. "Hey there, you're a pretty little thing. How do you do? I'm happy to meet you."

A sign hung from a piece of twine around the pup's neck. She reached for it.

WILL YU PLEASE FEED **G**YPSY? **G**OT NO FOOD.

The print was in various size letters on a piece of old newspaper. Whoever wrote it wasn't very proficient in the English language. She always noticed that due to the few years she taught school.

"Well, I'll be. Where is your owner, little girl?" Of course, she'd feed her, no question about that. She'd never turned away anyone or anything in need. Hobos were frequent visitors.

Sicily untied the animal and picked her up. "Gypsy, that's a mighty fine name. I never met a dog I didn't like. Even had one named Lure because he loved to go fishing. Fool thing would try to catch fish with his mouth. Caught one a time or two."

Gypsy licked her cheek and yawned.

Getting to her feet, Sicily scanned her yard and the edge of the woods surrounding her East Texas land that her father had left. Not a sign of anyone. Everything was still as though holding its breath. She turned her attention back to the dog and took it inside. No telling the last time the little darling had eaten. She pulled out some leftover stew she'd made the previous day and filled a bowl, setting it on the floor. A hungry dog wouldn't be particular. Some scrounging might uncover a better meal later.

"Here you go, Miss Gypsy."

The sweet animal didn't hold back, hurrying to the bowl and diving in. While Gypsy ate, Sicily filled another bowl with water and set it down then watched. The sweet pup would glance up occasionally to see if she was still there before going back to her food. Whoever had her must've been in a desperate place to part with the pet. The pet's bright eyes and shiny coat said

they'd seen to Gypsy's care as best they could. Maybe they'd fallen on harder than normal times.

The breed? The scruffy dog like most in the area was of questionable parentage. The way strands of hair hung down in her eyes reminded her of a beloved scamp.

Gypsy finished and lapped at her water bowl then danced on her back legs for her. The pup's antics soon had Sicily laughing.

"You're a regular show off. It's time for my walk. Want to come?" The pooch scampered to the door. "I take that as a yes."

Gathering her burlap bag that she'd fashioned to go over her head and sit on her shoulder, she opened the door and they were off to see what nature's medicine she could find. It was a lovely October day and the brisk air invigorated her. The pooch too it seemed. Gypsy scampered off to smell every weed, rock, and tree stump. Then the pup spied a squirrel and the race was on until it went up a tree out of reach.

The woods were alive in yellows, golds, and orange leaves each way Sicily looked. In her sixty years, she didn't think she'd ever seen a more beautiful sight. The trees reminded her of fancy saloon girls putting on a show for their audience. The breeze made the leaves dance and twirl up a storm. Overhead, birds flitted from one colorful branch to the next. Nature loved putting on a show. A graceful heron stood in a pond amid vibrant lily pads.

Sicily followed a well-worn path that she'd taken many times and collected some nice specimens of dandelion root, comfrey, and pennyroyal. Gypsy sniffed it all while she filled her bag. They climbed an incline, and she found some treasures in the dense carpet of needles and cones that she hadn't run across in a while—Indian Pipe and healing rattlesnake root. It was a good day. Satisfied, they continued their walk just for fun before turning back.

She'd grown up at her parents' side, learning all about herbs, roots, and bark they found in the Piney Woods. Being as how they'd come from Tennessee, they'd had tremendous knowledge of nature's remedies and gladly taught her. They'd been gone now for many years.

They neared the house when Gypsy raced ahead barking at the man sitting on her porch in the rocker. Drawing closer Sicily recognized her friend, Albert James, a regular visitor.

"Howdy, Albert. I reckon you came after more of my rheumatiz medicine."

Clad in patched overalls, he pulled his tall frame painfully from the rocker. Rubbing his knee, he grabbed his long walking stick. "Yes'um, I shore do need some." Albert glanced down at Gypsy sniffing his leg. "When did you get a mutt?"

"Found her on my porch this morning. Her name's Gypsy. I guess someone decided I needed company." Sicily removed the burlap bag from her shoulder. "Have I ever complained of being lonely?"

"No, ma'am. Ain't rightly heard you say so. Cute little rascal."

"That she is."

"Name's Gypsy?"

"That what the note said that I found with her. Do you know this dog?" she asked.

"Nope, sure don't. Maybe you need a pet. Keep you from being too crotchety." His wide grin flashed his toothless gums.

"Albert, you don't know the meaning of crotchety. Just you wait until I get a few more years on me. I might start carrying my rifle and shooting anyone sitting on my porch."

He threw back his head and laughed, shaking a finger. "Now I know why you ain't never found you a husband, Miz Sicily. You're meaner than a snake, old woman. You run off men with your sharp tongue."

"Good!" She didn't need a man underfoot. Nope. Those days were over. She held the door and Gypsy raced inside. Albert removed his floppy hat and followed at a much slower pace. "Who said I was old? Have folks been talking about me in Silsbee again?" she asked.

"Aw, you know how they are. Gotta keep the rumor mill goin'."

"That's the trouble with people. Got to be talking about someone. I reckon when they speculate about me, they're giving others a rest. Have a seat and I'll get your remedy."

He eased into a chair. "One of these days I'm gonna git too feeble to walk here."

"You can always find some kid willing to come after it." She patted her old friend's shoulder. "Or I might bring it to you when you get in a bad way."

"Thank you." He covered her hand with his callused one. "One thing I count on Miz Sicily is jawing with you."

Like many others in the Piney Woods, he had no family left. He'd lost his wife ten years ago to pneumonia and his only son had met with an accident one foggy morning right before Christmas. The life had seemed to go out of Albert in an instant, something she'd watched happen over and over with folks through the years.

"It seems strange that Christmas is creeping up on us," she threw over her shoulder as she rifled in a cabinet. "I love the season but, like you, I don't celebrate. We're too old for such."

"Ain't that the truth. Don't have no reason to nohow."

The sorrow in his voice made her swing around to look at him. "Why don't I come to your place and we can listen to the carolers and keep you from running them off?"

"Maybe. Beats the memories that always come around thicker than thieves."

Sicily handed him the remedy she'd made along with a spoon. "Want a cup of coffee?"

"Reckon that might taste pretty good. We can watch Gypsy entertain us. Did I tell you I once knew a woman named Gypsy? She didn't like to wear clothes and got arrested several times." He snorted. "I asked her to marry me."

She laughed, knowing he was pulling her leg. "You're always saying you almost married a scandalous woman. I don't believe you for one second."

"You're still a pretty woman, Miz Sicily, with your dark hair and girlish figure. Why is it a man ain't snatched you up?"

"I've outrun them all." The direction this conversation had taken brought more pain than she could bear. "And I can for sure outrun you so don't get any ideas, you old fool."

She quickly turned to make coffee and while they sipped on it out on the porch with the gentle breeze clinking the windchimes, Gypsy dog twirled and danced, putting on quite a show. Much better than a scandalous, half-naked woman that tempted Albert.

A practiced glance told her he was having a harder time breathing than usual. He looked older than Methuselah with thinning gray hair and long unkempt beard. Had to be in his seventies surely. Smoking and strong drink that he bought from a moonshiner when he had the money had ruined his health but what did he care? The man was only marking time anyway until he could leave the world and this infernal Depression with all its misery behind.

Wouldn't be too sad for her either. She got up and put a blanket on Albert and he kept right on snoring.

Chapter Two

ALBERT JAMES SPENT THE afternoon with her as was typical for lonely folks who needed a listening ear. He had just stepped off the porch to leave when he clutched his chest and turned white.

Sicily caught him and managed to get him inside to a chair. She hurried to her shelf of jars filled with all kinds of leaves and berries and took down the hawthorn, setting about making a tea. A glance at her guest showed his closed eyes and shallow breathing. There was no way he could walk home and the evening shadows were lengthening. Gypsy lay at his feet with her head on her paws, her dark eyes watching Albert. The pooch seemed to know there was a problem, which wasn't surprising. A lot of animals sensed when things were wrong with humans.

By the time she made tea and got some into Albert, it was dusk. He seemed a little better and the pain had subsided.

Keeping a firm grip, she led him to a cot she kept for folks too sick to walk back to town. "Get some rest. You can go home tomorrow." She covered him with a wool blanket and stood for a moment watching color begin to seep back into his face. Darkness came so early with the changing season and she felt weary to the bone.

Albert mumbled, "Don't you try to have your way with me, old woman. I'll have one eye open."

She snorted. "In your dreams. If I wanted a man, I'd pick one not all stove up."

"Just admit it, you're after my body."

"Goodnight. You can talk tomorrow." Giving him one last long look, she turned the lamp down and left the small room. She'd check on him during the night.

Satisfied Albert was okay for now, Sicily went to her alcove off the parlor. Gypsy hopped up on the small bed and laid her head on the pillow like she was the Queen of Sheba.

"If you aren't something, little dog. Give you an inch and you take a mile."

Unconcerned, Gypsy stretched big and yawned. Sicily took her hair down from the pins that held the dark strands with silver woven through it on top of her head and brushed it, putting it into a long braid. Then as she did each night, she opened the lid of a little box on her bedside table and lifted a necklace out.

She undid the catch of the locket to show the image of her true love. Jace Bonner had been the handsomest man she'd ever seen.

"Goodnight, my love." She kissed his picture then closed, and put it away. All this talk of marrying had released a flood of thirty-five-year-old memories.

The horrible things Jace's mother had said and the names she'd called her. Then Jace breaking Sicily's heart in a million pieces when he'd told her he had unfinished business to take care of before he could even think of taking a wife. But Sicily had known he was only protecting her. He simply couldn't cross his mother with her bad heart and his father dead.

They could've had a good life if Mrs. Bonner had stayed out of it.

Oh well, water under the bridge. The handsome Jace who'd stolen her heart was dead. The letter that came a six month's later had made it crystal clear—he was gone. There would be no more hoping and waiting.

With a heavy sigh, she lowered the wick on the lamp about the time Gypsy began to snore.

Good heavens! She scooted the little mutt over and climbed under the covers. But sleep was spotty and she tossed and turned then rose at midnight to check on Albert. She was up and down through the night and before she knew it, morning dawned all too quickly.

The man was now sitting in her kitchen with one over-alls suspender on his shoulder and the other hanging down, watching the chickens out her window.

"Good morning. How did you sleep, Albert?" Sicily let Gypsy out to do her business and pumped water into the coffee pot from the cistern outside that caught rainwater.

"Do you always sleep so late?" he grouched.

"The sun's barely up."

"I've been sitting here watching your hens. You sure have a big brood of cluckers."

"I'm going to take a bunch to town soon and hand them out to the starving folks. There're too many and they make good eating." Setting the coffee on the stove, she put flour in a bowl to make dough for biscuits. "Are you always this sour in the mornings?"

He ignored her question. "A couple of those mean roosters out there need to go in a pot too if ya ask me."

"Better watch it, old fool, or I'll put you in a pot."

"Humph!"

"As soon as we get breakfast over with, I'll feed and water my mule so I can take you into town."

"Aw, Miz Sicily, I could probably walk the two miles today."

"I have to make a delivery in Silsbee anyway so you might as well ride Jessie."

"Well, since you're going, I reckon that'll be fine. But I'll go feed him." Albert rose and reached for his floppy hat that had seen better days then pulled the other suspender up on his shoulder.

Sicily shook a floury finger. "Now, old man, you don't have any business out there with your heart. I'll do it."

"Shush. I know what I can do." He grabbed his walking stick and went out. Even though he walked slowly, he seemed better than last night.

She turned back to making breakfast, keeping watch on Albert out the window, and they soon ate. Gypsy wolfed hers down and looked at their plates with longing. Sicily gave her a bite or two from her plate as well. After washing the few dishes, she packed the bottle of liniment and tea herbs then helped Albert out and onto Jessie.

"Stay, Gypsy girl. You can't go. Stay here."

But the little dog had a mind of her own, and despite threats, followed them. After almost getting run over by one of those Model Ts in front of Albert's house, Sicily lifted the dog onto the mule, and they went to Mary Jane's place.

The woman in an old bonnet and faded flour sack dress took the offerings gratefully. "I'm in your debt, Sicily. This will help us. Only the mister hopped a freight this morning, going to look for work. We're starving to death here. He heard they're wanting grave diggers in Fort Smith, Arkansas. Folks are dying by the droves there."

Sicily laid a hand on Mary Jane's shoulder. "I'm so sorry. I hope he takes precautions. There must be some kind of disease running rampant."

The woman drew herself up, her mouth in a tight line. "My mister will do what he must."

That damnable pride. Sicily sighed and turned. "Fix a cup of that tea. It'll help your stomach."

"I will and I'll pay you when I can." With that, Mary Jane ambled into her abode that was sadly in need of repair like so many others.

Sicily and Gypsy headed home. A train stood on the tracks, blocking the road so there was nothing to do but pull behind a Model T and wait. Shortly, an exhausted line of children emerged from the passenger car and a sour-faced woman snapped at them to stop dawdling as they marched toward a church.

An orphan train. Her stomach twisted at the sight.

A woman in a dark hat with one droopy flower hurried from the place of worship waving her arms. "Go back. We don't want any orphans here. You'll have to get back on the train."

Sorrow pierced Sicily's heart at the thought of no one wanting the children or willing to take even one in. They were sorely in need of love and care. If she had the means, she'd take them all. Gypsy whined and looked up at her.

"There's nothing we can do, girl." She patted the cute dog's head. "One day this Depression will end and maybe folks will open their hearts." She could hope anyway.

One little boy probably eight years old broke off from the line and took off running, prompting some men having to chase him down.

"Please, let me go," the boy begged. "Don't make me get back on that train. I gotta look for my sister. Please," he sobbed. "I gotta find her."

"You're going where we tell you to go. Now get a move on," a man snapped, shoving the kid.

Tears filled Sicily's eyes. She itched to give the gentleman a good talking-to. Someone needed to teach him compassion. They were just kids, longing for some bit of love.

It took about an hour to get the children back on the train and the road open. Soon after, she left the squalor of Silsbee behind and inhaled the sweet, blessed smell of the forest.

"This is much better, isn't it, Miss Gypsy?"

The dog gave a sharp bark and snuggled in Sicily's arms.

Halfway home, a tall boy hobbled across the road with the help of a long stick, plunging into the thick brush. He appeared much older than the orphan train youngster she'd just seen. Her attention drew to his blood-soaked pant leg.

"Whoa, Jessie." Sicily stopped the mule and dismounted. Gypsy leaped from her arms and ran barking after the boy. She followed after the dog as fast as she could go.

Suddenly, the barking ceased. She thought it odd. Plunging through the last of the heavy brush, she found Gypsy in the boy's arms, the dog excitedly licking his face.

Now that she was face-to-face, Sicily could put the boy's age in the range of fourteen or thereabouts. He glanced up at her through shaggy hair as dark as midnight and swallowed hard.

"If I'm not mistaken, you must be Gypsy's owner," she said. "Did you tie her to my porch railing?"

The thin youth tried to rise, but he was either weak from hunger or his bloody leg wouldn't support him. He fell back, brushing a hand over his eyes. "I didn't see no other way, ma'am. Sorry."

"Why didn't you stay?"

A shake of his head moved the long, dark hair from his face. "I didn't want to burden you and if you fed Gypsy, that was enough. I could scrounge for nuts and berries." His voice started normal and went high, typical of a boy becoming a man.

"Good Lord, child. And just let your leg fall off? What happened?" She knelt and examined the wound. He'd lost a lot of blood, but his leg wasn't broken.

His shirt had been sewn from a flour sack and a large emblem with wording stating Columbia, America's Finest covered his back. He was a walking billboard.

"A hunter mistook me for an animal, ma'am. Can you just take Gypsy back with you? I'll be okay." Big tears filled his brown eyes and he sniffled. "She's better off at your place."

"Do you have a name, kid?"

"Tate."

He didn't volunteer more, and Sicily didn't press.

"Well, Tate, if you think I'm going to leave you here, you're sadly mistaken. Let me help you to my mule. Jessie will get all of us home and I'll fix your leg up. Then you can decide if you want to go or stay. But the choice will be yours."

"I reckon so, but I don't have any money."

"Few do these days. Are you able to work?"

"Yes, ma'am. I'm a hard worker."

"Good." She narrowed her eyes. "That is if you want to. I'll feed you regular and give you a place to sleep. What I have isn't the best, but it beats the hard ground of the woods." She put an arm around him and helped him stand. "My mule isn't too far."

Reaching Jessie, she gave him a boost into the saddle then lifted Gypsy girl up. She walked, leading the mule toward the only home she knew.

The afternoon sun filtered through the tall fragrant pines, dappling the dirt road. Sicily breathed deep of the fresh scent and considered her good fortune. She couldn't save every kid but if she could save just one that would make her the happiest woman alive. A smile curved her lips, and the birds sang a sweet song as they passed by.

This was the reason she'd awakened that morning. Someone needed her.

"Bye the way, I'm Sicily Rossi. And I think we'll get along splendidly."

Chapter Three

O NCE SICILY GOT THE boy home, she helped him down from the mule and into her humble little house, overseen of course by their four-legged friend, showing proper concern if all the whining and being underfoot meant anything.

Tate settled onto the little cot Albert had just vacated.

"When did this accident happen?" Sicily asked.

"Day before yesterday. I knew I couldn't take care of Gypsy, so I brought her here."

Sicily pushed the boy's pant leg up to his knee. She took extra care since the probability of him having another pair of trousers was zero. "How did you know I'd take her in?"

"I'd been watching you and thought you had a kind face."

"Sometimes looks are deceiving, kid." The bullet had thankfully missed the bone and gone on through. It was still seeping blood, but she could tell no major artery had been damaged and for that she was grateful. Also, it wasn't broken, another plus. Her only major concern was infection. Dirt had clearly gotten into the wound. She'd know more after she cleaned it.

"I've seen you for a good while and knew I could trust you by how you treated people. And once you helped a fox stuck in a trap. You were gentle." He winced when she examined the bullet hole.

"How long have you been living in the woods, young man?"

"About a year I suppose. I made me a lean-to with things I picked up here and there."

The pride in his words deeply touched her and told her of his determination not only to survive but improve his situation. That was what set humans apart, that drive to survive and thrive. She fetched a bowl of water and a clean cloth then carefully washed all the blood away, both fresh and dried.

"Where are your folks, Tate?"

"They died three years ago. I escaped an orphan train and hid out here in these wild Texas woods. Me and Gypsy. Ow, lady. That hurts."

"I'm sorry. I'll try to go easier." She'd been too saddened by the boy's story to pay attention. "From what I can tell, the wound doesn't appear too awfully bad except infection is starting to set in. That's always a worry. You need to keep this clean until it heals."

Tate propped himself on an elbow and squinted at her. "Did you mean what you said about me working for you?"

Sicily nodded. "Absolutely. I need some able-bodied soul to run errands, take my remedies into Silsbee for those too sick to come out here." She fixed him with a stare. "Can't pay much though so don't think you'll get rich. Like I said, I'll feed you and provide a bed in addition to a nickel each time you run things into town. You can use my mule. How does that sound?"

He pondered that a moment. Gypsy jumped onto the cot and prodded him with her nose as though begging him to accept. Finally, Tate gave her a smile. "Deal."

They sealed it with a handshake and she finished putting a bandage on the wound.

"Excellent." She glanced out the window at the sun sitting low in the sky. "I'll put Jessie in his stall and fix some supper. You lay here and rest."

As she picked up the bowl of water and turned to throw it out the door, Tate grabbed her arm.

He was fighting tears. "Thank you, Miss Sicily. I...I didn't expect such kindness. People don't treat orphans very well. Most run us off."

She laid a gentle hand on his shoulder. "If you watched me for a year, you knew you could trust me. What took you so long?"

"I had to make sure you were for real. Pays to be careful. You won't turn me in, will you?"

"That's fool talk, boy. I give you my word. What more do you need? You're safe here."

Tate finally relaxed and sank his head into the pillow. "Then you must be an angel. Before he died, my pa said angels would look after me."

"Nope, no angel. Just someone who cares."

"Ain't never met one like you."

Gypsy added her little bark of agreement before snuggling into Tate's side.

Sicily hurried into the kitchen before the boy could see tears glistening in her eyes. The boy's desperate need to trust deeply touched her. If she hadn't found him today, he might've lost his leg. Or worse. As it was, it still wasn't that good and would take all her knowledge to heal it.

Before starting supper, she made a poultice to put on the wound and applied that to draw infection out. The boy bore his pain well. Didn't say much about it but she caught him wincing when he lifted it off the cot and hobbled to the outhouse.

The meal was simple and made up of the last of the vegetables from her garden. No meat. But it was tasty and filled their bellies.

"Do you know how to read and write, Tate?" She kept the question casual.

"Some. I went to third grade and my folks taught me at home too. Why?"

"No reason. I was just thinking that it's important to be able to sign your name. I might have a few books left from my school teaching days if you'd like to use them while you're here. You'll need something to occupy your time." She took up the plates. "Of course, it's fine if you'd rather not."

"How long did you teach?"

"Five years," she answered quietly, the question bringing a lump to her chest. They'd fired her for teaching her students that blacks were their equal and just as good in addition to helping some black mothers learn to read. But it made the superintendent livid and he called a school board meeting. Next thing she knew, she was out of a job. Jace Bonner's mother had been one of the board members with the loudest voice, so it hadn't come as a surprise. It left her very sad that the same prejudices were continued in the curriculum. Normal in the south.

Tate rested his elbow on the table. "I heard the folks in Silsbee calling you the witchy woman."

"I know and I don't take offense." She pumped water from the cistern into her dishpan. "I'm just familiar with different things that grow in the woods that can heal people."

His eyes lit up. "Will you teach me? When I leave here, I want to know how to get along by myself."

"If you want to learn, I'll teach you." She put her hands in the soapy dishwater. "Will you take me to the place where you've been living?"

She was curious about the location and thought it odd that he'd been living in those woods for over a year, and she'd never run across him. He'd called the structure a lean-to. Very strange that she'd never seen it.

"Naw, I need it to be a secret. If those people from the orphanage come after me again, I can hide there."

Sicily fought the need to cry for this boy trying to make his own way as best he could. Freedom. There was so much to be said for being, for living, free. "I understand." She patted his shoulder. "That's all right. You keep your safe place. We all need one."

Even sixty-year-old women eaten up with regrets and loneliness. The woods, alive with birds, animals, and plants, were her sanctuary. Love and companionship had passed her by, and truth to tell, she wasn't sure she believed in romance much anymore. Seemed to her she was doing just fine.

And now she had Tate and Miss Gypsy dog.

When she finished the dishes, she fetched her old schoolbooks. Tate was excited and proved to be quite sharp, soaking up everything he could. His zeal was like a balm for her soul and teaching him at the kitchen table had awakened part of her that she thought had died. Before she knew it, the hour had grown late.

Sicily closed the books. "That's enough for tonight."

He spurned her hand to help him to his cot and hobbled on his own. However, he didn't refuse the blanket she laid over him and Gypsy. Or the quiet goodnight and pat on his chest.

Moments later, perched on her bed, she took the locket from the treasure box and gave Jace Bonner's handsome face a kiss then she put it away and lay down. But sleep didn't come. Tate had changed things and lifted the monotony of her life. He'd added laughter and joy to the house, similar to how her students did long ago.

Old people needed the young in numerous ways but mostly to make them feel they had something worth sharing. But the young needed them too. They needed the experience and wisdom that life had taught their elders.

Now, if she could figure out a way to make him want to stay. Just for a little while.

She brushed away a tear and made a list in her head of all she itched to show the boy.

TATE WANTED TO START on more lessons as soon as he got out of bed.

Sicily laughed. "Hold on to your horses, boy. Let me see to your leg and get some breakfast. Then I have to take care of the livestock and feed the chickens."

"Do you think I might study my letters while you're outside?"

She couldn't resist that winning smile that almost showed a dimple in his cheek and the gleam in the boy's eyes. "I don't see why not since you're not up to going into the woods with me yet. But you still have to eat your breakfast before I get the books down. I wish my students had been as eager to learn as you."

"Learning is fun," he declared, lifting Gypsy into his lap. "Everything I can master will help me be on my own." His eyes watered and he sniffed. "My parents are gone and ain't coming back. I used to think it was a dream, that I'd wake up and they'd be here. But

I'm not a kid anymore and that's wishful thinking. Reality is here. With you, Miss Sicily. A teacher of books and the woods."

She gave him a long stare. He'd had to mature way too soon. "Are you sure you're just fourteen?"

"Yes, ma'am."

"You talk like a grown man."

The boy turned red and rubbed his face in Gypsy's fur. She turned back to making breakfast, hiding a smile. "This is going to be a beautiful fall day. Like I said, I'll be going on my walk in the woods later to gather mushrooms and such, but I'll leave you with things to do."

"What do you use mushrooms for? Are they for eating?"

"Mushrooms are tricky and not all can be eaten. You have to be very careful to avoid the poisonous ones, yet they're excellent for making medicines with. When you're ready I'll teach you." Sicily put their eggs on a plate and set them on the table. "Mushrooms are very beneficial. They're excellent for the mind and help every part of the body to function well. Right now, so many starving people have no access to nourishing food and mushrooms. There's lots to learn."

Tate shook his head and picked up a fork. "I'll say."

Before sitting down, Sicily added two scrambled eggs to Gypsy's bowl.

"My folks always said a prayer over their food. Reckon we can do that, Miss Sicily?" Tate laid his fork down.

The request shocked her. His parents started him on the right path before they passed. "Yes, I'd like that. Would you lead?"

"Maybe you better go first this time."

Heads bowed and his young hand in Sicily's, she thanked their Creator. Tate was astonishing her at every turn. Just when she thought she'd seen and heard everything.

She decided she'd try to find something in the woods he'd never seen before.

"Miss Sicily, please be careful out in those woods. Hunters ain't too picky what they shoot. And I don't want to lose you."

"I appreciate your advice." She buttered a biscuit and added a spoonful of jam. "I don't need to be laid up with so many sick folks depending on me." Or this kid that had snuck into her heart.

Chapter Four

Sicily kept Tate healing at the cabin for a week before letting him go with her on walks to gather herbs and roots. You'd think she'd let the boy out of jail judging by the large grin on his face that teased the dimple trying to form in his cheek. Gypsy ran ahead, sniffing every rock and blade of grass.

"Everything looks so different," Tate exclaimed, inspecting a fallen log. "Almost like I've never been here."

He disturbed a long-legged burrowing owl sensing danger. Hissing like a rattlesnake, it rushed into a hole half hidden by the log where the ground-dweller had made a nest.

Tate leaped back. "Scared me for a minute."

"They get defensive, like people. Collect that mushroom there. It's a lion's mane."

"Looks funny. I never would've eaten anything like that." He plucked it up, handing it to her.

"It's one that's safe to eat and it makes very powerful medicine. Native Americans prized lion's mane."

They mostly stayed on the trail only venturing off once deeper into the forest. Gypsy stayed closer which was good. They wouldn't have to go searching for her.

"I'm looking for a fungus called Earthstars." She bent to gently brush aside damp foliage at the base of a red maple with magnificent red leaves right next to the golden leaves of a Florida maple. "Oh my goodness." She barely breathed the words. "Come here, Tate."

"What is it?"

"An indigo milk cap." She tugged it from the earth. "A type of edible mushroom. I don't see many of these. It's very healthy for you, good for fighting off infection and disease."

Tate squatted and picked several more buried under the fallen leaves. "They're pretty. Thank you for teaching me about these, Miss Sicily."

She patted his shoulder. "It's my pleasure. You're a good student."

They went a little farther and heard rifle shots.

"We'd better turn back," she said. "Time to go home."

Tate quickly picked up Gypsy and didn't have to be urged along. He found several other plants with his sharp eye along the way, and they didn't tarry but a second to collect them.

When they arrived back at the house, a thin young woman named Martha Ann was waiting on the porch under the windchimes. She pushed back stringy hair and rose from the rocker. "I knowed you'd be back sometime, Miss Sicily. I was enjoying the music the wind made tinkling your spoons an' such. I see you've been in the woods."

The poor girl had seen many a hard times and Sicily had given the friendship she craved like it was a thirst that couldn't be quenched. The Depression had stolen the life from Martha Ann's eyes as it had from so many others. If a person couldn't find a way to get through it, these desperate years would eat a body up. But the girl had other troubles that were far more serious, so Sicily had almost come to see her as a daughter that she'd never had.

Sicily smiled. "I have. This is a student of mine staying here. His name is Tate."

"How do, Tate." Martha Ann folded her arms nervously, her swollen left eye twitching noticeably. Her arms were black and blue.

Only twenty-three, she had a bad case of anxiety to the point she often couldn't function. Her husband's beatings didn't help the situation.

"Come inside, dear." Sicily gently took her arm as Tate held the door. "I'm going to make you some calming tea and massage your neck."

"Thank you, Miss Sicily." Tears filled Martha Ann's eyes. "You're always so kind to me. Like my mama. Leroy..." She couldn't finish for the sobs.

Tate silently took the burlap sack from Sicily and set Gypsy down. Then boy and dog both went outside.

"You sit right here, honey." Sicily pulled out a chair at the kitchen table. "I'll get the water on."

Martha Ann nodded. "Sometimes I think my head is just going to fly off."

"I'm glad you came." Sicily winced at the closeup of the fresh bruises. "I want you to come anytime you need a friend."

"Leroy would be boiling mad if he knew I came here," Martha Ann mumbled. "He's run off all my friends and said he'll kill me if I come back to your place." She released a troubled sigh. "But I had to."

"We won't let him ever find out." Sicily patted the woman's shoulder and reached for the jar of lavender. "Have you been working on that quilt like I told you?"

"I was but Leroy—" Martha Ann's lip quivered. "He yelled at me to fix him something to eat then yanked the quilt down from my frame and threw everything out in the yard. When he left, I brought it back in. Why does he do that? It ain't hurtin' nothin'."

The man drank too much and was jealous of anything that took attention from him and everyone in town knew it but did nothing to help. Martha Ann started taking in washing and ironing a while back for extra income. He made her give it to him, but she managed to hide some of it as Sicily had advised her to do and buried it in the woods.

Sicily shook her head. "I don't know, child. Men are peculiar."

When the lavender tea was ready, she pressed a cup into Martha Ann's hand. "Drink this and think of a place that made you happy."

"My granny's. She 'pert near raised me."

While Martha Ann sipped on the tea, Sicily stood behind her and massaged the knots from the slender neck, telling funny stories of her early life as a teacher. Slowly, the tension left the young woman.

"Kids always make me laugh." Martha Ann finished the tea. "I wish I had a baby but I'm glad in a way. Leroy would just be mean to the little thing. Best I don't wish for one."

"You don't want to bring a child into your life at the moment."

"Leroy blames me for that. Says I'm not fit to be a mother." Martha Ann whispered, "But it's him. He's always drinking and can't make his Johnson work."

God's blessing if Sicily ever knew one.

Suddenly, Martha Ann jumped to her feet, her eyes wide. "I've gotta get home. It's late and Leroy will be back."

All the calming tea in the world wasn't going to fix this sad situation.

"Let me get Tate. He'll take you home on my mule. It'll be faster."

"No! If Leroy sees him, he'll—" Martha Ann ran to the back door then turned, wringing her hands. "Miss Sicily, I'm scared. Give me something that will make Leroy go to sleep and not ever wake up. Please."

Sicily's gaze went to the poisonous mushrooms on her shelf and she took a step before swinging around. As dire as Martha Ann's situation was, she couldn't be an accomplice to outright murder. "I'm sorry. I can't."

The desperate young woman rushed to her and took her hand, kneeling on the floor. "Please. I won't tell a soul. I'm so scared."

Taking in the bruises and black eye, Sicily again considered it. If ever anyone needed killing, it was Leroy. She pulled Martha Ann's trembling body up and smoothed back the woman's hair. "I can't. But I can offer you a place of safety. Stay here and let me look after you."

"It won't help. He'll find me." Martha Ann continued wringing her hands, her eyes wild.

"Then go to your mama's."

"She told me never to come back. She doesn't want me, and she has my brothers and sisters to feed. No, killing Leroy's the only way."

Before Sicily could say another word, Martha Ann whirled and ran out the back door as if the devil's hounds were chasing her. And maybe they were.

Tate came in from the porch. "Has she left?"

"Yes." Sicily wearily picked up the teacup, feeling a hundred years old. Why did she feel such a burden to fix everyone's problems for them? Some things were unfixable in life and Martha Ann's situation was one. Leroy deserved to die, no question about that. Dark evil rolled off him in waves. But only Martha Ann could make the decision to leave and until she did, Sicily's hands were tied. She hated to contemplate the grim outcome that she'd seen multiple times before where the women either plain disappeared or ended up in the cemetery.

Why couldn't life be simple and uncomplicated? But maybe it never was meant to be.

Tate put an arm awkwardly around her shoulder. "Sit and I'll make you some tea."

And as quickly as that, Sicily felt better. The boy really was a dear and read her like a book.

Chapter Five

THE FOLLOWING WEEK PASSED with no sign of Martha Ann and Sicily grew more concerned with each passing day. Nor had she seen Albert and wondered if his bad heart kept him at home.

After breakfast, she took up the plates. "Tate, can you run some of my remedy into Silsbee please?"

The boy glanced up from his books. "Yes, ma'am. I'll get old Jessie ready."

Sicily looked out the kitchen window, still holding the dirty plates. "I also need you to go by Martha Ann's place. It's odd I haven't seen her. She usually comes out once a week. Make sure her husband isn't home then give her a note for me. But be very careful."

"Don't worry, Miss Sicily." He grinned. "I've learned how to sneak. Maybe I'll pick up some news from town. Do you need anything from the store?"

"I don't believe so." She took two nickels from her purse and handed them to him. "Just in case you want to get you something. One is for our agreement and the other is fun money."

"Thank you but you don't have to give me more than we shook on."

"Well, you deserve it. You've been a big help in gathering herbs and plants for my medicine."

"I enjoy it. Thank you." He eyed her burlap bag hanging on a nail. "Do you mind if I take that bag? Gypsy can ride in it and won't be underfoot."

Sicily laughed. "She does like to get under me even though I've stepped on her a few times. No, I don't mind. We need to make you one next time I buy livestock feed or flour."

Tate grinned big. "My very own sack. Miss Sicily, I'd like that a lot."

She got it down and went outside with him. While he readied the mule, she wrote a short note to Martha Ann then stuck it inside the saddlebags with Albert's heart remedy.

Before Tate rode off, she cautioned him, "Now be careful and don't take any chances."

"I won't."

The place seemed deserted with the boy gone. Was it always this quiet and she never noticed? That boy and his dog gave her home so much life, sending the ghosts running.

She sat on the porch under the sweet music of the tinkling windchimes and thought about children she might've had. She'd talked about it with Jace all those years ago and they'd even gone so far as to pick out the name of what their first would be. A boy of course and his name would've been Noah after her father. It seemed a lifetime ago. If she'd had children, they'd be grown now with families of their own.

But thinking back, she'd seen Jace's reluctance at having offspring. He'd not really wanted any for some reason. There had been other warning signs that they weren't suited to one another as well that she'd chosen to ignore. She was lucky that God had other, much deeper plans for her. Helping people was her true calling.

Martha Ann's panicked face in her kitchen sprang to memory. Her young friend had known stark terror so thick she must've tasted it on her tongue. Maybe she should've given Martha Ann a concoction. No one would've blamed her—except the sheriff, a lazy good-for-nothing who turned a blind eye to the plight of bruised and battered women. And since he and Leroy were cousins, the man sure wasn't about to help Martha Ann.

After thinking everything over, she rose to get busy. She had more than enough to do. She was chopping weeds from her winter garden and was down to the last rows when she heard the mule. She leaned on her hoe and turned to see not only Tate but Albert as well. Good Lord! What was he doing here? She'd sent the remedy just so he wouldn't have to come over.

She met them at the porch and held Jessie while Tate eased off favoring his wounded leg before helping Albert.

"Miz Sicily, I come to visit a spell," Albert declared, stumbling over his own big feet.

Catching him, she said, "I have lots of work to do today. I can't sit and keep you company."

"I know that. It's young Tate I come to see. Did you know he's on his own now?"

"Yes, Albert. He's been here a while. How's your heart?" She held his arm and helped him onto the porch and into a chair.

"It's doing fairly good for a man about ready for the bone yard." He cackled and slapped his knee. "But back to the boy, I need to teach him some things."

"Now, Albert, don't you start in on telling him to chase women. He's too young for that." She turned to Tate. "Did you see her?"

Tate shook the hair out of his eyes. "Yes, ma'am, and I gave her the note. She had lots of bruises, but she smiled and said to tell you not to worry."

Not to worry? What did that mean? That she had a plan to run away? Or that she'd found a way to rid herself of Leroy? It didn't make sense.

"Did you see her husband, Tate?"

"No, just her."

Maybe she'd finally gotten her nerve up to rid herself of the sorry excuse for a husband.

"Okay. Thank you."

"I'll go put Jessie in his stall."

Her gaze followed the boy until he rounded the house.

"Were you talking about Martha Ann just now?" Albert asked. "Cause if you were, I can add what I know."

"And what's that?"

Albert was always full of town gossip. It seemed to thrill him to know things to tell her.

"Martha Ann was found wandering the streets in Silsbee in half a daze earlier in the week. Only had a cotton under thing on. What do they call those thingamajigs women wear under their dresses?"

"A slip?"

"Yeah, I reckon. She was bloody of course. Sheriff Bledsoe took her home and I hear he told Leroy to lock her up. Folks wonder if she ain't quite right in the head from those beatings."

"She very well might've. A person can only take so much." Now it made sense why Martha Ann hadn't been out. Sicily rubbed her arms then folded them across her chest. How could folks keep watching this and not lift a finger? "But she's alive?" she asked.

"Reckon so. Ain't heard any talk of her kicking the bucket. Lots more been going on too."

"You don't say?"

"Willis Carson and his wife were seen boarding the train with their belongings in cardboard boxes. Goin' west we heard. They were starving flat to death here. This country's in poor shape. Nobody's got any food much and few ways to make a living." Albert shook a finger. "California is where ever'body's headin'. They say that's the land of milk and honey. Yes, sir."

"Too bad about the Carsons. I hope they find things better out there." Sicily rose. "You sit here and enjoy the breeze. I have some work to do."

His bony fingers wrapped around her arm. "Wait, I ain't even got to the boy."

"What boy?" Her work forgotten, she sat back down.

"An orphan. Came through on the train an' Peevy and his wife took him."

The Peevys never had a kind word or a smile for anyone. Sicily's stomach twisted. "How old is he?" she asked quietly.

"Looked about eight or so. Younger than Tate. Wore raggedy clothes and just as skinny as a rail. Peevys are gonna work that kid to death and feed him out of the slop bucket most likely."

Dear angels in heaven! "Probably so but what can we do, Albert?"

"Nuthin'." He cut his eyes around. "Just thought you'd want to know since you took in Tate and all."

"Appreciate it. I truly do." She might just wander over toward the Peevy place and check on the boy. And then what? She put a hand over her eyes. It was too much. She'd be in the same situation as with Martha Ann—caught between a rock and hard place. She mumbled something and left Albert sitting on the porch with Gypsy and trying to teach the dog to play dead. It was more like the dog teaching the man who was already half that way.

Later, she heard Albert's voice and moved closer while staying out of sight.

"Tate, now you listen good. Avoid old women at all costs. They're mean as the dickens and they know a hundred ways to hurt a man. Take Miz Sicily. She can poison you if she took a notion and that's for dern sure. Don't never cross her, boy."

She heard no reply from Tate so he'd either gone to sleep or was just nodding. An hour later, Tate told her he was taking Albert back to Silsbee.

"I just can't take anymore. That old man is as crazy as a loon."

"You're learning, son. Take him with my blessing." The man had gotten on her nerves too. Usually she could take him with a grain of salt but today she needed the whole shaker full and the pepper too. To be fair though, she was worried about Martha Ann. Especially when she was eaten up with guilt and concern, the old windbag got on her nerves.

TWILIGHT HAD CAST PURPLE shadows across the land, promising darkness soon. Sicily and Tate had just finished eating supper when a pounding sounded on the door. Gypsy barked and ran toward the noise.

"Who could that be, Miss Sicily?" Tate asked, reaching for the last biscuit.

"I don't know." She hurried to find out who would come at this hour.

Martha Ann burst inside the moment Sicily opened the door. "Help me."

The woman's nose and mouth were bleeding badly and had colored her dress scarlet.

Sicily hurriedly shut the door and led Martha Ann to the kitchen. Tate scooted back his chair and pushed it toward the girl.

"Sit down and hold this dishtowel to your face, child. I'll get water to clean you up." Sicily hurried to pump water from the cistern and grabbed a clean rag. "I take it Leroy is on a tear again."

"He was out with his friends and visited a bootlegger. Came home stumbling drunk. I knew better than to say a word, so I curled up on the bed out of the way. But that made him mad too. He just started in with his fists. Said I thought I was better than him. When he passed out, I got free and ran."

"You're safe now." Sicily wet the cloth and began to clean her up.

"I got your note." Martha Ann looked up, tears in her eyes. "You're always so kind. It helped to know you were thinking of me." She raised her chin a little before dropping it again to her chest. "I can't keep running to you. I'm trying to figure how to get out of this mess myself. I feel real bad I asked you to…" She glanced up at the shelf. "…to give me something. I ain't your problem."

"Now listen here, you're like a daughter to me and I'll do everything I can except break God's Commandment."

Tate had backed against the wall, chewing on a fingernail, not knowing what to do.

"Tate honey, can you go outside and watch for visitors? Keep out of sight and come tell me the moment you see someone."

"Yes, ma'am."

"Leave Gypsy girl in here or she'll give you away."

The boy slipped out of the back door and quickly closed it before Gypsy could escape.

Amid the dog's soft whines, Sicily gently washed Martha Ann's mouth and nose. "Girl, how long are you going to take this? You can change it whenever you want and you'll have my full support. I have a little money saved that will take you far from here."

"Miss Sicily, I ain't strong like you. And where would I go that Leroy wouldn't find me?" She took in a shuddering breath. "I'm trapped."

Of course, she was right. That sorry excuse for a man would hunt her down and kill her most likely for daring to defy him. This wasn't a simple matter and would require a lot of thought.

Leroy would find Sicily a little harder to get rid of. But time? It didn't seem on their side. The violence was escalating.

Suddenly, a loud bellow reached them. "Martha Ann, you'd better come out or I'll tear that witchy woman's house down. Hear me?"

Tate burst in through the back door with eyes wide. "He's here. Caught me off guard. I'm sorry."

"It's all right. We'll handle it."

"No, I gotta get out of here!" Martha Ann sobbed, jumping to her feet.

"Let me hide you, girl. Go out to the barn and bury yourself under the hay."

"Martha Ann, you can't keep embarrassing yourself this way!" Leroy hollered.

"Oh God, oh God! I'm sorry, Miss Sicily." Martha Ann stumbled for the back door.

"Then run, girl. Run as fast as you can. I'll try to keep him here." She could do that much. As the flash of Martha Ann's blood-stained dress disappeared into the night, Sicily's gaze again swung to the jars on her shelf. She had the means to end this.

But she couldn't fight Martha Ann's battles for her. What would that teach her?

The voice in her head whispered, "Not a blamed thing if she's dead."

The air seemed to be sucked from the room as Sicily struggled to breathe. Go after Martha Ann or stay rooted? She had Tate to protect and wouldn't leave him. If she left, she was taking him. She moved toward him and saw his firm jaw and a steadiness in his eyes. A man where there was a boy.

"We have to do something, Miss Sicily. You know it."

She wasn't sure if he'd spoken or if it was the voice in her head.

The crack of the screen door shredded Sicily's raw nerves. Before she could move, Leroy Vaughn, ugly and mean, stood in her kitchen with Gypsy snarling and racing around him. With his dirty hair flying in all directions and fury in his eyes, he resembled a bloodthirsty madman.

"Where's my wife? I know she's in here so don't deny it, old woman!" Leroy screamed, his face livid. Spittle flew from his mouth, and he reeked of liquor.

Tough, terrified, and shaking, Sicily faced him, her chin raised. "She's not here. Why do you keep beating on that poor girl? There's only so much a body can take. You're going to kill her one of these days."

Leroy opened his mouth to say something as Gypsy sank her teeth into his leg.

"Ow, you little mutt!" Leroy kicked at the dog, but she easily evaded the foot.

"Tate, get her and hold her until this unwelcome caller leaves," Sicily said calmly.

Clad in a pair of dirty overalls with no shirt, Leroy's wild gaze lit on the bloody gauze, rags, and bowl of red-tinged water on the table. "That proves she was here. Get her or I'll set fire to this shanty like I should've a long time ago."

Sicily's mouth dried and she swallowed hard as she searched for an answer. Truth or a lie, it didn't matter.

Chapter Six

EVERYONE WENT SILENT IN the house on the edge of the woods except Gypsy. The little dog was barking fit to raise the dead and fighting to wiggle from Tate's arms.

Tate spoke, his voice clear. "Those are mine. My leg's bleeding. Got shot."

"Show me," Leroy barked.

The boy lifted his pant leg where he'd been shot, and the wound was indeed bleeding. Sicily didn't know how or why but it seemed a miracle. He must've hit it and knocked the scab off.

Sicily jerked up her broom and brandished it like a weapon. "You have your answer." She thrust the broom like a spear toward him. "Now get out of my house and don't you ever come back."

Surprise crossed Leroy's face for half a second before he flared his nostrils and sucked in a raspy breath. He rolled his shoulders back, pointing a dirty finger and snarled, "I could break you in half, uppity woman. I'm gonna find my wife and when I do, there'll be hell to pay. And if I find that dog outside, it's dead."

"You could kill me, but I'd think about that first. Getting rid of the only doctor anyone's got here would rile a whole lot of people, including your cousin the sheriff. Get out of my house. Martha Ann is much too good for the likes of you." Seething, Sicily marched to the back door and held it open. "Get out! If you barge in again, you'll find yourself facing my shotgun."

Leroy gave an angry snort and stomped out. She slammed the door after him and threw the bolt then made sure the front door was secured as well after which she got her shotgun from the bedroom.

"We gotta do something, Miss Sicily," Tate said putting Gypsy down.

The little dog promptly ran to the door, barking and snarling.

"Let me think on it. I do agree that this is putting us in his crosshairs." Sicily lifted a weary hand to her forehead. "But the solution might become very complicated. Leroy has friends and his cousin is the sheriff." She turned. "What happened to your leg to make it bleed?"

"I caught it on the door in my hurry to get inside." He sat in a chair at the table and raised his trouser leg. Blood had covered his leg.

Gypsy finally wound down and parked herself next to Tate, licking his hand.

"It sure saved us. Let me get some clean water and rags." She threw the bloody water out the door and pumped some fresh then knelt to tend to the wound.

"Where do you think Martha Ann went?" Tate asked.

"I don't know. I'll check the barn when I finish here." Sicily prayed that wherever she was Leroy never found her.

"I'd tell her about my hideout in the woods if she'd go there."

"We'll keep that in mind." Sicily finished doctoring Tate's injury thinking how odd it was that women in Martha Ann's situation rarely left their abuser. They were just too frightened to leave and most really had nowhere else to go. Very few honorable jobs existed for women which was a real shame.

Most simply bided their time before death claimed them, whether by a husband or their own hand. Everyone had a breaking point, and she was never more aware of that.

Sicily finished her second, and hopefully last, doctoring job for the night and grabbed her shotgun. "I'm going to go see if Martha Ann is in the barn. I'll be right back. Lock the door after me and don't open it until you hear my knock."

Tate stood quickly, his face a mask of worry. "Let me go with you. It's too dangerous."

"No, I want you safe." She placed her hands on his shoulders facing him. "If something happens, you can survive without me."

Cautious and listening to every sound, she went out and crossed the space to the barn. Though she searched every inch, she found no sign of Martha Ann and the same with the outside. She could only conclude that the girl had gone back to town or had sought shelter in the woods. Her heart ached for the girl. Tate was right. They had to do something. This couldn't go on.

THE FOLLOWING WEEK PASSED without much to interrupt it and Sicily found quiet comfort in her woods with the animals and her roots and plant collecting. One thing had changed though. She began taking her father's rifle along each time she went away from the house.

She'd sent Tate into town with some of her chickens to give away. "Just give them to whoever looks the hungriest."

"They all are, Miss Sicily."

"I know. Just do your best."

That might prove helpful in finding out information about Martha Ann without asking questions. Maybe Martha Ann had found a way to patch things up with Leroy. At least she hoped so. But it was a powder keg and just needed one spark to go off.

Meanwhile, she tried to keep her mind occupied stockpiling food as well as her remedies for the winter months when sickness grew worse.

Gypsy loved the late October outings and exploring whatever came into her little doggie head. Sicily wished she could live totally in the moment as animals did, not worrying about yesterday or tomorrow. They didn't even think five minutes in advance.

The days were getting cooler and there was a bite in the air. Nights required a fire to chase away the chill. She'd sit by the warmth and Tate would lie on the floor with his nose in the books, learning. Always learning.

He'd returned from town after giving away the hens. "Folks sure were tickled to get them. I imagine they'll eat well for one day. No one knew anything new about Martha Ann."

"Okay, son." She turned back to plucking weeds from her garden.

On a brisk morning excursion, Tate stuck different varieties of mushrooms and roots into her sack. "I want to show you where I used to live and will again if things get desperate."

"Are you sure?" she asked quietly, stopping her search underneath the brightly colored leaves and pine needles on the ground.

This was the first time he'd said much about his hideout in a while and the fact he offered to show her meant he trusted her and that brought a warm feeling. She was curious to see where he'd survived on his own for almost a year.

He shrugged. "You might need it sometime, especially if Martha Ann decides to live in the woods. Or that orphan boy you keep thinking about living with the Peevys."

Clearly, he'd also been thinking a lot about that orphan boy. "Okay, point made. Maybe we can make use of it. Show me."

Tate led the way through the thick tree growth that now bore the breathtaking autumnal colors and crossed a small stream with stepping rocks. They'd traveled deep in the forest where the absolute silence created eerie tingles up her spine. The tall loblolly pines, blackjack oaks, and other trees cast mysterious dark shadows over everything.

Abruptly he stopped. "Here we are."

She glanced around at the natural rock overhang with small trees lining the front. "I thought you said it was a lean-to. I'm not seeing it."

"Closer." He pointed toward the outcrop.

She crept under the rock ledge and Tate removed what appeared to be a crude door, consisting of small saplings strapped together with vines. It blended so perfectly with the surroundings she had to squint to make it out. The saplings in front of the overhang added an extra layer of camouflage. Grinning, he stood aside. There stood a crude shelter of sticks, dried mud, and branches. She was immensely impressed with his ingenuity.

"This is pure genius," she said. If a body didn't know exactly where to look, they wouldn't see it. She turned and patted his arm. "You have quite a special instinct of how to protect yourself."

"No one ever found me here," he said proudly. "My dad showed me how to make something like this one day before he died. Just in case I ever needed it."

"I'm simply amazed." She crawled into the shelter and noticed a book or two on a neat stack of blankets. Curious what a boy with a third-grade education treasured, she picked up a tattered book and scanned the title—*The Call of the Wild* by Jack London. "I take it you liked this story?"

His grin stretched wider. "I've read it about a hundred times. I didn't understand some of the words, but I'm like him, struggling to survive. Buck was a special dog."

"And so was Thornton a special man who took him in and nursed him back to health."

"That's why I taught Gypsy how to dance and do tricks." He picked the dog up and snuggled her close. Gypsy licked his face in a show of affection.

"You never told me where you got the sweet dog."

"I found her here in the woods yelping to beat all. Her foot was caught in a trap. Me and her have been together ever since."

Sicily smiled and put an arm around Tate. "A match made in heaven. You're both scrappy."

Tate glanced up at her. "I'm glad you saved me and Gypsy. It's almost like I have a mother again."

She brushed his hair back, her heart overflowing. "That's the best compliment I ever got. If I had been fortunate enough to have a son, I'd want him exactly like you."

He ducked his head. "Aw, I ain't much."

With red creeping up his face, he moved away from her and began putting branches and things across the shelter. She'd embarrassed him. Easy to do, she was finding out.

They'd started back and Tate was leading the way when two men burst from the trees, setting Gypsy off in a frenzy. Sicily was a little ways behind but saw it all. Her heart in her throat, she hurried to catch up.

"Where you goin' boy?" a mustached man in hunter's clothing asked.

"Heading home." Tate answered.

The man's companion wearing a hat with flaps in similar clothing grabbed Tate. "Are you the one messing with our traps?"

"No, sir. I haven't even seen them."

"I say you're lying," he snarled. "And we think you stole our muskrat out of one."

"You're mistaken, mister."

Sicily parted the brush, her shotgun pointed at them. "I advise you to leave my son be. Let him go and be quick about it. He's been with me the entire morning."

"Well, someone stole our muskrat," spouted the man with the mustache. He kicked at Gypsy but she was too fast.

"I give you to the count of three to release your hold on my boy and go on your way." Sicily's angry voice sounded frightening in her own ears. "One. Two."

"All right, don't get your bloomers in a wad." The hunter with the hat shoved Tate away from him. "I bet you're that witchy woman that lives over the way."

"Could be. Tate, collect Gypsy. We wouldn't want her biting a hunk out of these two." Sicily didn't take her eyes off the two men, nor did she breathe easier, until they disappeared into the trees.

She and Tate walked home in silence, the ordeal stealing conversation. Sicily had never been more aware of the danger lurking from everywhere. The Depression had made people very desperate—the kind of desperation that kept them awake at night, their bellies growling with hunger. It drove them to do things they wouldn't otherwise. A fragment of an idea began to form. The empty lots in Silsbee could be turned into community gardens and everyone could grow food. No one would have to go hungry.

Only problem was, that would require everyone's cooperation and likely the sheriff would try to find a hundred ways to stop them. Maybe there were laws preventing people doing for themselves. She could hear Sheriff Bledsoe spouting such nonsense.

She'd think on it some more. It would work. Where there was a will, there was a way.

Reaching home, she unpacked the various things they'd collected then she turned to Tate. "We're going into town after we eat a bite. We'll take the wagon so I can haul some feed back. And we'll see what we can find out. I'm sure Albert is about to bust a gut to give me all the low down."

"He's sure a talker, Miss Sicily." Tate gave Gypsy a scrap of food and affectionately rubbed her head. "I think it makes him feel important, don't you?"

She laughed. "I know so. Old folks always need something to keep them connected with what's going on around them."

"I guess." He grinned like a donkey eating briars. "I'm really gonna get a sack like yours?"

"You really are." She brushed back his long hair, noticing he'd gotten a little taller than her. "And we're getting you to the barber. If not, you're going to go blind."

"I'll get the wagon ready." He started to go then stopped. "Do you think I can drive?"

"Yes, you can drive."

He went out the door whistling with Gypsy at his side. It took little to make him happy.

She turned to the sink to wash her hands before she made them some lunch and suddenly realized she was whistling also. Her life was especially full and meaningful since the boy came.

Sudden guilt swept over her. Why couldn't women like Martha Ann have this same sort of peace deep in their souls? It wasn't right. Life was all about choices and consequences and a woman had to be strong and god-awful determined to break free of dangerous situations.

She didn't say anything to Tate, but she wanted to check on Martha Ann and ask a few people about Leroy and if he'd shown his rear more. Time was growing short and if she was going to help that poor woman at all, she had to come up with a plan.

Chapter Seven

Out on Sicily's place, the days all bled together which made it hard to keep track as she went around the business of scratching a living. The town of Silsbee seemed a beehive of activity, baffling Sicily until it dawned on her it was Saturday. Tate proved to be a good driver and stopped for cross-walkers, horses, and the few automobiles that had found their way. The town was kind of tucked into an out-of-the-way part of Texas so not a lot of travelers passed through. Today it seemed was the fall festival when folks brought handmade goods to town to try to get a few dollars. Something else Sicily would've remembered if her head hadn't been filled with so many problems.

With this many people, she was glad they'd left Gypsy at home or she'd bark until she lost her voice.

They had a lot of things to do and began at the farm supply. The familiar smell of manure, baby chicks, grains, and everything else tickled her nose and she blocked a sneeze.

Dan Williams rushed forward to wait on her. "Miz Sicily, seems a coon's age since I last saw you. Those hens were sure welcome. How you been?"

"I'm doing fine for the most part." She put an arm around Tate. "I have me a helper now and he's a godsend. Name's Tate."

Tate shook hands with the farm supply owner. "Nice to meet you."

"He'll be making some of the medicine deliveries here to my patients, Dan."

The owner propped himself against a counter and stuck a toothpick in his mouth. "He looks like a fine, strapping boy. That's good. You need someone to do your running for you."

"I'll take a sack of feed, Dan," Sicily said, keeping the man on track.

"Sure thing. Tate, just go grab a sack." Dan rang it up and she paid him.

In the back, Tate was looking the sacks of grain all over. They had several different company logos on them and she supposed he was looking for something special even though the sack she was giving him was the empty one in her barn at home that had America the Beautiful on it from the Farmers Fidelity Feed Company. That would be his.

Dan handed her the change. "I heard Miss Winnie took a fall, but she seems none the worse for wear. That sure is a spry woman."

"I guess if she'd needed me, she would've sent someone." Sicily snapped her purse shut. "She's what now? Seventy-five?"

"Yep, if she's a day. Still up every morning before dawn feeding her chickens."

"It's good to stay busy." Sicily noticed Tate had selected and loaded the feed. "Well, we need to be running. Lots to do."

They said their goodbyes and next drove slowly past Martha Ann's place. No one was out and the curtains were shut. She told Tate to keep going.

At the corner, she said, "Stop the wagon please."

He did and she stared at the vacant property that encompassed two lots. With the drought it was down to dirt and weeds that stood knee-high. The incessant wind had dried the soil out but as she looked, she envisioned neat rows of fresh vegetables. Her father had taught her ways to keep drought from stealing all the moisture and she itched to put them to use. Such a shame to not use this land when folks were so desperate for food.

"What is it, Miss Sicily?" Tate asked.

"What do you see here?" she asked.

"Nothing. What am I supposed to be seeing?"

"Not much yet, but with luck maybe you will in the spring. I'm thinking of getting some folks together and putting in a community garden for everyone to use. No one will go hungry."

"That's a good idea. I'll help."

She patted his knee. "I know you will. You're a visionary like me. I noticed that when I saw the shelter you made for yourself.

You're smart." Taking one last look, she said, "You can go on now. I'll have to find out who owns that property."

"Shouldn't be too hard." Tate flicked the reins to get the mule moving. "Where to next?"

"Let's visit the barber."

When they arrived, she got out and went inside with Tate to introduce him to Art O'Neil. The place was empty, and Art had stretched his bones out in a barber's chair reading the newspaper.

"Miss Sicily, what brings you in today?" He put the newspaper down and came forward to shake hands.

"This is Tate," Sicily said, smiling. "He's living with me now and as you can see, he needs a trimming. He'll tell you how short he wants it." She took money from her purse and handed it over. "Keep the change."

"Thank you, ma'am." Art slipped the money in his pocket and grabbed a cape. "Sit down, son, and let's talk."

"I'm going to run an errand and will be back for you, Tate."

"Thank you, Miss Sicily. You probably don't want to listen to man-talk."

"Not today. I need to deliver some remedy. You two have fun."

Art was a talker on any given day and if he'd had few customers, the length of conversation more than doubled. When that happened, he wouldn't even stop to take a good breath. Poor Tate. She didn't allow herself much pity though because she had things to do that would be best if he wasn't with her.

She had a list of clients on her errands. Albert came first. She could probably find out more from him if she could keep him on task. Of course, that wasn't easy for the creaky old Romeo who had it in his head that every woman itched to marry him, especially the very young and beautiful. To hear him tell it, those were chasing him all over Texas and half of Louisiana. She stopped at his place, grabbed her burlap sack, and knocked before sticking her head in.

"Albert, are you asleep?"

He roused from his chair and glanced at the door. "Miz Sicily, that you?"

"Yep. Did I wake you?"

His sparse white hair sticking forty ways from Sunday, he stretched his creaky bones. "I've told you over and over I don't nap in the day. I'll have you know I was resting my poor knees. Been trying to outrun Lucy from over at the bank and my tongue was lolling out. She's already got the wedding day picked but I told her she oughta know that I have a long list of guests we gotta invite."

"That so? Wonder why it is I hear she's set to marry that nice man she's been seeing."

"Aw, that's just a ruse to throw people off. You know how they are." He rubbed his wrinkled face. "What's in that sack?"

"It's your rheumatiz remedy. I figured you were about out."

"Well, have a sit down. Yes, ma'am." Albert reached for a spoon off a little table next to his armrest and breathed on it then rubbed it on his shirt to clean off the residue on it.

"Now, go easy. This batch is real potent," she cautioned.

He unscrewed the lid and dipped the spoon in it, putting it in his mouth. "I feel better already."

"It doesn't work that fast," Sicily said dryly and leaned forward. "What do you hear about Martha Ann?"

He shrugged. "Folks ain't seen her and they say Leroy is keeping her under lock and key in the house. Customers cain't even get in to pick up the washing and ironing they brung her."

That could be likely. Sicily was persistent. "But has anyone seen her?"

"Not that I've heard but they have heard her yell out that she's taken sick and cain't open the door." Albert got another spoonful from the jar and smacked his lips. "That's mighty good, Miz Sicily."

"You're not supposed to eat it like candy."

Well, if people had heard Martha Ann, that meant she was alive. That relieved her somewhat.

"What about Leroy? Has he been raising Cain with his buddies?" she asked.

"Sure the hell has and shootin' that gun of his at everyone. Folks stay inside at night." Albert started to put the lid on the jar. "Think I'll have a little more."

Sicily tried to grab it, but he stuck it down in his chair. "Albert, you beat all I ever saw. You don't listen to a word I say. I'm going to get on my way. No use trying to talk to you. I have better things to do."

"My friend Toots said he heard that a group went to the sheriff and told him to calm Leroy down or he'll soon be out of a job."

"I'm afraid that won't do a lick of good. Leroy does all Bledsoe's dirty work and makes the disgruntled toe the line. He's not about to get rid of Leroy."

She was almost to the door before Albert hollered, "Wait. I remembered something."

"What's that?"

"Leroy has taken up with the moonshiner's daughter. Acts like he don't have a wife."

Not a new wrinkle on his behavior but worrisome all the same. She placed a steadying hand on the door.

Albert went on, "Folks say Beth, a pretty little thing, has no say in the matter. Leroy takes what he wants and that's that."

Oh Lord, someone else to fret over. Sicily released a troubled sigh. She couldn't save everyone. Someone else would have to help young Beth.

Without turning, she said, "Thanks, Albert. Might better keep that old pistol you have handy."

Hurried steps took her to the wagon, and she sat there trembling. When were others going to step up and protect their own? Shuffling footsteps sounded.

"Miz Sicily, I remember something else," Albert called, waving his stick arms.

She glanced up. "What's that?"

"I was supposed to tell you that Mabel has pleurisy and needs you to stop by."

Mabel Bonner was a snooty woman and rarely gave her the time of day. She was Jace Bonner's persnickety aunt and sister-in-law to the woman who ruined her wedding plans.

"Thank you, Albert. Message delivered." She shook the reins and got the mule moving before Albert made her promise to go by Mabel's house. She'd leave her to the last and if she ran out of time, that would be a sign from God.

She made several more planned stops then circled back around to Martha Ann's, parking down the block. She quietly made her way back, slipped into some tall brush next to the house, and rapped on the window of what she vaguely recalled from a visit there once as the bedroom of the small dwelling, praying Leroy wasn't home.

There was no response, and she was about to turn away when a blood-stained hand poked through a bed sheet they'd hung on the window in an effort to keep some of the dirt out like so many others did. It seemed as though the fingers were grasping for something.

Sicily placed her mouth against the windowpane and whispered, "Martha Ann."

The door of the house suddenly flew open. "Who's out here?" Leroy yelled.

Her heart hammering, Sicily ducked out of sight, barely breathing. Making herself small, she shrank into the colorful fall ground foliage, willing the man to go back inside.

"I know someone's snooping around! Show yourself!" he yelled, stomping around the corner of the dwelling.

How long Sicily huddled there, she didn't know. Finally, after poking around, he went back into the house, slamming the door.

She still didn't move for the longest, knowing he'd be watching for movement. To find her would be disastrous. Silent tears ran down her face as her heart broke for the woman who'd become like a daughter. But the only avenue open to her was leaving. Tate would be waiting and wondering where she was.

At last, she circled the house, keeping in the tall brush, and darted to the wagon.

She had no choice but to leave her young friend and it ripped her heart out. "It's not over yet, Leroy Vaughn," she whispered. "I'm not going to let you win."

But the fear that Martha Ann was hanging on by a fingernail gripped her. If she could just find enough strength to hold on a little bit longer.

Chapter Eight

SICILY ALMOST DIDN'T RECOGNIZE Tate as he waited outside the barbershop. The shorter hair gave him a manly look and he just seemed different. She could actually see his sensitive brown eyes now that they weren't hidden beneath the shaggy bangs. He stood with a kid around nine or so and not in the best of shape with ragged clothes and dirty hair. He must be the orphan the Peevys took.

It was good that Tate was making a friend. The young man was far too serious and mixed up in adult problems when he should be catching frogs and playing marbles. Even now, Tate's shoulders slumped as though he had the world on them.

Sicily pulled to a stop alongside the pair and grinned though she didn't feel like it. Martha Ann's fingers on the bed sheet were burned into her brain. For a moment, she considered going to Sheriff Bledsoe, but being Leroy's kin made that impossible. He'd just tell her to mind her own rat killing.

No, the folks in Silsbee had to take care of things themselves and that was a sad fact. They might as well have no law as Bledsoe who had Leroy at his beck and call to terrorize folks and put the fear of God in them whenever he needed.

Sicily forced herself to relax the tight hold on the reins and noted the protective arm Tate had draped around the young kid. "I like your haircut, Tate. Makes you look like a grown man. Did Dan talk your ear off?"

"Pert near. He sure is a talker." Tate patted the boy's shoulder and Sicily quickly caught the wince before a mask dropped over the kid's face. "This is George, Miss Sicily. He's staying with the Peevys."

She was right. "Nice to meet you, George. I'd like you to take supper with Tate and me."

A man, Peevy by the sour face under the slouch hat, hurried out of the general store and clamped down on the poor boy's arm, yanking hard. "We don't allow him to go places. He's got work to do. Come along, George." Peevy stalked toward a wagon, practically dragging the boy. "I told you not to talk to anyone. Can't you listen?"

"Have a good day, Peevy," Sicily called, noting the disagreeable man's stiffening shoulders. Kill a person with kindness she always said. Even though the sourpuss wouldn't know a kind word if it bit him on the rear. And too, it would irritate the man even more.

The wagon shifted with Tate's weight when he climbed in. "I only talked to George for a few minutes, but he hates where he's at. That much I know. He said they make him sleep out in the barn at night and padlock the door."

"Poor kid. But that's probably welcome relief from the Peevys. Living in the same house with them would be pure torture." Sicily let a horse and wagon go by before she pulled in behind them.

"I saw big bruises on his neck," Tate said low. "I told him how nice it was living with you and tears came into George's eyes."

Her stomach twisted and it took a few heartbeats to answer. "I'm sorry for what he's going through. I wouldn't wish it on my enemy."

"What can we do, Miss Sicily?"

"We have to stay out of that—for the moment anyway. Just be a friend, Tate. When you get to be my age, you figure out real quick you have to pick your battles. And right now, Martha Ann is in worse shape." She patted his leg. "I'm ready for the quiet of my woods. How about you?"

"Me too. I'm sure Gypsy will be glad to see us."

"I have one more stop then we'll get back to that sweet little dog." A moment's silence passed. "Why were you picking over those grain sacks back there at the farm supply?"

"I wanted the best in case I need to make a quilt or curtains for my hideout. I've seen quilts made out of 'em. Course, we'll need more than just one or two."

"That's a great idea." The boy was always thinking of ways to make life a little better.

On the outskirts of town, she stopped at Mabel's fancy house. At least it was one of the best in town, not that it was saying that much anymore with everyone short of money. Upkeep had long since went by the wayside with the Depression dragging on, not only for this one but everyone's. The housekeeper, Corrine Gray, in a black dress and white apron answered the door.

Sicily gave her a smile. "I heard that Mabel's sick, and a friend asked me to stop by."

"She ain't here, ma'am. She's gone over to Woodville to the doctor. You want I should tell her you called?"

"No, Corrine. Just say that Sicily Rossi came by." She started to add more but decided that was enough. "Have a good day."

Well, it seemed the good Lord took that chore out of her hands.

As the mule plodded toward home, Sicily took some deep breaths and hurried old Jessie along the path to her sanctuary where the breeze through the windchimes made of spoons and pieces of metal brought such peace to her weary soul.

THE FIRST THING SHE DID when they unhitched the wagon and put the mule in his stall was to have Tate carry the new sack of feed to the barn. She emptied the used one into the feed bin and handed it to Tate.

"Here you go, son. Make it the way you want."

He fought tears as he reached for it. "I want it like yours," he managed, ducking his head.

"There's a sharp knife over there on the shelf."

Instead of rushing to it, he stood there silently biting the inside of his jaw. Then he put his arms around her and gave her a hug. The affection surprised her, catching her off guard. But she, too, had tears as she hugged him back.

"Thank you." His voice caught as he spoke quietly. "Thank you so much."

She pulled back and met his eyes. "You don't know it, but you're very special to me."

Tate couldn't manage a reply and she knew he must have a lump blocking his throat because she did too. Gypsy must've heard their voices and began yipping inside the house.

"I guess I'll go let her out." Tate sniffled, his gaze on his feet. "She's about to tear the door down."

"It does sound like she's anxious to see you. Go on and then start making your bag so you'll have it tomorrow when we walk."

"Thanks again, Miss Sicily. This is the best thing anyone did for me in a long time."

She wiped her eyes and watched him disappear out the door. He was going to be a fine man. One of the finest she'd ever seen.

Before she'd finished brushing old Jessie down, Gypsy was dancing under Sicily's feet, so happy they were back from town.

"You'll live over it, girl. Get used to it. You're not the only pea in the dish."

The dog yipped and went to pester Tate sitting on the steps of the back door.

Sicily laughed, thinking how good it was to hear that sound. She put the brush down and went to stand in the barn door. The screech of an owl made her jump as it swooped down at her from the rafters. A chill ran gooseflesh up her arms as a big gust of wind took her breath.

Trouble was coming. She didn't know when or from where, but it was coming.

THEY HAD FINISHED EATING supper that night and Tate was helping her with the dishes when she heard a thump on the back door. Drying her hands, Sicily hurried to see what caused it.

As the door swung open, a woman's battered body clawed her way inside. Only after she wiped the blood from the face did she recognize Martha Ann.

"Mama, help," Martha Ann managed through swollen lips.

Remembering the owl, Sicily sucked in a breath. "Tate, can you help me get her inside?"

Between the two of them, they managed to carry the woman to Sicily's bed.

"I'll need some water, Tate. Then can you fetch clean clothes?"

"Yes, ma'am." He picked up Gypsy before she could jump on the bed and hurried out.

Sicily grabbed her scissors and cut the dress off. Ripped and torn, it wasn't worth saving anyway. She saw the broken arm immediately and though she took extra care, Martha Ann gave a blood-curdling scream.

As she worked, Sicily made a vow that the abuse would end here and now. This was it and Leroy wasn't going to get her back. She met Tate at the door and took the supplies. "Wait out there for a little bit."

"Will she be all right?" he asked quietly.

"God willing, eventually." As he turned away, she took his arm. "Get my Winchester and keep watch. Leroy will come."

"I'll shoot him if I have to."

"It may come to that I fear. What did you do with Gypsy?"

"I put her on my cot and shut the door. Best to keep her out of the way."

"Good boy." Turning, she went back to her young friend who'd suffered far more than anyone ever should.

Martha Ann was in and out of consciousness as Sicily cleaned her up and very carefully got her into one of her nightgowns. Her arm would have to be set but that would come later.

"I love you, Mama," Martha Ann muttered, her eyes closed.

"Child, I'm Sicily." Tears ran down Sicily's face as she smoothed back her hair.

"I know, Mama."

Brushing tears away with an arm, Sicily hurried to the kitchen to fill the kettle and put it on the stove. Then she reached for the willow bark to help with the pain, praying she could get Martha Ann to drink it. When it was ready, she added some feverfew to the willow bark tea. Fever was a concern with the broken arm.

An hour after getting the tea down her, Martha Ann settled and appeared to rest.

Tate appeared at the door, his face white. "I think you need to come. There's a bunch."

She shook her head when he tried to hand her the Winchester. "Keep it. I have another." She opened a trunk and took out a rifle, loading it.

With Tate following, she hurried to the front window, pushing the curtain aside. A Model A idled in front of the house with armed men standing on the running board.

Leroy jumped off and stalked forward. "Witchy woman, I demand my wife. Now!"

"What are we going to do?" Tate whispered.

"He'll get her over my dead body. Can you ease out the back door and come around the side? They won't be expecting you. Don't shoot until I do then let's give him something to think about."

"Yes, ma'am." The lines of Tate's face set, and he aged fifteen years. "I'm ready."

He turned and went into the kitchen. Sicily opened the front door, taking a bead on the spot between Leroy's eyes. "Get off my land. You're not welcome here."

"I want Martha Ann, you old woman. I know she came here," Leroy snarled, weaving on unsteady legs. He ratcheted a cartridge into the chamber of the rifle.

"She's half-dead and here she'll stay," she replied in a strong voice. "Now leave."

Leroy laughed. "You're crazy."

"What'cha waitin' for? Shoot the old biddy!" yelled one of his buddies.

Leroy jerked the rifle up and it went off barely missing his foot. He jumped back with a curse.

"Go home and sober up," Sicily advised. "There's nothing for you here."

Instead of returning to the car, he stumbled to the porch. His buddies climbed out of the car and formed a circle behind him. Things were about to get ugly.

A voice sounded off to her left. "I'd listen to her." Tate's voice held steel and instead of going high and low then back again, it was deep, like a man's. "Get off her property."

Evidently surprised to find Sicily with help, Leroy released another curse. He shaded his eyes, squinting. "Who's there? Who are you?"

"Doesn't matter. I told you to leave," Tate said.

"I ain't going nowhere without my wife." Leroy placed a foot to the bottom step.

Sicily fired, the projectile nicking his shoe.

"The next one will go in your knee," she warned. "You'll get in my house over my dead body."

"She's bluffing," said one man with a scraggly beard.

"I guess we'll see about that." Sicily's gaze moved over Leroy's lackeys. It was odd how different these were and how emboldened they became in a group. But one alone never made threats like this.

"Yeah, show her how we handle her kind," said another. "She's just a woman."

Tate moved behind the knot of angry men. They glanced around nervously. A sudden explosion of gunfire rent the night air.

The pungent smell of gunpowder burned Sicily's nose, and no one had to tell her this took things to a new level from which there would be no turning back.

Chapter Nine

SICILY TRIED TO SWALLOW but the spit had dried in her mouth and her heart raced a hundred miles an hour. Focus, she told herself, straining to pierce the darkness and the smoke in search of the one who had fired the shot. She dearly prayed that it wasn't Tate. He was young but she thought he had more sense.

A voice rang out, "Everyone just hold your fire!"

Carrying a long gun in the crook of his arm, Sheriff Bledsoe strode through the gaggle of drunks to the bottom step of Sicily's porch. His voice was gruff and he seemed irritated to have to deal with this. "Care to explain what's going on here, ma'am?"

Tate moved up the porch to her side and his presence bolstered her.

She lowered her rifle. "Leroy beat poor Martha Ann half to death, and she came here for help. I washed the blood off and put her to bed."

"She wouldn't let me inside to see about my own damn wife," Leroy interrupted. "I want her arrested."

Sicily stiffened her spine. This could go two ways. She hoped to avoid a confrontation with Bledsoe, but she wasn't about to let him take Martha Ann. Exactly how to keep him from it, she didn't know but she'd fight with everything she had. "Martha Ann's not able to go anywhere, Sheriff. Half the bones in her body are broken. What's that kind of drunk going to do with her? He's trying to kill her and doing a good job of it, too."

Leroy tried to push his way past Bledsoe, but the sheriff grabbed his arm, yanking him back. "Go sit in the car."

"I want this witchy woman arrested and taken to jail. She tried to shoot me. Tried to shoot the whole lot of us." Leroy insisted.

Bledsoe gave him a shove. "Go to the car. The rest of you too. I'll handle this."

When they finally retreated to the Model A, Bledsoe turned to Sicily, his face carved of stone. "I want to see her."

Sicily's chin rose a notch. "You can look but I won't let you take her."

"You'd stop me?"

He towered over her by a good six inches, but she didn't back down. "However I have to. She's staying here for now."

Bledsoe pushed back his black hat, his eyes not seeming as hard. "I have to see her, Miz Sicily. You understand."

"I reckon I do." She stepped back. "Come on in, Sheriff."

He removed his hat, and she led him to the small bedroom where she put her rifle down. Martha Ann's swollen eyes were closed. Her face and arms were a mass of dark bruises.

"He broke her arm, Sheriff. And nose. Not sure what else. Could have internal injuries. I did what I had to do keeping Leroy out. No one should be allowed to beat anyone this bad."

Bledsoe gave her a nod, not speaking. He pulled the quilt aside for a moment before letting it fall back into place and turned. His voice dropped an octave. "I'll have a talk with Leroy and take him home. Lock your doors. I can't guarantee that he won't be back."

Couldn't and wouldn't. If Bledsoe had some backbone, he could lock his cousin up which he wasn't about to do. Pissants stuck together.

They walked toward the front door. "Thank you, Sheriff. Believe me, I will bolt my doors and windows but liquored up men like him..." she paused. "Sometimes nothing short of a bullet will stop them."

He jerked around. "I hope I won't have to be back to arrest you, Miz Rossi."

Sicily gave him a sweet smile. "I'm a law-abiding citizen. Always have been. Those lines we all draw are often mighty difficult to undraw." She raised her gaze to his and looked him in the eye just so he'd not mistake her words. "I plan to keep him out of my house by whatever means necessary. Goodnight, Sheriff. I won't hesitate to protect what's mine and I won't back down." She held the door for him, making the message clear his time was up. After he went through, she threw the bolt then leaned against it, her hands trembling.

Tate came from the kitchen area, his face troubled. "I hope that sheriff can make those bullies leave. I think they planned to do something real bad to all of us."

She put a hand on his shoulder. "I'll keep watch to see if they return since I'll be up anyway with Martha Ann. I'm sorry you had to see that but I'm really glad you're here."

"Me too, Miss Sicily. You probably could've handled it by yourself but I'm glad you didn't have to."

Gypsy scratched at the door where Tate slept.

Sicily smiled. "I think your little friend wants out. Thank you for putting her out of the way for the time being." A moan came from the bedroom. "My patient calls. Maybe I can get more tea down her. Check the doors and you go on to bed. Did you get your bag made like you want it?"

"Yes, ma'am." Tate smiled shyly.

"Good. You'll have to go by yourself to the woods tomorrow. You know what to look for though and I'll want you to gather a list of things."

"I don't know the plants that well."

"I'll show you what each looks like." The moans were gathering steam. She gave the boy a quick hug. "Now go get some sleep. I'll make sure you're safe."

"Goodnight, Miss Sicily."

They headed in different directions. In the bedroom, she found Martha Ann twisting in the sheets.

"Mama. Mama, I can't find you," Martha Ann cried through swollen lips. Her eyes appeared open in the tiny slits.

Sicily leaned close, pushing back the strands of hair. Her forehead was feverish. "I'm right here, child. I won't leave you."

Immediately, the woman settled. She had to be in tremendous pain. "Will you drink more tea?"

"Awful."

"I know but it helps with fever and pain. You need it. I'll put the water on and be right back."

The night passed slowly, measured in weak heartbeats and cups of tea. Each time she went to the kitchen, she checked the windows but saw no sign of Leroy, thank goodness.

Tate rose at dawn and dressed. The kitchen door squeaked as he went out to care for the livestock and feed the chickens. Such a good boy. Her heart swelled with pride as though he belonged to her.

When he brought the eggs in, he stopped in the bedroom. "How is she?" he asked.

"In pain and she has a fever. I've given her willow bark tea and other things to help. You and I will set her arm today and that'll be even more painful."

"Can it wait until she's a little better?" he asked, shifting the egg basket and blocking Gypsy from the room.

"Maybe. It'll start knitting back together in a week and we'll have to set it before then. Might be best pain-wise to get it all over with at once rather than have to put her through more agony later. I'll think about it."

"I'll fix mine and Gypsy's breakfast so you don't have to worry with that. I can cook eggs and we have plenty today. I'll cook you one too," he offered.

"Thank you, I'd like that." Sicily brushed a weary hand over gritty, tired eyes that had seen too much of the bad side of humanity.

"Will Miss Martha Ann want to eat, do you reckon?" Tate asked.

"Honey, I truly doubt she'll take a bite of food and I won't force it. If she wants something later, I'll fix it. But thank you for thinking of her."

He glanced at the woman on the bed. "I feel sorry for her, you know? It ain't right."

"No, it isn't." Sicily rested a hand on the girl's chest, thankful to find steady breathing.

Tate went out and softly closed the door then pans rattled in the kitchen. The boy was very capable, but then he'd lived on his own for so long and learned how to take care of himself. Self-sufficiency used to be taught at home but with fathers off looking for work and mothers stressed to get through each day, children weren't getting much direction anymore. She couldn't count the number of young ones left alone to fend for themselves these days.

Pushing away sadness, Sicily changed her clothes and combed her hair, all the while thinking about what she wanted Tate to gather. She'd need the bone-knit plant comfrey for sure. A lot of it to make into a salve and poultices. Nothing better for broken bones and swelling.

He'd just put two eggs on a plate for her when she entered the kitchen. "That smells good. I didn't realize I was hungry until you started cooking."

Gypsy girl did a little dance around Sicily's feet as though very happy to see her. The dog jumped into her lap and Sicily buried her face in the soft fur. She didn't mean to cry and tried to keep from it, but all of a sudden, a sob tore through her and the waterworks started. The stress of everything had become too much. Gypsy licked her hand and stayed still as though sensing Sicily needed her. A hand touched her shoulder and stayed there.

Moments passed in silence and when at last she looked up, Tate stood beside her, tears also filling his soft brown eyes.

He quietly handed her a dish towel to wipe her eyes and she achieved some semblance of her calm, orderly self. "Thank you, Tate. We're a fine mess, aren't we?"

The boy cleared his throat, pulled his hand from her shoulder, and stepped back. "I think the eggs have gotten cold. I can cook some more."

"They'll be fine. I'm not particular. But cook yourself another batch." She hugged Gypsy and the dog jumped down.

"I eat them cold just fine. Might still be a little warm. I sliced some bread." He sat and offered a short blessing.

Sicily pulled her plate closer and lifted a fork, taking a bite, grateful for the food. Too many people had nothing, so she wasn't about to waste anything.

Once they'd eaten, Tate did the dishes while she made a list of things for him to collect in the woods. "Be sure to get some comfrey," she said. "Do you remember what it looks like?"

"It has purple flowers on it I think."

"That's right. It's a little late in the year for the blooms but you should still see a few. I also need some of the roots." She sketched a picture of the prickly leaves. "I'm drawing it in case you don't find any still flowering."

"Yes, ma'am. I'll get it."

"Willow bark too. I think I'm running low." She finished her list about the time he dried his hands and folded the dishtowel.

In no time, he got his new bag, and she handed him the list as well as the drawing of the comfrey leaves. "Get what you can find of these. Some may have already died off until spring."

He nodded and stuck the paper into a shirt pocket then called to Gypsy. The pair went out the door, leaving the house quiet and still. Sicily sat there a moment in the silence before going to check on Martha Ann.

Her young friend was awake. She turned questioning eyes on Sicily.

"You might not remember much about last night but you came here. How, I don't know seeing the shape you were in. The way your knees are skinned, you might've crawled." She arranged the quilt. "Your nose and left arm are broken. We'll have to set the arm sometime today. I'll wait for Tate to return from gathering in the woods because it'll take two of us and I won't lie. It's going to hurt bad. Real bad. But it has to be done if you're ever to use it again."

Tears leaked out of the girl's swollen eyes. "Leroy—"

Sicily waited for her to complete her thought, but that was all she said. "I know. That man of yours came here rip-roaring drunk with friends. I wouldn't let him in." She smoothed back Martha Ann's hair and dabbed at the tears. "You're not going back there. He'll kill you. He almost finished the job last night."

"Water," Martha Ann croaked.

Filling a glass about half-way, Sicily raised her head and held it to her lips. "Go slow."

The girl took a few sips and Sicily laid her head back on the pillow. "I'll make some willow bark tea and maybe you can take a little food."

"No food," Martha Ann whispered, closing her eyes.

"That's probably a little soon but you do need the tea."

"Awful."

"I know, girl, but it'll help with the pain. You need it. Just rest and I'll be back."

Martha Ann said nothing but cried in pain as she tried to get comfortable.

The morning passed as Sicily tended her young friend and soon Tate returned, his bag filled with everything she'd requested.

"You did good, boy." Sicily beamed. "I'm going to turn you into a healer before you know it."

Tate grinned. "I like knowing what things can make a sick person better. And even what to do for a headache."

She unloaded the burlap sack. "The woods are full of plants that can treat just about everything. All you have to do is get out and look."

"My mother knew a little bit but not as much as you. When I used to get a sore throat, she made me drink some real bitter stuff, rubbed a salve on my throat and wrapped a warm cloth around it. It always made me feel better."

"Most folks do know some things. That's important with doctors few and far between."

Tate nodded and glanced toward the bedroom door. "How is Martha Ann?"

"She woke up and drank some water and tea. Mostly sleeping which is best. But, after we have a bite of lunch, I'll set her arm and I'll need you to hold her down."

They ate and Sicily ground the comfrey root to pack around the break that would harden with time a bit and keep the arm stable. True to her word, it took both of them to get the girl's arm back in place. Unable to take the horrible pain, Martha Ann lost consciousness and that was a pure blessing. They finished up in silence then let their patient rest.

"Miss Sicily, I'm going to move out to the barn so you'll have a place to sleep," Tate announced. "You can't rest sitting in a chair."

She studied his eyes and found caring there. His parents had done a good job of raising him. "That's very thoughtful, but I hate to put you outside."

"I don't mind." He gave her a flicker of a grin. "Besides, I'm thinking I need to keep watch. This way, it won't wake you when I go out."

The day crept along and that afternoon with two hours of sunlight left, they made a soft place for Tate to sleep in the barn. Sicily was relaxing on the porch, humming an old tune, when a rusted Model T puttered down the road. It stopped in front of the house. Stiffening, she picked up the rifle from beside her chair. She'd been expecting a visitor, so it was no surprise.

Leroy climbed out along with two buddies. All carried rifles. An empty liquor bottle rolled from the open car door, clattering to the dirt. They hadn't seen Sicily yet.

They'd only staggered a few steps when she got to her feet, bringing the rifle up. "That's far enough, boys."

The group jerked to a stop. "We come to fetch Martha Ann!" Leroy yelled. "B-bring her out and there won't be any t-trouble." He hiccuped.

"See, there's a problem with that. She isn't quite up to walking just yet." Sicily watched their hands and if they twitched a finger, she'd open up, drunks or not. "And even if she could, she wouldn't spit on you if you were on fire, Leroy Vaughn."

"You've p-poisoned her against me, old woman." He hiccupped loudly again.

"No, she's finally had enough," Sicily answered, seeing a reassuring shadow at the corner of the house. "You're so drunk you can't even talk. Now, get in that car and get off my land."

Fury lined Leroy's face and his fists clenched. "No damn woman is going to tell me what to do," he growled.

With his next step, Sicily aimed for his feet and the bullet kicked up dirt next to his boot. His buddies moved back but Leroy took another defiant step.

Tate moved into view, standing tall and looking every inch a man. He fired the Winchester, the bullet knocking Leroy's hat off. "I'm not a woman. Martha Ann is through with you and your kind so get used to it. Get gone and don't come back!"

The drunk trio stared. Sicily held her breath, praying they'd do the right thing. But with men in their condition, it might be a toss-up and could go either way. While they couldn't hit the broad side of a barn, they could get lucky. The air crackled with a dangerous current.

How to end this standoff without anyone dying.

"Don't do anything stupid, Leroy," she murmured to herself.

Chapter Ten

THE LATE AFTERNOON SUN reflected off the Model T windshield creating a circle on Sicily's porch. Leroy cussed a blue streak, fumbling with the rifle. Her eyes narrowed as the man dropped it. More curses spewed and a buddy picked it up for him. Finally, Leroy lifted it up, pointing it at her. The thing could go off any second.

Sicily readied to fire. She didn't want to shoot him, but she had to do something.

A sound reached her, gaining steam by the moment.

"Bringing in the sheaves, bringing in the sheaves," a group of men sang. "We shall come rejoicing, bringing in the sheaves. Sowing in the morning, sowing seeds of kindness, sowing in the noontide, and the dewy eve."

All eyes fastened on the trees where three men appeared in view, singing the old hymn. They stopped, glancing around. The leader came forward holding a Bible. "We were on our way to a revival and it seems we got lost." The shirt and trousers he wore were common for the area and nothing fancy by any means. But the clothing was a step above patched overalls that Leroy's group showed up in minus shirts.

The speaker with light-colored hair strode up to Sicily's porch as though they didn't have rifles pointed at each other. He removed a slouch hat. "Howdy, ma'am. I'm Reverend Stover. Is your soul right with God?"

"I reckon it is, Preacher." Sicily's gaze shifted to the men flanking Stover and found them focused on Leroy and his henchmen. They didn't just wander up. They came to help, and she was happy they did because they needed something to diffuse the situation.

Reverend Stover turned to Leroy. "Why would you want to shoot this good woman, son? I hear she's helped everyone in town when whatever sickness befalls. Folks are quite fond of Miss Sicily and wouldn't take kindly at all to you hurting her. You might think about that." A moment's silence passed. "Are you saved, young man?"

"If I wanted to go to ch-church, I'd damn sure go." Leroy started leaning sideways and his friends propped him up.

Sicily wanted to laugh but stopped herself. He made a pathetic drunk. But sober, he was as mean as the devil.

"You seem to be treading a rough sea there, Mr. Vaughn. Why don't you go home and sleep it off?" Stover said. "Then think about what you're doing."

One of Leroy's cronies yelled, "Why don't you mind your business!"

Stover turned to him. "Your wife and kids need you more than Leroy. God sent me to tell you to go home."

"Or what?" Leroy asked belligerently. "You ain't the law."

"That's true. My brother asked me to clean up the town a bit and turn to more godly ways. Maybe you haven't heard that he owns that sawmill where you work." The preacher paused, letting that sink in.

Why hadn't Sicily ever heard that Leroy worked at that lumber mill? She stored that tidbit away.

"I suggested to my brother that he start by employing more God-fearing men who treat their wives and others with respect." Stover moved closer to the threesome.

Maybe he was about to say something he made sure they needed to hear. Sicily noticed they'd begun to quiet down and watched the preacher nervously.

"It makes for a real nice town when people care about each other and band together as the good book teaches." Stover flipped open the Bible and Leroy and his lackeys jumped back like it might be a snake. "These are tough times. It makes for a real nice town when folks care about each other." He peered into their faces. "Don't you think that's a better way to live?"

Leroy put his hands on his hips and cocked his head to the side. "How come you know me? I ain't never seen you."

Sicily wondered too. She'd never heard of Reverend Stover. But then she didn't go to town often and when she did, she made quick work of it.

The reverend answered, "I haven't been here that long, but I've seen you around town, always shooting your mouth off or trying to scare some poor soul. Now, I hear you've put your sweet wife in a bad way. Progress is coming and people don't let bullies run roughshod over them anymore. I've seen it before when bad apples spoil things. The Lord catches up with them or a bullet does. Either way, no one sheds a tear over them, and no one even remembers them the next day."

The cronies behind Leroy began to fidget and looked down. The two men with Stover moved forward, watching them carefully. Now that she could see them better, she recognized Art the barber and Dan from the farm supply. Both carried rifles.

"I ain't here for any preaching. Don't want any either," Leroy snarled.

"Suit yourself." Stover swung around to Sicily. "Do you mind if I pray for Martha Ann?"

"I don't mind, preacher. She can use any pull you have with the good Lord."

"Thank you, ma'am, but He listens to every prayer. Mine don't carry any more weight than yours." Stover turned to the sullen threesome. "Where do you want to spend eternity, brothers?"

"Let's get outta here," Leroy's friend said, pulling on his arm. "I ain't gonna lose my job for you. I need that money."

Leroy collected his hat and the trio staggered to the car. Sicily breathed a relieved sigh as she held the door for Stover. Dan and Art waited on the porch with Tate as they watched the vehicle tear toward town.

Martha Ann didn't stir a muscle during Preacher Stover's visit but appeared to breathe easier. If only she knew how much a few people in town cared for her. And maybe they all did but were scared to show it.

Preacher Stover's face tightened with pain as he took in the girl's bruises. Tears filled his eyes. To Sicily, it was clear he truly cared for her. He knelt down, took Martha Ann's palm and offered a comforting prayer.

Afterward, Sicily escorted Stover out to the porch where Dan and Art waited. "Thank you all for coming," she said. "I wasn't sure how that was going to end. It's hard to predict drunk behavior."

"Miss Sicily, you would do the same for us," Dan answered. "And has."

"It was the least we could do for you and Martha Ann," Art added. "Maybe we haven't shown it much, but we are concerned. Folks are fed up with Leroy and we're ready to vote the sheriff out at the next election."

"Who's going to run against him?" she asked.

Dan chuckled. "Don't know yet but even the dog catcher would do a better job."

"Your help was much appreciated." Sicily put a hand on Dan's shoulder. "This would've ended a whole other way if you men hadn't come." Immense gratitude washed over her, stinging the back of her eyes. The shift in attitude was wonderful to see.

The men said goodbye and off they went.

"Do you think Leroy will leave us alone now, Miss Sicily?" Tate asked quietly. "Maybe he won't want to lose his job."

She patted his hand. "Time will tell, boy. I've given up trying to predict tomorrow. He may not even remember anything the preacher said. Rotgut whiskey has pickled that man's brain."

It didn't hurt to hope for change even though it would take a miracle. A leopard didn't change his spots. Ever. Deep in her gut, she had to plan for the worst.

THE NEXT WEEK FLEW BY with no sign of Leroy. Tate had gone to the woods alone each day and was becoming quite adept at identifying the plants but was still learning their uses. Martha Ann improved a little more with each sunrise. She still jumped at even the slightest noise but that would take time.

Saturday morning found her and Sicily sitting in the sun. Gypsy dozed between them. Tate was delivering some remedies in town, so it was just them. Martha Ann was recovering well and able to walk unassisted a little as long as something was nearby to hold onto if needed.

The woman tilted her face to the sun's rays. "This feels heavenly." A smile tilted one corner of her mouth. "Do you know how long it's been since I've enjoyed this kind of easy quiet?"

Sicily glanced at her. "I'm sure it's been a while."

"Before Leroy, it was my daddy. He was never happy and took it out on my mama and me because I was the oldest child." Martha Ann's forehead wrinkled in thought. "So I think I must've been just a child the last time I knew peace like this. Why do men always want to raise hell and hit?"

"I don't know, child. I was never married but my father was a kind man." Sicily realized that five nights had gone by without telling Jace Bonner's face in her locket goodnight and somehow it felt right. If they'd married, he might've turned out angry and mean like Leroy. Perhaps she was lucky. She had to forget him and move on, say goodbye to the past.

Sicily listened to the windchimes, loving the soothing sound. "It is nice. Leroy seems to have gotten the message and your trouble is over."

"Nothing ain't ever over with him," Martha Ann murmured low as though saying it louder would conjure him up.

She said it with such certainty that Sicily knew it for the truth. The little niggling in her head spoke of something dark and ugly waiting. They had to stay ready and not get lulled by the quiet. The train whistle blew in the distance, sending a message to stay on their toes.

A woman on foot appeared in the distance coming toward them. When she got closer, Sicily shaded her eyes. It looked like those of Mabel Bonner's housekeeper, Corrine Gray.

The housekeeper arrived out of breath. She appeared younger than her thirty-five years. It was the way she'd pulled her pretty blonde hair back from her face with simple combs that gave her the younger look. Sicily rose, offering a chair.

"I can't, ma'am. It's Miz Mabel. She's in a terrible bad way and wanted me to fetch you."

"What seems to be the problem? Didn't she go to a doctor in Woodville?"

Corrine nodded, her green eyes brimming with tears. "Yes, ma'am, she did. He told her she has a cancer growing inside that causes a lot of wrenching pain in her stomach."

Cancer was usually a death sentence. "I don't know what I can do except give her something for pain."

"Anything would be welcome, Miss Sicily. I fear she isn't long for this world."

"I'll get my bag." She picked up the rifle next to her chair and turned to Martha Ann. "Let's get you inside, dear."

Old Jessie nickered as the mule carrying Tate came into view. Good, it relieved her that the boy was back since it didn't pay to leave Martha Ann alone.

Tate reined to a stop and dismounted.

"I'm glad you're back." Sicily quickly filled him in on the situation. "I don't know how long I'll be gone so you'll have to guard the place."

"Yes, ma'am." He took the rifle from her. "I'll make sure she's safe."

Martha Ann gave a long sigh. "I hate to be so much trouble."

"Let me worry about that. This is what friends are for."

With Tate on one side and Sicily on the other, they got Martha Ann inside and settled in a chair. Tate took Sicily aside and talked low. "Albert said Leroy's got the moonshiner's girl living with him and she's bearing the brunt of his anger. Folks notice lots of bruises."

Where was the end to all this misery?

"Her father needs to step in. That's his duty." Sicily couldn't take on anything more. "Keep this between us for now."

"Understood."

She gathered her bag and filled it with jars and willow bark. "I'll have to ride the mule, so no need to unsaddle him."

Old Jessie carried Corrine and Sicily to Mabel's house and cries of agony came from the upstairs bedroom. With her bag of remedies in hand, Sicily followed the sound.

Mabel clutched Sicily's hand. "Please help ease this. I can't stand it."

"I'll do what I can," she assured the woman, patting her arm. The past mattered little when someone was dying.

Mabel licked her dry lips, her face feverish. "We've never been friends you and I but I'm begging you to help me."

"I'm not here to rehash the past. I'll make some willow bark tea and get started." Sicily nodded to Corrine beside the bed and went down to the kitchen.

An hour later, Mabel's face that was twisted in pain began to relax. However, it was clear that the end was near.

Mabel clutched Sicily's hand and spoke weakly. "I have something to tell you before I die, a secret I've kept. A confession."

Curiosity prickled Sicily's arm. "I'm listening."

"Bernice and I fostered a lie. My nephew Jace did not die. He's alive, living down in Beaumont." Mabel choked and began to cough.

Shock raced the length of Sicily's body and her heart pounded. "Alive?"

When the coughing passed, Mabel went on but her voice was very weak. "We paid for the lie. Bernice died a very painful death and now I am too. God is punishing us."

Her eyes closed and she pictured his handsome features on their last day together. By now, his sandy hair would have streaks of silver, but his eyes would sparkle and the cleft in his chin would deepen with a smile.

"I'll love you forever," he'd said long ago in his deep voice before kissing her.

They'd both known then on some level that forever would only be as long as his mother let him.

Tears filled Sicily's eyes. *Jace was alive.*

Chapter Eleven

H OW COULD IT BE? Sicily's head spun and her knees buckled as she collapsed on the edge of Mabel's bed. If Jace was alive, why hadn't he come in these forty years? Was he not the least bit curious about the life she'd made without him? Questions circled in her head like a flock of vultures looking for their next meal. Her mind went back to the brief letter she'd received from Mrs. Bernice Bonner six months following their breakup.

I regret the news I must tell you, the letter had read. *My Jace met with an accident, and it took his life. He's gone. I buried him in the Magnolia Cemetery.*

The blow had come out of nowhere and she'd never gone there to find his grave because the finality of that would've brought added pain to deal with.

"Mabel, I don't understand. Why did Mrs. Bonner, Bernice, go to the trouble? We'd called off the wedding," Sicily said, her voice sounding distant in her head.

The woman's weak words were hard to hear, and Sicily had to lean closer. "It was Bernice's idea. She knew Jace would never love another woman the way he loved you. You, my dear, held the power to ruin her plans for her son. He'd married a local girl that she handpicked but she knew you'd come and mess that up. See? Jace never got over you. Bernice swore me to secrecy, but I can't die with that on my conscience." A shudder ran through the woman, and she paused to gather the strength to finish. "You can find him in Beaumont on Remington Street, across from the Baptist church."

As though in a dream, Sicily rose and stared out the window at the dark shadows falling. Behind her, she could hear Corrine trying to coax some water down her employer.

Twenty-something miles separated them but Beaumont might as well be on the other side of the world.

The train could take you, a voice whispered.

No. She wouldn't seek him out. That part of her life was over. Done.

Bernice Bonner must've really feared her to do a thing like that. Questions swarmed like locusts. Secrets were like that—the why of it all. Sicily dragged air into her lungs. How was this revelation going to affect her? She trembled with anger, stung anew at how quickly he'd cast her aside.

Sicily stopped herself, flinging away angry tears. That was the thing—he hadn't wanted her enough to stand up to his mother. He was weak, spineless.

But the main question was, what did her heart say? Jace always let his mother run his life, not showing any strength of character forty years ago. Reality hit her. She liked the life she'd made for herself. What would she even say to him?

So many unanswered questions and she still wondered about the why of it all.

Mabel drifted in and out of sleep and revealed details of how Jace had married another woman. "His wife died not even two years into the marriage," she mumbled. "No offspring. Everyone needs children to look after them when they grow old. I wish I'd had some to care for me now." Tears ran out the sides of Mabel's eyes.

Sicily gently wiped them away. "You have friends."

"You're the lucky one, Sicily. Very lucky. Bernice would've made your life miserable. My sister knew how to do that." Mabel met Sicily's gaze. "She did to me what she did to you. She didn't like the man I was going to marry. I loved Mitchell so much and we made plans to marry." The woman struggled to talk, and her voice became weak. "But Bernice said he wasn't good enough and sent him packing. My sister killed everything she touched."

Poor Mabel. Sicily felt truly sorry for her. "Maybe you should rest a bit," she suggested.

"You were the lucky one, Sicily. My sister would've made sure Jace never loved you more than he did her."

Lucky? Yes, maybe she was. She surrounded herself with peace and beauty and her soul found contentment.

Mabel cleared her throat. "I married Harold, but I never loved him the same way. He had a mistress. I followed him once and saw her. I never told him, and I never mentioned her."

"How sad," Sicily murmured. She was right about Bernice.

A sudden thought turned her back to Jace. Did he get lonely? Did he say goodnight to her when he went to bed? She gave a soft snort. That was a flat no. The forty years since without nary a peep said he never gave her a thought.

Mabel tossed restlessly. "Money is its own cage," she mumbled. "I'm glad Bernice died. And Harold. I wouldn't want them here."

So Jace's mother was dead? Sicily couldn't dredge up any words of sympathy.

Mabel jerked awake, her eyes darting around the room. "Where are you, Sicily?"

"I'm right here." Sicily leaned over the woman so she could see her.

"I beg your forgiveness." Slender fingers grabbed at the air, finally finding Sicily. "Please forgive me so I can get release from this earth. I need that to set me free."

The clock in the room ticked loudly, breaking the silence. Time was slipping away but Sicily had it in her power to give Mabel a peaceful crossing.

"Sicily?" Mabel croaked.

Tears trickled down Sicily's cheeks. "I'm here. I forgive you. Go on and make your peace with God."

An hour later around midnight Mabel drew her final breath. Sicily and Corrine worked quietly, taking care of washing the remains and placing her in a freshly made bed. Sicily inhaled a deep breath. She'd done what was right and good. In freeing Mabel from the lie she'd kept, it had also freed her in a lot of ways. She'd grown as a person, becoming confident in herself and her abilities. It had also freed her to learn about plants and roots that went into the remedies she made that helped the sick. Yes, her life was full and interesting.

The two women went downstairs to the kitchen.

Corrine released a soft sigh. She was a pretty woman with soft blonde waves. Though Sicily knew she was around fifty, she'd aged gracefully and looked far younger. "That's all we can do tonight. Miss Mabel gave me all the instructions for her service, and I'll relay those to the preacher come daylight." She touched Sicily's arm. "How are you? What you did took a lot of strength. I didn't know the depths of Bernice and Miss Mabel's vengeance. You were very gracious to forgive my mistress."

"I'm fine. Nothing I learned tonight will change me one way or another." Sicily patted the hand on her arm and wearily sat down at the table. "I saw no reason to withhold absolution. That would make me no better than those two, and I learned a long time ago that holding grudges robs a body of living." She yawned and stretched. "If you don't need anything else, I'm going home."

They said goodbye and Sicily climbed on the mule. Guilt washed over her that she'd left the poor animal saddled all these hours, right by the door. But she hadn't expected to be there all night either. She was used to folk not wanting her to stay long. Although it was 1930, so many were anchored back in the hills and hollows where they came from, halfway believing her to be a witch who cast spells and put hexes on people. It had taken a long while to educate them and prove herself.

The homeplace looked peaceful in the early morning light with the sun filtering through the trees. It's times like this she could almost see her mother and father, hear their voices. She really missed them today and she guessed it was hearing that Jace Bonner was alive.

The shock had knocked her off her feet and she was still absorbing it in degrees.

Forty years ago, she was young and believed that love conquered all. The last decades had taught her that while love was important, human behavior often circumvented the best of intentions and purest of emotions.

The backdoor sounded and Tate bounded out grinning. "You're back."

"I didn't expect to stay there so long." She dismounted. "Is everything all right here?"

He stuck his hands in his back pockets. "We're fine. I've been looking out after Martha Ann and making sure she ate." He lowered his voice. "She disappeared for a bit in the afternoon and I don't know where she went. I left her on the bed napping and went outside to do some things."

Sicily paused, frowning, her hand on the burlap bag hanging from the saddle horn. "How long was she gone?"

"Beats me because I didn't know when she left. I reckon it was about an hour after I discovered her missing. I went out looking for her and when I got back, she was sitting at the kitchen table and swore I was mistaken about her leaving." He blew out a ragged breath of air and ran a hand through his hair. "I know I wasn't crazy."

"No, don't think that. She's used to having to sneak around and pretend she's one place when she was another." Sicily glanced at the house. "I'm just glad she came back."

"Me too. I didn't want to be the one to lose her."

She laid a hand on his arm. "You aren't responsible for her. Get that? Martha Ann makes her own choices. If she wanted to go somewhere, you couldn't stop her. Understand?"

"Yes, ma'am. I'm glad I didn't mess up."

"You couldn't if you tried." She gave him a smile. "Been up all night. Can you unsaddle Jessie and put him in the barn? I promised the poor old thing some oats to make up for leaving him saddled all night."

"I'll take care of him." Tate patted Jessie's withers. "What happened to your patient?"

"She passed on I'm afraid."

"That's too bad. I'm sorry."

"Thanks. Mabel was tired of living." Sicily had seen too many folks die because everything seemed so hopeless, and life filled with pain and suffering. "Did you and Martha Ann eat breakfast?"

"Yes, ma'am. I fixed it. She didn't eat much though."

"Okay." She went on to the house and got quite a welcome from Gypsy. The dog yipped, danced around, and wagged her little tail almost off. "You're a cute little mess." She rubbed the dog's ears affectionately.

Martha Ann looked up from the table. "Miss Sicily, I'm glad you're back. I missed you."

After giving Gypsy the proper attention, Sicily hung her burlap bag on its nail. "I'm glad to be home." She noted the girl's unkempt hair and the flour sack dress that hung on her thin frame. "Today, we're going to give you a bath and wash your hair. It's time to start living again."

With her staying most of the time in bed, Sicily had waited until she was better to give more than basic soap and water.

Martha Ann's lip trembled. "How do I do that? Where will I go…I mean when I leave here?"

The girl's eyes shone bright with tears, giving her a little lost puppy look. Sicily pulled her up into a hug, mindful of the broken arm. She held her for a long moment until Martha Ann's quivering stopped.

"After we clean you up, we're going to go to the woods. Now I know you can't walk that far yet, so you'll ride old Jessie. Breathing some good fresh air is the first step to living again." Sicily smoothed the girl's hair. "Would you like that?"

"Yes, ma'am." Martha Ann smiled. "Can you teach me a few things about the plants?"

"I'll be glad to. The woods are filled with wonderful things. When I'm troubled or worried about something, the quiet peace of the woods soothes my soul."

"I wish I could find that."

Though she was bone tired, Sicily attended to Martha Ann and soon had her looking much better. With her hair washed and combed, the young woman was very pretty.

Sicily gave her an admiring glance. "Much better. I never knew the true color of your hair. It's beautiful."

"You think so?"

"I certainly do."

"Leroy always told me I was homely and should be lucky he took me."

"Don't believe a word that man says. He only wants to hurt you and he's expert at knowing how."

"Thank you, ma'am. It's good to be really clean."

Nodding, Sicily glanced at the clock. Two hours left 'til noon. "Come, let's go to the woods then I'll sleep a while."

Tate saddled Jessie and they all followed the worn path into the woods with Gypsy girl leading the way. Sicily stopped now and then to show Martha Ann a particular plant or mushroom, sharing its uses for different things. The girl proved to be a good student and excited to learn. Not as much as Tate was but close.

One thing that struck Sicily was the girl's intelligence. She was extremely smart. She had to dumb herself down to be on Leroy's level. Another thing that struck Sicily was the girl was far more agile than she'd thought. At times Martha Ann forgot herself and took off walking just fine.

It's possible she did walk into town when Tate missed her. But why? That was the question.

By the time they returned home, the two women were exhausted. They ate a quick lunch and climbed into bed, leaving Tate to greet any callers.

It only took a second for sleep to claim Sicily. She had a crazy dream of Jace Bonner. He was riding a tall, white steed and wearing the clothing of a knight. He bowed low over her hand, kissing her palm. "Come away with me," he said quietly. "We're destined to be together."

Before she could speak, the dream switched to a garden, and she was planting vegetables alongside Leroy.

She woke up shaking her head. That was the strangest dream she'd ever had and was not ever gonna happen. She looked in on Martha Ann and found the battered girl still napping. She poured a glass of water and stepped out onto the porch. It was no surprise to find Albert entertaining Tate. The boy seemed to enjoy it, judging by the laughter. The man was quite an embellisher and swapped ends with the truth on a regular basis.

Albert heard the door and looked up. "Miz Sicily, I brung news from town. Mabel's funeral is set in two days on Thursday at the Baptist Church."

That seemed rather quick but why dally? Better to get it over with. Mabel had no relatives except Jace and he wouldn't be coming from Beaumont.

"I appreciate you letting me know." She sat down next to Tate. "I doubt too many will come. She wasn't too popular with her blunt talk and demanding ways."

"You never know about these things." Albert folded his hands in front of him. "There's something else that will interest you."

"You might as well tell me before you bust a gut." Sicily made herself comfortable.

The man craned his skinny neck at the door. "My neighbor Francine said she thought she caught a glimpse of Martha Ann in town. She was wearing a large hat and hid her face, but Francine swears it was her. Course, she can only half see and can't hear anything."

It was becoming pretty clear that Martha Ann had gone into town. Curiosity rose.

Before he could take a good breath, Albert continued, crossing his legs. "That young gal that Leroy moved in is now gone. Her daddy got mad at all the bruises on his daughter and threw a gasket. There was a mighty big ruckus at Leroy's and Bobby Earl pulled a gun. Came near to putting Leroy six feet under. Too bad he missed."

"You are full of news all right," Sicily said. "Tate, are you keeping up with all this?"

"I'm trying but it's hard. I think I need to write it down."

Albert blew his nose on a large handkerchief. "My friend Amos told me Leroy's boss at the lumber mill warned him that the next time he comes in drunk, he's fired. They're fixin' to lower the boom on him."

Now that would work Leroy into a tizzy.

An uneasy quiet settled over Sicily and she swore the breeze, the birds, and her breathing stopped. This meant the man would renew his efforts at getting Martha Ann home. She was going to have to rush her plan. The urge to hurry pounded in her head.

As God was her witness, Leroy would never get another chance to kill the sweet young girl. They'd move her as soon as she woke up.

Chapter Twelve

SICILY WONDERED IF ALBERT was ever going to wind down. Each time she thought he'd reached the end he started back up again and rattled nerves that were already shot. However, to be generous he had shed some light on Martha Ann's mysterious disappearance and keeping her up to date on Leroy proved helpful. Still, enough was enough.

Sounds in the kitchen came from inside the house indicating the girl was up. Gypsy went to the door and whined. Tate rose to let the dog inside then he returned to sit down.

"Well, I'm glad you stopped by, Albert." Sicily gave him a pointed stare.

"Miz Sicily, now don't rush me. I ain't gotten to Mabel's dying yet. What do you think she'll do with that big house and all her money?"

"Albert, that's none of my concern and it shouldn't be yours either," Sicily scolded.

Refusing to heed her chiding, Albert leaned forward, his hands on his knees. "Folks in town said Mabel left everything to the housekeeper. What's her name? I clean forgot."

"Corrine."

"That's right." His face brightened. "I heard Mabel left her that big house and everything in it. What do you suppose Nadine'll do with it?"

Sicily grabbed a broom and began sweeping all around his chair. "It's none of our business. Lift your feet. And it's Corrine, you old fool. Corrine."

"That's what I said. Josephine. A pretty thing and still in the bloom of life."

What was the use? Albert couldn't hear and couldn't find his rear with both hands.

"Why are you so interested in Corrine?" Tate asked.

Sicily stayed busy with the broom and even swept under his feet a second time.

"Why, I'm thinking of asking her to marry me." Albert chuckled. "She'd get a good deal. I probably won't live too much longer anyway, and I need a woman to take care of me."

"You'll outlive all of us, you old codger." Sicily turned at the sound of the door. Martha Ann came out, pushing back her hair. Sicily put the broom in a corner and asked, "Albert, don't you need to get back to town?"

He gave her a blank look. "Well, it's a mite early yet. You got the porch spic and span I got to say." He glanced at Martha Ann. "You're looking better. How's your arm?"

"It's fine," she mumbled. "Miss Sicily, I thought I heard you say we have some things to take care of this afternoon."

Sicily could've kissed her. "That's right dear. Yes, we have lots to do before night. Albert, I'm sorry but we can't sit here entertaining you. And Tate can't either. You'll have to come back another day." She thrust his hat in his chest and Tate took his arm.

"I reckon I'll be going then." Albert got his long walking stick and shakily navigated the steps off the wide porch.

Tate put a steadying hand on Albert's arm, helping the old man and his creaky bones to safer ground.

She waved him down the road. When it was safe, she turned to Martha Ann. "Albert said the moonshiner saw bruises on his daughter and took her out of Leroy's house. Plus, he's gotten a warning at the mill about drinking and they're about to fire him."

The color left Martha Ann's face and her hand trembled as she looked around. "Oh no! He'll be blood-boiling mad. I gotta go."

"Yes, you do, and we have a hidden spot in the woods where you'll be safe. I'll gather some supplies for you, and Tate and I will take you there. I have a bad feeling about Leroy."

"Yes, ma'am. He'll be fit to be tied all right." Martha Ann's eyes widened, and she put her hand over her mouth. "He can't catch me here. Oh God. I wish I'd found a way to kill him so he can't hurt anyone else. And now I only have one good arm."

"Take a deep breath," Sicily said. "He'll not find you."

Within the hour, they were heading into the woods with Martha Ann on the mule. They showed her the path and marked it with signs so she could find her way out if she needed to.

Once there, Tate showed her where everything was while Sicily made her a nice bed on some fresh hay.

"You'll have enough food for a few days." Sicily gave her a hug. "We'll bring more and leave it inside that hollow trunk by the creek a ways back. I'll let you know what's happening and you can leave us a note that you're all right."

Tears bubbled in Martha Ann's eyes and her lip quivered. "I can never repay you. Do you care if I call you Mama Sicily? Please. It would mean so much."

"Honey, you can call me anything you like. I'm glad you think that much of me." The request deeply touched her.

"Yes, ma'am. You're more like a mother than my own." She cleared her throat. "Just watch out for Leroy. I don't want him to hurt you or Tate."

"I won't let him." Sicily glanced at the slice of sky through the trees. "We need to get back now. You'll be safe here. Light a candle when it gets dark and close the door to keep the animals out."

"I'm not afraid of animals or the dark."

"Good." Sicily hugged the girl again and pulled some small canvases and paint out of her bag. "To occupy your time. There's not much you can do with one arm, but I think you can manage to paint pictures. Remember, I'm not too far away."

Martha Ann's smile widened. "You think of everything, Mama Sicily. I used to paint before I got married and I always found it relaxing. Maybe I'll paint you a picture."

They said goodbye and she and Tate left. Relief washed over her, and her heart was lighter that she was giving Martha Ann a chance to live free of abuse.

THAT EVENING, SHE WAS RELAXING by the fire with Gypsy in her lap and Tate was stretched out on the floor with his books when she heard a motor.

Boots sounded on the porch and a heavy fist pounded on the door. "Martha Ann! I'm tired of fooling around!" Leroy shouted. "Get your sorry butt home where you belong!"

Gypsy jumped down with a growl and clawed at the door, barking her head off.

Tate sat up, closing his books. He got to his feet.

Sicily inhaled a big breath of air. "Here we go." She went to the door empty handed. If she needed a gun, it was next to the fireplace and easy to reach.

"It's late to be out calling," she said, opening the door.

For once, he was stone cold sober, which brought even more nerves.

"I've come for Martha Ann." He glanced around Sicily. "I'm taking her back home."

"I'm sorry, Leroy, but she's not here." She had to tread carefully here. The sober Leroy was much scarier than the drunk one. This one could murder without batting an eye.

"What do you mean? Where the hell did she go?" He brushed past Sicily and came inside only to have Tate stop him with a hand on his chest. Gypsy released a vicious snarl and bit at his ankles.

"Get out of my way, boy!" Leroy grabbed Tate's shirt and drew back to hit him.

Gypsy went berserk, biting at Leroy's legs.

Sicily's voice grated out, low and deadly. "Hit that boy and it'll be last thing you ever do. Now turn him loose."

Surprise swept Leroy's face and he must've known she meant every word. He dropped his hold and stood back. "I'm going to find my wife one way or another."

"Look your fill. I won't stop you. But I told you she's not here." Sicily swept her arm wide, inviting him to search. "Go ahead. Look all you want."

Leroy tore through the rooms like a crazed man, hollering for his wife.

When he stopped in front of Sicily again, she asked him, "Satisfied?"

"She's gotta be out in the barn. I know she's here somewhere." He raced outside.

Tate glanced at her, whispering, "I'm glad she's not here."

"Me too."

Leroy returned from his search, much calmer but deadlier. "Witchy woman, better tell me where my wife went," he growled.

The unspoken threat in his low voice was unmistakable. A warning zigzagged up her spine.

Sicily wet her lips and tried not to show her fear. "You know, she was feeling kinda homesick. She didn't say where she was going though. Have you checked the trains? She might've gone home to see her folks. Better start there."

He snorted. "Do you think I can drive clear over to Deweyville?"

She stared at him. "I don't know, Leroy. If you want her bad enough, I guess you might."

His eyes wide, he glanced around the room. "Did you put a hex on me?"

The quiet question caught Sicily off guard. "I don't deal in hexes. I'm more in the doctoring business. I don't practice voodoo."

"You must. Everything is going wrong." He ran a hand over his bloodshot eyes. He didn't appear to be sleeping much. There was a dangerous light in his face that she hadn't seen before. His raspy breathing filled the room. "If you hear from her, tell her I need her home. If not, there'll be hell to pay when I find her."

"I don't expect to ever see her again, but I'll give her the message if I do." Her heart racing, she watched his expression and the creepy smile that slowly formed terrified her.

"Goodnight." She held the door for him and once he was out, she shut and bolted it.

Tate moved the curtains aside just a tiny bit to look out. They heard the car start and breathed easier as it went toward town.

"Oh my!" Sicily dropped into a chair. "I didn't know what he was going to do." His behavior was typical for someone who was losing everything but trying desperately to hold on.

Desperate and filled with rage.

Served the louse right after what he'd done. Hexes? He was sure superstitious. If she knew one, she might use it on him.

"Tate, let's move you back in the house. I don't like you being out in the barn by yourself."

He looked relieved. "If that's what you think best, Miss Sicily. I'll go get my things."

THE NEXT TWO DAYS AND NIGHTS were peaceful with no sign of Leroy. On Wednesday, they went for their daily walk in the woods and took more food for Martha Ann.

Tate ran ahead and pulled a note out of the hollow tree stump, waving it. Sicily hurried to him. "Read it."

Doing fine. Love it here. So quiet. But I miss you.

"That's good." Sicily had hoped the girl would be happy living here for a bit. She took paper and pencil from her pocket and wrote a reply, telling her about Leroy coming and that it was too dangerous to come out. But soon, Sicily promised. *I have a plan,* she wrote.

She handed the note to Tate. "Put the food in there with the note and let's move away from here."

To tarry with the food could cost them if anyone had followed. She imagined Leroy was still watching when he wasn't at work. In any event, it was better to be safe than sorry. Besides, Mabel's funeral was that afternoon and she didn't really want to go but felt like she had to for Corrine's sake. The woman had been so distraught over her mistress's death. If it was true and Mabel did leave her the house and money, she'd need a friend. Everyone she ever knew would be hounding her for a piece of that good fortune.

They went home and had lunch then Sicily changed to a better dress and left Tate there to keep watch. Folks were filling the church when she arrived, so she slipped into a seat near the back. Mabel must've had more friends than she knew.

Preacher Stover led the service, and it was nice. He seemed very caring, and her thoughts went back to the night he and the other two men from town appeared to send Leroy home. She hadn't seen him since. But she knew he was watching Leroy and took comfort in that.

The funeral was over in short order, and she stood for Corrine as she followed the casket out. But the tall gentleman walking beside the housekeeper looked familiar. The distinguished bearing and handsome features sent her memory roaring back along with a sick whirl in her stomach.

Jace Bonner.

She looked for an escape route but there was none except straight ahead through the open doors. She'd almost made it when Iris Russell stopped her.

"Miss Sicily, I just love the remedy I got from you for my arthritis. It's helped tremendously." Iris waved to a friend. "But I'm needing more. I can come get it tomorrow."

"That'll be fine, Iris. I'm glad it's helping." Sicily turned her attention back to escaping unnoticed, but the throng made it impossible to turn back. It swept her along toward the doors.

Suddenly, she stared up into the face that had occupied many of her dreams and her tongue seemed glued to the roof of her mouth.

"Sicily, I was hoping I'd see you today." He took her hand in his, those mesmerizing gray eyes staring into hers. His deep voice sent a quiver up her spine. "You're as pretty as ever. I've missed you."

"Jace, I just heard you were alive from Mabel before she passed." Sicily crooked her head to one side, staring. "You look good for a dead man."

He winced, color creeping into his face. "That wasn't my doing and I knew nothing about it until my mother confessed before she died. That was a despicable thing to do and I'm ashamed of her."

She shrugged and gently pulled her hand free. "Everyone makes decisions—your mother, you, me. Then we have to live with our choices. Sometimes that's the difficult part."

He rubbed the back of his neck, his gaze lingering on her. "True, and I've sure had to live with mine. Why is it we hurt the ones most that we love? I know I caused you immense hurt and I'm very sorry. I stayed away because I didn't know how to fix it. Will you forgive me?"

He was sincere, no doubt about that. But it didn't erase his actions. He'd known she was alive but did nothing to find her. Not once in forty years. She couldn't get past that.

"Nothing to forgive. We're living the lives we were supposed to and I'm very content. It's far too late to turn back." She glanced around at the crowd, knowing most came out of curiosity and to try to get in Corrine's good graces before they hit her up for money. "When are you going back?" she asked.

"Tomorrow or the next day. I have some things to do for my aunt." He paused, holding his hat in his hands. "Do you suppose I could come see you? I'd like to see where you live and these remedies you make from plants and roots in the woods. My aunt told me about you."

"I see." She smiled and waved to a friend. "If you have time drop by. I can't guarantee I'll be there though. I spend most mornings in the woods." She spied Albert alone with Corrine and groaned. "I'm sorry, I need to rescue Corrine."

"That's fine. I have to get to the cemetery anyway. I'll see you again before I leave."

He walked toward a Model A and got in. Her knees still shook at the unexpected encounter. She never thought in a million years that he'd come. And now that he had, what did it mean for her?

One thing she did know. This surprise meeting wouldn't change her life one way or another.

Chapter Thirteen

Sicily had almost made it to Corrine and Albert when she heard him say, "Miz Corrine, would you marry me?"

"What?" Corrine asked, shock on the poor woman's face.

"Albert, there you are." Sicily was a little out of breath after coming face to face with Jace. "I've been looking for you."

Albert had spit combed his hair, parted it in the middle, and wore his best overalls. "Not now. I'm busy." He shooed her away with a hand and moved to block her progress. "Miss Corrine and I have important things to discuss."

She linked her arm through his. "I want to get your ideas for that community garden we're planning."

"A community garden?" Corrine's eyes sparkled with interest. "Where?"

"On the corner of Poplar and Elm. It's perfect. I'm trying to figure out who owns it."

Beside her, Albert fidgeted and fumed. "You can yak about that another time. It's my turn. Go mind your beeswax."

But Corrine went on as though she didn't hear him. "I think that lot belonged to Mabel. I'll have to make sure it's the same one you're talking about but if so, it now belongs to me. Mabel kept that lot in town even though she didn't do anything with it. I think maybe she forgot about it since it wasn't close to her house."

"Oh, Corrine, that's wonderful. Do you have any plans for that land?"

Albert yanked his arm from Sicily. "I was here first. You just wait your turn."

Corrine hid a grin. "Albert, I'm flattered that you think of me as a wife but I'm not looking for a husband. No, thank you. What you're needing is a nurse and I'm not that either." She turned to Sicily. "Let's talk later about that land. I'm very interested."

"Yes, it can wait." Sicily patted Corrine's shoulder. "You have to get Mabel in the ground and the funeral director is looking over this way."

"I've got to go. Albert, Sicily, we'll talk more in the coming days." Corrine hurried across the church yard to the hearse.

Preacher Stover appeared at Sicily's side. "It's a beautiful day for a send-off."

"Yes, it is. That was a lovely service."

Albert stalked off muttering, "She ruined it. She ruins everything."

Stover stared after the disgruntled man. "Was he talking to you or me?"

"Me, I'm afraid. I did ruin his plans, but someone had to rescue poor Corrine. He was making a fool of himself, proposing marriage to the new heiress."

"I'm sure he'll get over it. He doesn't appear to be in the best shape to take on a wife."

"That's true but it doesn't stop Albert. He proposes to every woman who crosses his path."

"I've heard that. Such a strange man." He chuckled low. "How are things at your place these days, Miss Sicily?"

"Can't complain. Leroy left us alone for about a week but he's now back looking for his wife. I have a good idea that he won't be a problem for much longer."

"Now, Miss Sicily, I hope that's just wishful thinking."

"You never know."

They parted ways and Sicily began the walk home. Her thoughts were in a turmoil, twisting around in her head. While Jace was charming and very nice, his appearance unleashed a hundred memories that she'd spent forty years trying to bury. And thought she had. But now he was back from the dead as it were.

One particular memory took hold and burrowed inside her head. He'd shown up with flowers in her classroom at the small school where she'd taught. His eyes had twinkled with mischief as he presented them to her with a flourish in front of her students. He knew such a display made her want to sink through the floor. But that was the first time she'd seen love shining in his eyes.

She couldn't deny his charm. He'd had that in spades. Still did.

And now he was driving out to see her tomorrow. Why? Was it simply a friendly visit? Or was it more? Did she want it to be more?

Before she could address that, Gypsy saw her coming and raced to meet her. Sicily scooped up the little dog and buried her face in the wiggling fur ball.

"Hey, girl, did you miss me? Just between us, I wish I'd stayed home."

Gypsy yipped and licked her face. She carried the dog the rest of the way.

Tate stood and met them. "How was it?"

"Okay as far as funerals go. Lord, I'm tired." She sat down in the shade of the porch and Gypsy hopped off her lap to go chase a red leaf tumbling across the yard in the breeze.

"I'll get you some iced tea," Tate said, going into the house. He returned, handing her a glass.

She thanked him and took a sip. "I don't think we'll be bothered with Albert for a while. He's mad at me."

"What did you do?"

"I interrupted his proposal of marriage to Corrine. The man was furious. Why he thought a funeral was the right place, beats me."

"He'll get over it as soon as he starts to hurt."

"You're so right." She glanced over her neatly kept yard and beautiful trees along the boundary line. "I'm proud of this place," she said. "I've made a good life for myself."

"Who wants to argue with you?" Tate threw a stick for Gypsy to fetch.

"Maybe no one. At least not yet. We're going to have a visitor tomorrow and I guess I'm getting prepared." She released a sigh. "The caller is Jace Bonner, Mabel's nephew. I knew him a long time ago." She glanced over at Tate. "We were set to marry, but his mother stopped it, and he didn't have the gumption to go against her which led to us parting ways."

"You haven't seen him in all these years?"

"Forty to be exact and no, today is the first time since then. I was told he'd died."

"Does it make you nervous?" He threw another stick.

"A little I guess because I don't know what he wants."

"If you want, we can go hide out in the woods all day."

Sicily laughed. "Tempting, but no. This is something I can't hide from."

"You can always consider it."

"I do need to go look for some henbane and ginger root tomorrow. Iris Russell needs some tincture and I'm out." She rose. "I need to change and make use of the rest of the daylight." There would be time later to worry about Jace Bonner's visit.

THE MORNING DAWNED UNDER a gray sky that quickly changed to sunny by noon. Sicily and Tate had to wear light coats for their walk in the woods. The wind had a definite chill. November was on their doorstep. It had been two weeks since Martha Ann came. Didn't seem possible. They stayed longer than usual because of the peace it brought. Tate spied some goldenrod and tall rattlesnake root.

"I even know their names," he told her.

She smiled. "Let's hear it."

After he identified them correctly, she patted him on the back. "You're going to make a fine healer if that's what you want."

"I do. I want to make people well like you, Miss Sicily."

That pleased her to no end. Her thoughts went to Jace, and she imagined what kind of life she would've had as his wife. Miserable. She murmured to herself, "This is where I belong."

Her peace lasted until mid-afternoon when Jace drove up and got out. Her knees turned to jelly. He still had that effect on her after all these years. Or maybe it was the black Stetson he had on that added to his good looks.

Jace smiled wide. "Sicily, I hope I'm not interrupting any-thing. You must keep very busy."

"I do but I set aside time for your visit." She pulled Tate forward. "I want you to meet a very special young man. This is Tate. We sort of found each other."

Gypsy scampered around them, stopping to sniff Jace's pant legs.

He picked the dog up, rubbing her ears then stuck out a hand to Tate. "Jace Bonner. It's nice to meet you, Tate. I'm sure you're a big help to Sicily."

"Yes, sir. She's teaching me about plants and stuff that grows in the woods. I like learning."

"Then I hope you stay with her," Jace answered, putting Gypsy down.

"Would you like to see the place?" Sicily asked.

"I can't wait. Everything is very well-kept. But then you were always orderly as a school marm. Do you miss your students?"

"Sometimes, although I'm now teaching Tate." She patted the boy's shoulder. "He's a little behind in his studies but a fast learner, though, so it won't take him long to catch up."

"I like knowing things." Tate tossed a stick for Gypsy. "Go ahead and take Mr. Bonner around. I'll wait here in case someone comes for any of your tonics and things."

"Thank you, Tate." Sicily swung to Jace. "Are you ready?"

"Lead the way." He fell into step with her. "This was your folks' place if I'm not mistaken."

"That's right. My dad bought the land way back when he married my mother."

"How many acres do you have?"

"Ten. It's plenty for me to take care of. What do you do, Jace?"

"I bought a ranch outside of Beaumont and run some cattle. I also kept a house in town." He scanned the chickens, barn, and other outbuildings, nodding. "Nice."

So he was a rancher which explained the black Stetson and deep tan. A cowboy stayed outdoors a lot. She could see him gravitating to something like that to escape town—and his mother.

Sicily opened the door to a shed. "This is where I dry various plants I collect from the woods."

He stepped inside to look at the rows of plants hanging from a low beam and spread out on the tables. "You have a great operation here."

"I do okay, and it makes me happy to help so many people with their ailments." She touched the goldenrod Tate had found that morning. "I don't make much. Folks trade with whatever they have. Sometimes it's a chicken or something they grow but mostly they have nothing. This country is in pitiful shape and people are starving."

"That's the truth. Miss Corrine was telling me last night that you have a plan for some kind of community garden in town on an empty lot that belonged to Aunt Mabel."

"I do and I'm itching to get started. We can put in a winter garden that can help a lot of people. Then in the spring we can go bigger, encompassing an entire lot."

"That's a good plan. Have you thought of where you'll get the seeds?"

"I hope I can work out some kind of deal with Dan at the farm supply."

Jace met her gaze. "I'd like to help. Will you accept a donation?"

"I won't turn anything down, but you don't have to. I'll find a way." She studied his eyes and saw his interest.

"I've seen the same need in Beaumont and a garden like this will feed a lot of starving people." He took her hand and squeezed it. "I want to help you succeed."

Sicily pulled her hand back and they walked a short distance into the woods, finding a seat on a log. It was nice to see him after such a long time but the feelings she once had for him were gone. Old folks had a saying that you could never go back, and she saw the wisdom in that.

"I have a lot I want to say. I just never thought I'd get the chance." His voice deepened. "I know I hurt you very badly and I'm sorry for that. Sorry that I let my mother ruin our plans. I loved you then and I still love you now. I never stopped."

"But why did you say you didn't love me anymore?" she whispered, an ache for all they'd lost filling her. This was something no plants, roots, or jars of remedy could fix.

"I couldn't let my mother destroy you as she vowed to do. I had to shield you from her vicious jealousy that took over." He dragged air into his lungs. "I watched her helplessly as she destroyed my father, and I couldn't let her do that to you. I loved you too much."

Suddenly weary of rehashing the past, Sicily got to her feet, arms crossed. She stared at him. "There had to be a better way, Jace. Lying to me wasn't right and it still isn't."

He shook his head. "Night after night I looked at it from every angle and couldn't find an answer. There was no way to get my mother out of our lives. I even fantasized about running away with you and going somewhere but she'd have found us. And I would've left with nothing. I wasn't strong enough back then to live without money." He got to his feet and stood close, tucking a strand of hair behind her ear. "You were so beautiful and sweet. I couldn't watch your love eventually turn to hate as it would've."

She turned away, unable to believe his pitiful excuses and actions that had destroyed her. "But we could've tried." If he'd found the strength to follow his heart. Only he hadn't.

"For how long?" he asked gently. "And then what? Divorce? Believe me, you would've been hurt far worse."

Sicily picked a ladybug off her sleeve and let it fly away. "I loved you, Jace, and I wanted to spend my life at your side."

"I know. What we had was special. I was so proud of you. Sometimes I'd go to the school and listen at an open window. No one had your kindness and skill at shaping young minds." Jace took her hands. "Is it too late for us? Do you think we can try again?"

There it was. She had the marriage, a handsome husband, she'd yearned for in her hands. Thoughts swarmed of Tate and Martha Ann, not to mention the people in town that depended on her. What would they do if she up and moved to Jace's ranch? She'd have to give up her community garden idea. Give up this plot of land that she loved and her woods that sustained her spirit. The list of what she'd give up was longer than the gains.

The pull of him wasn't nearly as strong as she'd expected it would be. There was no desire, no appeal left.

"Jace, I can't. I've made a good life here for myself and I don't want to give it up. All I can offer is friendship and I hope you accept that."

He paused for a moment, staring at his hands. "I will treasure your friendship and I understand. Timing is everything. The window has closed. Still, I had to ask." He gently kissed her cheek, squeezing her fingers. "You're a special woman, Sicily. As beautiful as the day I met you."

She chuckled. "Except for all the wrinkles and saggy skin."

"I see none of that when I look at you. I see the young school-teacher with stars in her eyes and a need to help others." He paused. "Can I kiss you? Just once more."

At her nod, he took her in his arms and placed his lips on hers. The kiss took her back in time when she thought life was perfect and love healed all things.

Sicily thrust a hand in his hair and found it exactly as she remembered. His breathing became rough and uneven. The kiss was nice, but it seemed very sad. Maybe because they were saying goodbye to the past. She had no regrets about her decision. They were friends. Nothing more.

She'd lived a good life since and, while romantic love was truly glorious, it wasn't the only thing to fulfill a person.

They broke apart and she glanced at the woods she loved. This was where she belonged and here she'd remain. She'd felt it in her bones as soon as she'd told him no. If this wasn't confirmation from her heart, she didn't know what was.

Chapter Fourteen

Jace's absence spread a blanket of relief over Sicily's heart. While her mind had always wondered "what if" all those years, the reality of what it might have been like to be his wife seemed much less appealing now. She had been honest with him today, and thought he was honest with her. They both deserved that at the very least. Now she could let go of those old dreams, happy in the life she'd made here for herself.

Jace's fervent kiss swept into her thoughts. If he'd caught her in a moment of weakness, that might've convinced her to try marriage. His lips had settled on hers so tender and sweet. In all these years, he hadn't forgotten how to kiss. But maybe he got practice with another. Just because he hadn't married, didn't mean he wasn't seeing someone. She hoped he was. Despite that it hadn't worked out for them, maybe there was a nice woman in Beaumont to ply kisses on.

A cowboy. He'd sure looked handsome in that black Stetson.

She and Tate dove into making the remedy for Iris Russell, finding enjoyment in the task.

After a while, Tate broke the silence. "Miss Sicily, I liked Mr. Bonner. He was nice and he seems to be right fond of you."

"He was at one time and I of him." She stirred the various juices and pulp together. "It's strange how life makes you think it's going one way only to suddenly turn and you're swept another."

"Do you think you'll marry him now?" Worry lined Tate's face. "I mean, maybe me and Gypsy should go back to the woods."

Of course, he'd be worried about this tenuous situation. Sicily would have to reassure him.

But before she could, Gypsy got to her feet at hearing her name and whined. The dog had gotten drowsy watching them and closed her eyes. Now, she was wide awake and wanting to be noticed.

"I'll play with you in a minute, Gypsy," Tate said rather irritably which wasn't like him. "Wait 'til I get finished."

All of this talk of an old love and such seemed to be bothering the boy.

Sicily stopped what she was doing and laid down her spoon, facing him. "Son, stop worrying. I'm not going anywhere or marrying anyone and don't mention going back to live in the woods. Ever. This is your home now. Understand?" When he nodded, she continued. "There will not be a wedding, nor will I leave here by my own free will. This is my home and I love what I'm doing. Jace

Bonner understands that clearly as well as the fact that a friend is all I'll ever be. That part of my life is over."

The worry lines vanished from Tate's face, and he smiled. "I only want you to be happy, Miss Sicily. I can go wherever. Shoot, I'm used to just drifting around."

"I am very happy with our arrangement and you're staying." She glanced at Gypsy. "I can finish up here. Go play with her before it gets dark."

Soft laughter bubbled as she watched the boy and his dog romping and playing. Tate little resembled the young man who'd held the shotgun with such ease and would've shot Leroy if he'd have hurt Sicily. She turned back to a second vial and filled it from a different pan then slipped the vial into her pocket before Tate returned.

I have a good suspicion that Leroy won't be a problem for much longer.

The statement she'd made to the preacher reverberated in Sicily's head. She shouldn't have voiced that thought out loud and didn't think she had, but there was nothing to be done about it now. She screwed the lid on the jar of Iris's remedy and removed her apron, hanging it on a nail. Thoughts turned to Martha Ann as she closed the door to the drying shed and went into the kitchen.

Not long after, she and Tate sat enjoying turnips grown just a few feet from her backdoor and carrots stewed to perfection. The root vegetables tasted so sweet after the first frost.

"I'll have to take Iris Russell's remedy by her house in a bit," she announced over supper. "I won't be gone long."

"I'll take it, ma'am. There's no use in you getting out," Tate answered.

"Thank you but I really need to do this myself if you don't mind."

They finished and she put on a coat and hurried out to the barn, leaving Tate with the few dishes. She saddled the mule and took off toward town, her thoughts on the chore ahead. The pink and purple dusk gave way to nightfall. A half-moon was peeking over the trees to light her way and she said a prayer.

A falling star streaked across the sky, leaving a trail. Sicily took that as a sign she was doing the right thing.

When she arrived at the Russell home, Iris answered her knock. She was a nervous woman by nature and clasping her hands together at her reed-thin waist. "Come in and I'll pay you. I had a little bit left after selling my eggs."

Sicily stepped into the warmth but declined to sit. "I don't have but a minute."

Iris paid her what she had, and Sicily left, glancing at the moon now high with a halo around it. She pulled her coat tighter and inhaled a deep breath that fogged in the air then climbed back on old Jessie. Her nerves were frayed tonight but that was neither here nor there. She slid a hand into her pocket and closed around the vial. One more task, then she'd hurry home.

TATE SEEMED RELIEVED WHEN she finally walked in the door an hour later. Gypsy went to meet her, tail wagging. "I'm glad you're back. I can unsaddle the mule."

"Thank you, son." Her hands trembled as she laid the vial, now empty, on the sideboard. She went into the living area, dropping into her chair by the fire. "I'm beat. It's going to get cold tonight."

"Just rest, Miss Sicily. I'll be right back."

She heard the door sound when he went out. Such a dear boy, so compassionate.

After Tate got Jessie in his stall and brushed him down, they both sat companionably by the fire. Gypsy curled up by Tate. The train whistle sounded, that and the rumble of iron wheels carrying farther in the cold night. Such an eerie sound that sent prickles along her spine.

Sicily raised her head to listen.

"What is it, ma'am?" Tate asked.

"Just the train. I've always loved the sound. Most of the time we can't hear it out here." Gypsy jumped into her lap and she held the little dog up close. "Tomorrow, we need to take more food to Martha Ann and see if she's warm enough. The nights are getting colder."

"I think there are enough quilts, but we can ask next time," Tate said.

A heartbeat passed then she said quietly, "It's best if she stays hidden." She wasn't sure if she voiced that aloud or was only thinking it.

"Do you need some hot tea?" Tate asked. "I can fix it."

She glanced up. "That sounds nice."

Suddenly a knock sounded on the back door. Gypsy came awake, barking.

"I'll get," Tate said, getting up. "I'm going to the kitchen anyway."

"Be careful. Ask who's there before you open it."

"Yes, ma'am."

He hurried to the kitchen. "Who's there?"

Sicily couldn't hear the reply, but Tate unbolted it and swung the door open.

"It's Martha Ann," he hollered.

Sicily rose, panic gripping her. "What's wrong, girl?"

Martha Ann released a horrible sounding cough and came in by the fire. She was shivering. "I'm sick. Can you give me something to help?"

Sicily felt her forehead. "You have a fever. How long have you been ill?"

"I started feeling puny yesterday." The girl coughed again, and Sicily pulled a chair closer to the fire for her. Martha Ann sat down, stretching out her hands to the flames.

"Tate, add another cup of hot tea for Martha Ann," Sicily called. "I'll have you feeling better in no time. You'll stay here in the house tonight, but we should take you back tomorrow."

"Whatever you think, ma'am." She went into a terrible coughing fit, the sound deep in her chest like the croup. By the time she settled down, Tate brought the tea.

"I made willow bark for her, Miss Sicily, just like you would do," he said, handing each of them a cup of steaming liquid.

"You seem to be reading my mind, son." Sicily took a cup from him and set it beside her chair. She went into the bedroom and brought back a blanket, wrapping it around Martha Ann. "There. You'll be warm soon. I'll rub some thick mentholatum salve on your throat and chest in a bit. You can have my bed tonight and Tate can sleep here by the fire."

"Gypsy and I will be comfortable in here on the floor." Tate went back to the kitchen for another cup. "Hot cider," he said, sitting back down with Gypsy in his lap.

"This is nice." Sicily glanced around at the faces. "I'm glad we're all together again on a cold night like this. All safe and sound." She was happy to note that most of the facial bruises had faded from the girl's features and the broken nose was healing nicely. She'd check the arm before they took her back to the woods, but it was probably healing too.

"Yes, Mama." Martha Ann yawned. "I'm not used to staying up this late."

"Finish your tea and I'll help you into bed." Sicily rose again and put a brick close to the fire to heat. "This will feel good on your feet."

"They're ice cold," Martha Ann said, nodding. "I'm sorry to come but I had to."

"I'm glad you did, child." Sicily resumed her place and finished drinking her tea. She felt a hundred years old tonight and prayed she wasn't getting sick also. The air was so cold and humid. She shouldn't have gone out herself, yet she had no choice.

And now it was done. Peace drifted over her.

An hour later, she had everyone settled in their beds, Martha Ann with a warming salve on her chest and the brick at her feet.

She covered Tate with a couple of soft blankets. "Are you warm enough?" she asked.

"Yes, ma'am. I'll keep the fire going through the night since I'm right here." Tate smiled up at her. "Goodnight, Miss Sicily."

"Pleasant dreams." She went to the small cot and got under the cover. Things were going to be better tomorrow. She didn't tell Jace goodnight and never would again. She liked it better when she thought he was dead. That had seemed final. Now that he was flesh and blood, she must get the past straight with no pretending it had been something better. She sighed, closing her eyes. Being dead was less messy for those left behind.

Morning dawned before Sicily knew it, realizing it was the best sleep she'd had in a while. She hadn't even gotten up once to check on Martha Ann. She rose and dressed then went to the kitchen, surprised to find Tate coming from the living room with Gypsy behind.

"You beat me up. How did you sleep?" She opened the fire box on the cookstove.

He grinned. "Like a bug in a rug. I was warm, and no bad dreams. I'm late getting up."

She threw in some kindling and lit a match, watching the flames catch the wood. "Do you have those often? Bad dreams, that is."

"When Leroy came around a lot, I had a bunch of bad ones of him hurting us." He set Gypsy down and filled the dog's water bowl.

"I hope that's a thing of the past. We'll see. Want to go collect the eggs?"

"Sure." He reached for the basket.

"Get your coat."

"Yes, ma'am." He reached for it and thrust his arms in the sleeves then he went out with Gypsy. Sicily went to check on Martha Ann and found her already dressed.

"How do you feel, girl?"

Martha Ann smiled. "That salve worked wonders. My cough is much better, and I don't think I have a fever."

"Sometimes a body just has to get good and warm. Do you feel like eating?" Sicily asked.

"An egg sounds wonderful." When the girl pulled a wool sweater on, something fell out of her pocket.

Sicily picked up the oblong card. It was the train schedule. Before she could ask anything, Martha Ann quickly took it and stuck it in her pocket.

What did a train schedule mean? Was Martha Ann thinking of running? Except the poor girl didn't have any money. She wanted to ask her questions but wasn't sure it was any of her business. One thing was clear though. Martha Ann had been in town several times lately. Still, she wasn't her keeper. She had to remember that.

"Eggs coming up." Sicily smiled and patted the girl's shoulder. "I'll get coffee on and fill your belly then we need to take you back to the woods."

"I know, but maybe I won't have to stay for much longer." She hugged Sicily. "Thank you for fixing me up, Mama Sicily," she said softly.

"I'm glad I could. I want you to be well and happy. You've seen too much sadness." With her arm around Martha Ann, they went to the kitchen.

After they ate and the dishes washed, Tate saddled Jessie and Martha Ann climbed on. The forest was awash with golden sunlight that streamed through the mostly naked branches. Gypsy romped through the multi-colored leaves and chased squirrels.

Sicily stopped and glanced around at the beauty. A slight breeze at times sent a shower of leaves tumbling down around them. This was her world and she felt at home here.

As they went a little farther, heavy mist from the night's humidity rose from the forest floor, making shapes shift between the tall trees like dancing ghosts.

They made several stops to collect plant and root specimens and arrived at Martha Ann's hideout. She slid off the mule.

Minutes later after unloading a few things and stashing them in the small confines of the hideout, Sicily asked, "Are you sure this is all you need?"

"Yes, Mama Sicily. I mainly just needed medicine for my cold."

"Now, rub the salve on your chest every night and heat the brick we brought to put in the bed with you."

"Yes, ma'am. I will."

"Okay. Give me a hug. We need to be getting back."

The two women hugged. "Be safe and I'll see you soon," Sicily said.

"You too, ma'am." Martha Ann kissed her cheek. "Don't worry about Leroy."

"I won't. We're going to be fine." Sicily turned and Tate helped her onto the mule.

When they arrived back home, they found Albert waiting on the porch. "I got big news."

Something in his voice and worry on his face meant it wasn't good. However, the miffed attitude at the funeral seemed to be gone just like Tate had predicted.

"Did you walk on this cold morning?" Tate asked.

"I hitched a ride on Aaron Freeman's wagon. I couldn't dally."

Sicily dismounted and Tate took the mule to the barn. "We had things to do. What is so important you're busting a gut to get over here to tell?"

"You won't believe this. Better sit down," Albert said, his eyes about to pop out of his head.

"Just get it out. What's happened?" Sicily could've strangled him for being so slow. "And it better not be about you getting married to some poor woman."

His eyes glittering, Albert put his hands on his knees and leaned forward. "Leroy is dead. He got run over by the train."

Chapter Fifteen

IT SEEMED THE WORLD stopped turning in that instant. The birds that had been merrily chirping and flitting about the porch disappeared and a hush fell around them. Albert sat as still as an old worm-eaten woodpecker, staring straight into Sicily's soul.

Everything inside her froze. "Dead?" She dropped slowly into a chair beside Albert. "I shouldn't speak ill of the dead, but he had it coming. I'm glad Martha Ann is free of him."

"Wherever she's at, she needs to stay there a while. The sheriff is looking for someone to pin this on and it makes him no nevermind who it is." Albert wiped his nose with a dirty handkerchief then folded it all neat before stuffing it in his pocket.

"How do they know Leroy didn't just get crazy drunk and lay down on the tracks?" she asked.

Albert slowly swiveled, his strange expression set in stone. "I never said he laid down on them. How would you know?"

"A guess, Albert. Just a guess. Drunks do weird things and you said he got run over by the train. Does Sheriff Bledsoe honestly think someone murdered him?"

"Yep. He said Leroy would never have done that willingly. He believes someone poisoned Leroy and put him on the tracks. He came to that conclusion because of some white stuff around the mouth."

"That's hogwash. It was probably vomit." Sicily remembered the train schedule that fell out of Martha Ann's pocket last night. Could she? No, not possible. "I'm sure there are lots of suspects. Except for his cronies, everyone in town hated him. And maybe he got into a fight with them and one had enough. I could go on all day."

"Miss Sicily, the sheriff knows you were in town last night right before this happened. And so was Martha Ann."

Sicily's head jerked around. "Martha Ann? Did someone see her?"

"Several people." Albert leaned back in the chair and crossed his spindly legs.

"Even though she'd be justified, you'll never make me believe Martha Ann did this. First of all, she has a broken arm. She couldn't lift a sack of potatoes, much less a grown man. Besides, she's sick with a bad cold and coughing her head off."

Albert raised both hands. "You don't have to convince me. It's the sheriff. Just wanted to warn you before he showed up at your door." He swiped a sleeve across his sweaty forehead. "Frankly, the town's gonna be a whole lot better off if ya ask me."

Sicily sat back in the chair. "Agreed. I, for one, won't shed a tear."

"Doubt anyone will. They might throw a party. The moonshiner is also a suspect after what Leroy did to his daughter. And don't forget, the man tried to shoot Leroy." Albert glanced over at her. "I don't reckon I could trouble you for dose of rheumatiz medicine."

"I'll get some in a minute. I have to think about this."

A whistling proceeded Tate as he came around the corner and stopped. "Who died?"

"Why do you say that?" Albert asked.

"Your long faces. Makes me think someone died."

Albert patted a chair. "Come on up and sit with us and we'll tell you the latest about poor old Leroy."

When Tate took a seat, Sicily spoke. "Leroy died last night. Apparently, he laid on the train tracks and got run over. Or, depending on who you ask, someone placed him on the tracks."

"Those big wheels cut off his head," Albert added, his arms waving about like a windmill with a broken sucker rod. "His head went one way and his body another. Made a terrible mess I heard."

Tate's face dropped. "Wow. I never would've guessed he'd end up that way but I ain't surprised. He wasn't very good at making friends. Or keeping them."

"It seems the sheriff suspects me and Martha Ann." Sicily stared at the road that led to town. "I expect he'll be calling on us before long."

"Better get your story straight," Albert warned. "The sheriff likes to trip people up and put words in their mouths."

"All I have is the truth. There's nothing to get straight." Sicily rose. "I'll get that medicine for you, Albert. I didn't figure to see you for a while after Mabel's funeral. You were pretty mad at me."

"You were messing in my business. But I decided to forgive you since we're friends and all."

Sicily caught Tate's gaze and winked. Pain could change a person's view of things in a big hurry. She went inside, her thoughts on Leroy and the sheriff. In the kitchen, the empty vial on the shelf stole her attention. She crossed the room and put it in a drawer. No need for the sheriff to see it if he went poking around. She'd have to send Tate to the woods with a note for Martha Ann about the news and to stay put for now.

Just because Leroy was dead, didn't mean they were in the clear.

She took the medicine back to Albert with a spoon. "Do you believe in ghosts?"

"I sure do! I see them all the time." Albert peered around nervously. "Do you think Leroy will haunt us?"

"He might. His presence hangs over the town like the Headless Horseman." And just for fun, she added, "Leroy might be out for revenge."

"I'm gonna have to start wearing garlic around my neck." Albert swallowed the medicine in a big gulp and got to his feet. "Gotta be going. Don't want to be near you long since you were the one Leroy hated most."

"Need help?" Tate asked, watching him stumble down the steps.

But Albert didn't answer in his hurry to get gone. The levity helped send the gloom away.

QUIET DESCENDED AND WITH IT came a peace they hadn't had in a while. A day passed before the sheriff came calling. Sicily and Tate had just returned from their morning walk in the woods with their sacks filled with various plants and mushrooms. They had left a note for Martha Ann in the hollow tree. Sicily prayed the girl would stay put, even though that was anyone's guess. She seemed to have come and gone a few times since being at the hideout.

Gypsy raised holy hell and tried to bite the man. Tate hurried to pick her up.

"There you are," Bledsoe called from the back porch where Gypsy had run him. "I need to speak to you, Miss Sicily."

"One moment, Sheriff. Let me put this sack in the drying shed."

"I'll do it, ma'am," Tate offered.

"I appreciate that, but I'd like to spread the plants out on the table." She needed time to sort her thoughts.

"I understand." Tate read her perfectly and winked, handing her his sack as well. "I'll take the sheriff into the house then and keep him occupied while you put those away."

Half an hour later, she joined them in the living room. "A glass of apple cider, Sheriff?"

"Don't mind if I do, Miss Sicily. You do make the best around." He rubbed his big stomach.

"I'll get it," Tate offered. "Need to put Gypsy in the bedroom for now anyway."

After the boy left, Bledsoe stared at her. He'd removed his hat and hooked it on one knee of his crossed legs. "Miss Sicily, you know why I'm here. I'm sure you heard about poor old Leroy, and I need to ask you some questions."

"Sheriff, I don't know anything much about that night. A pure shame what happened to your cousin."

"Let's start with why you were in town so late. I've only seen you deliver your medicines in the daylight."

She met his gaze full bore, wondering if some folks believed what came out of their mouths. "People get sick at night too. Illness isn't bothered with the time of day. I go whenever I'm needed and since we have no doctor, folks depend on me."

Tate returned with the cider then sat down.

"Thank you, son." Bledsoe took a big sip. "Man, that's good." He set his cup down. "But, Miss Sicily, you're not a doctor, are you?" Bledsoe reminded her with a smirk. "Folks call you the witchy woman. What exactly is this service you provide?"

Sicily swallowed a scathing retort and gave the irritating man a tight smile. "I use what the good Lord gives us to help people feel better. My remedies are all the relief some of these folks get. Now if you'll excuse me, I have things to do." She started to rise.

"Sit down. I'm not through," he barked. "Do you ever put curses or hexes on people you don't like?"

Good Lord! What was he trying to say? That she put a curse on Leroy and made him lay down on the train tracks?

"Sheriff, do you know what a dumb question that is? It's hardly worth answering but I will assure you I have never dealt in curses or hexes and frankly wouldn't know where to start."

"Leroy mentioned it, ma'am." Bledsoe took a small notebook from his pocket and wrote something down then glanced up. "What were you doing in Silsbee night before last?"

"Not that it's any of your business, I delivered some medicine to Iris Russell for her arthritis. You can ask her."

"I will. Then where did you go?"

Tate made a disgusted sound and patted her hand.

She smiled. "You're taking a long time to get around the same bush, Sheriff. I didn't give Leroy anything or put a curse on him if that's what you're trying to get at. I was home by the time the train went through town. Tate and I were sitting here and I remarked on how far the sound carries on a cold night." She glanced down at her hands then raised her gaze. "Are you accusing me of something?"

"There was bad blood between you so you can't blame me for asking."

"She's telling the truth, Sheriff," Tate interrupted. "We were sitting right here when the train went through that night."

Sicily gave the sheriff a hard scowl. "I know where I was and when." She paused until the man's narrow-set eyes met hers. "The fact is that cousin of yours made a lot of enemies. Dangerous ones. Much more dangerous than an old woman growing herbs and making tinctures for sick folk." She paused again, allowing the silence to fill the room. "Go down on main street in town, throw a rock, and you'll hit two or three. Have you asked the moonshiner and his daughter? I hear they had the best reason to get shed of him."

"I intend to." He looked at his notebook again. When he raised his eyes to her once more, they were as hard as granite. "Where is Martha Ann? Don't insult me by saying you don't know. Tell me where she is."

"In a safe place and that's all you'll get from me. Her arm and ribs are still broken. She can't lift anything with the broken one and she sure couldn't lift her husband's dead weight with only one good arm. The poor girl's still fighting to recover after that last beating that came near to killing her. You saw the shape she was in."

"I still have to speak to her," he said coldly, all friendliness gone. "I know she was in town the night of the murder. Don't deny it. People saw her."

"Sorry, I can't help you. That girl has been through sheer hell over and over and not once did you lift a finger to stop Leroy from beating her senseless." Sicily lowered her voice. "The way I see it, you bear as much guilt as anyone for letting it continue. Shame on you. Folks are fed up with you. Leroy would still be alive if you had done your duty." She got to her feet, her voice full of righteous fervor. "Furthermore, who said anyone did one thing to him? The man was a drunk. He probably stumbled on a rock and hit his head but instead, you're bothering honest hardworking people with these ridiculous accusations. He died because of sheer stupidity, and you seem to have no proof to the contrary."

"Enough!" He stood and jerked his hat on. "Have Martha Ann in my office tomorrow or I *will* arrest you." The lawman shook a finger. "Is that clear?"

"It's clear, but I won't guarantee she'll be there. Folks won't stand for much more. Lock me up and you might have a riot on your hands."

The two stared each other down. The sheriff blinked first and stuffed his little notebook back into a shirt pocket.

Sicily squashed a smile. She'd gotten to him at least a little. "I believe you can show yourself out."

He slammed the door behind him and stomped down the front steps. Sicily wondered if Gypsy hadn't had the right idea. She'd like to bite him herself, but he'd probably taste like rotted meat.

Tate put an arm around her. "Do you think he'll arrest you?"

"Who knows? I left my crystal ball in the closet." She softened her expression and smiled. "Let's forget all about the sheriff and make some oatmeal cookies. I haven't made any since you've been here, and I think I have enough molasses and oatmeal."

"Could we?" Tate's expression turned wistful. "My mother used to make them a long time ago, but I haven't had any since."

Sicily got out the oats. "They were a favorite of my mother too. My father loved cookies, pies, and cakes, but we seldom had sweets and learned to really appreciate them."

Gypsy's pitiful whine came from Tate's room along with scratching.

"Go let the little thing out," Sicily said. "She's been in jail long enough."

Tate opened the door and Gypsy ran to Sicily for pets. She dropped everything to give the dog some loving before letting her outside.

She and Tate turned back to making cookies and he got a mixing bowl out.

"We sure miss a lot of things that we used to have, don't we, Miss Sicily?" His voice dropped lower. "Sometimes I have a hard time remembering my mother's face and it makes me sad."

"Time tends to steal what we never want to forget. It does it to everyone."

"But does it make me a bad son?"

She stopped and put an arm around the boy. "No, not at all. The love you have for your parents never fades even if you sometimes forget their faces."

Most of the worry seemed to leave Tate's eyes. She gave him an affectionate squeeze, emotion putting a lump in her throat. How empty life would be without him.

They got the batter mixed up, dropped spoonfuls onto a pan, and put them in the oven before they said much more. And it was Tate who came back around to the sheriff.

"Are you going to the woods to get Martha Ann?" he asked.

"I'll go talk to her in a bit but she's not ready to face the sheriff." Her thoughts went again to the train schedule that had fallen out of the girl's pocket. She'd been thinking about running, that's all that could be and would be.

"But the sheriff will arrest you. He said so."

"Honey, that sheriff is all bark. He likes to threaten but doesn't follow through. I'm not worried about going to jail. What proof does he have that I did anything? What proof that anyone did anything? Leroy was a known drunk. His favorite saloon hangout was right there by the tracks. He probably had too much whiskey, stumbled out, fell onto the tracks, and that's the end of it."

"I guess. At least it's possible. The saloon is right by the tracks."

She patted his hand. "Stop worrying. It's going to be all right."

And somehow, she'd make sure of it. Leroy had done his best to destroy them while he was alive. He sure wasn't going to from beyond the grave. They simply had to ride the investigation out.

Tomorrow, she'd go into town to ask around to see what she could find out and who saw Martha Ann. The more she knew, the better she could run interference.

The cookies turned out and the big smile on Tate's face made her glad she'd suggested it. Gypsy girl loved them too. She quickly ate hers then wanted more. Typical dog.

That night, she got into bed, mulling over the day's events. It was another cold night and just before she went to sleep, the train's faint whistle carried from town. A smile formed on her lips.

Chapter Sixteen

SICILY WOKE RESTED AND energetic. Her thoughts went to plans for the day as she dressed and met Tate in the kitchen. He was feeding Gypsy a fried egg he'd just made.

"Good morning." She tied an apron on. "I don't know why you're always beating me out of bed. Guess I'll have to buy us a better rooster. Mine has gotten lazy."

Tate smiled, plopping an oatmeal cookie into his mouth. "It was these cookies. I woke up smelling them. They're sure good."

"I'm glad I could bring a taste of home to you. We all need that from time to time, me included." She glanced at a full egg basket sitting on the sideboard. "You already collected the eggs too."

"Yes, ma'am." He reached for another cookie and shrugged. "You got a lot to take care of around here and I like helping."

She patted his shoulder, noting that he was three inches taller than her. When had that happened? Had she been so wrapped up in the Leroy trouble she'd failed to notice? "You spoil me, son."

"Ain't I supposed to?" he asked with a lopsided grin. My, he was going to be a handsome man when he finished growing. His sandy hair had gotten darker and his voice deeper.

"Sorry, spoiling me is not your job." She gave him a quick side hug. "We'll go into town this morning unless you have other plans. I need to talk to a few people, and I also want to look at that vacant lot again. We need to get some things like beets, turnip greens, spinach, and cabbage planted for winter. As a matter of fact..." her words trailed as she thought.

"What, ma'am?" Tate asked.

"I was just thinking that we wouldn't be as limited as I thought if we use cardboard, sheets, tarps, and things to make covers over them when the weather gets real cold."

"I've seen that done!" Excitement shimmered in Tate's eyes. "I could make those round things from willow to hold the covers up off the plants. There's a bunch of it along the creek."

"Exactly. It's a little more work but doable. Of course, I'll have to speak to Corrine to find out if that belonged to Mabel. I figure to stop by her house on the way."

"And maybe I can talk again to that orphan boy at the Peevys." Worry crept into his face.

"What was his name?" Sicily asked. "I've forgotten."

"George," Tate supplied. He held the back door to let Gypsy out. "Do you worry about the sheriff locking you up?"

Bledsoe was sure looking to put Leroy's death on someone so yes it concerned her, but Tate didn't need to know that.

"No, he's not going to do that, but he sure wishes he could. Nope, not worried."

Sicily had just finished sweeping the kitchen when a knock came on the front door. Tate was out in the back, so she opened it to find Corrine. "Come in. I was telling Tate that I needed to stop by your house on the way to town."

"I hope I'm not too early." Corrine had arranged her short hair in becoming waves. She had a nice smile, except now she chewed on her bottom lip.

"There is no such thing as too early for your company. Have a seat. Or would you rather go to the kitchen, and I can fix hot tea?"

"I just drank several cups this morning, so I don't need more. This won't take long." Corrine sat in a chair in front of the fire. "These mornings have gotten cold lately. The fire feels good."

Sicily sat in a nearby chair. "What's on your mind?"

"I wanted to assure you that the vacant lot in town did indeed belong to Mabel and now it's mine. We'll have to wait until the deed changes over to my name but there's no reason you can't go ahead and start getting things in the ground. I couldn't wait to come tell you."

"That's wonderful news, Corrine." Sicily clasped her hands together over her heart.

"But there's one stipulation," Corrine added. "You have to let me help you. I want to do something for these poor starving people."

"The more the merrier I always say." Sicily's smile couldn't get any wider. Her idea was taking off. The more folks she could involve the better.

Corrine's eyes twinkled. She looked so different from the housekeeper she was when Mabel died. "I've also been toying with an idea, and I want to see what you think."

"The world needs more ideas. I'd like to hear it."

"Well, you know how big Mabel's house is—six bedrooms plus a sitting room and large kitchen. I'd like to open it up to the homeless, young and old."

Martha Ann flashed into Sicily's mind. Maybe the girl would even like to help Corrine. She took the woman's hand, blinking back tears. "That's a splendid idea."

"Mabel kept a room locked up tight while she was alive, and I always wondered what was in it. Since I couldn't find a key in any of her things, I called a locksmith to come out and open it and you won't believe what I saw." Corrine laughed. "Mabel had hoarded men's and women's new shoes, bolts and bolts of fabric, canned goods you wouldn't believe, and other things. She hoarded everything that was in short supply even though she never needed it."

Sicily pictured that. Mabel was such a miserly woman who never thought about anyone but herself. "That's amazing. What are you going to do with it?"

"I'll give to folks who need and can use it."

"Good. The need is truly great. Would you like to go into town with me and Tate? We're going to look at that lot and talk to Dan at the farm supply. He carries seeds and bulbs. We'll see if he can give us a deal."

"I'd love to." Corrine squeezed Sicily's hand. "I haven't been this excited in a long time."

"Me either."

"Mabel's car is running like a top and we can go in that."

In minutes, they all piled in, even Gypsy, and took off toward town. Sicily hadn't ridden in very many automobiles so she gripped the dashboard. But the ride was so smooth she soon relaxed and enjoyed it. They'd just passed the curve when they saw two carloads of travelers parked just off the road down by a little creek. Corrine slowed and went past, then turned around and went back.

Two men in worn overalls met the car when it stopped. The tallest one offered a smile. "I'm right sorry about trespassing but it was dark when we got here and couldn't find anyone to ask. We'll move on within the hour."

Corrine and Sicily opened the doors and got out. Tate volunteered to wait in the car with Gypsy girl.

Sicily's heart went out to the ragged group who'd tied everything they must've owned onto two old cars. One of the women looked to be about seven or eight months pregnant. Both women wore a haggard look of exhaustion. A little boy and girl in rags played quietly, occasionally glancing up at the adults with pinched faces. All of the group were very thin. Who knows when they last had a decent meal.

Sicily and Corrine shook their hands and introduced themselves. The men didn't offer their names which was common these days until they knew they could trust you.

"Where are you headed?" Sicily asked.

"Nowhere in particular." The first man removed a hat that had seen better days and scratched his forehead. "We're hoping to find some work. Heard there's a sawmill around here."

"That's right," Sicily answered. "Only I don't know if they have any openings."

Just then Gypsy jumped out a car window and ran up to the men, begging to be petted. The speaker of the group picked her up. "Now aren't you a pretty thing?"

"Her name's Gypsy and she's wrapped everyone around her finger," Sicily offered.

"A puppy," the children cried. "Can we see, Daddy?"

He showed them the little squirt then set her down to play with the kids. Gypsy was in hog heaven. She jumped on them and licked them to death. Sicily watched the show, relaxing. If the dog trusted them, so would she. Animals were the best at judging character.

"How about a place to rest up and get some food in you?" Corrine glanced at the two women. "You're not trespassing here but my place is nicer and has beds."

Hope sprang into the women's eyes. One pushed back a scraggly strand of hair. Sicily could hardly bear their silent pain. They were the distraught faces of America's Depression.

She smiled at them. Then turned to back to the men. "What did you do before misfortune set in?"

"We were farmers. And then the dust storms came and didn't stop. Lost everything. We're brothers by the way. Our wives and kids are worn to a nubbin and need the rest." He paused and drew himself up straighter. "What you ladies offer is a godsend, but we'll have to do some work in exchange."

His companion finished, "We're handy around a yard or fixing things in a house. My wife is due to have our first child soon and she's not doing well. I'm worried about her."

Corrine and Sicily exchanged glances. They could use these men in their big project.

"Then, let us help. As it turns out, we're needing someone with planting experience for a large community project. I'll tell you more about it later." Corrine gave them directions to her house. "I'm going into town for a little bit, but I'll be home in an hour. Go on down there when you get ready, and I'll be there shortly."

"That's a deal, ma'am." Tears filled the man's eyes. "You don't know what this means to us."

Sicily laid a hand on his shoulder. "We just want to help. This is everyone's problem, and we'll only get through it by helping each other."

"Yes, ma'am. We're truly grateful," said the second brother, a younger man, who was hatless. "I'm Nick Justice and my brother is Quentin."

"Glad to meet you." Sicily spoke to the women who'd sidled closer. "I'm the healer in these parts and maybe I can help you feel better. I'll sure try if you'll let me."

"Thank you, ma'am," the pregnant woman said shyly.

The other woman, the mother of the children had tears running down her face. "We came to a fork in the road a little ways back and Quentin flipped a coin. God must've had a plan."

"Yes, ma'am. He always does." Sicily rested a light hand on her arm, appalled at the skin stretched over bone.

"I'm Josie and my sister-in-law is Etta."

"We're looking forward to getting acquainted." Corrine patted her hand.

Explaining that they needed to go, Sicily and Corrine collected Gypsy. Waving goodbye, they got back in the car. Corrine started the engine and pulled back out onto the road.

The travelers confirmed what Sicily had always believed—that hard times made people more of what they were and those with nothing were often the kindest and most grateful.

Tate spoke first. "They seemed really nice. The women were scared at first."

"The men were too. They've had to deal with rude people that kept them moving." Corrine shifted gears and the engine purred, carrying them to town.

"Corrine, it appears your house won't be empty long." A warm glow settled in Sicily's chest. "You know, maybe they'd like to help us break ground on the community garden."

The woman nodded. "I had the same thought. It feels good to help our fellow man."

Sicily sank back in the comfortable seat. "There's nothing better. Let's go check out the lot again, if you don't mind, Corrine, then we'll go talk to Dan at the farm supply."

The town of Silsbee only had one paved street and that was Main. Hard packed dirt made up the rest except when it rained. Then they were mud pits.

When they drove up to the lot on its unpaved street and killed the motor, everyone got out. Sicily liked the vacant lot even better than when she first saw it. She bent to pick up some black, rich soil and let it sift through her fingers. It was excellent dirt for growing food.

"I see your smile, Sicily," Corrine remarked. "I take it this is first-rate dirt."

"It is. We'll have no trouble growing whatever we plant."

"Even herbs and mushrooms?" Tate asked, putting Gypsy down to sniff.

"That's right, son. Anything we want."

"I've always been too busy keeping a house to have a garden and Miss Mabel never wanted one either," Corrine confessed. "Too much work she said. Or it was too hot. She always had an excuse. I'll have to rely on you for advice."

"Nothing much to it. You'll catch on fast." Sicily stared after Tate who'd walked off a ways, no doubt looking for a patch of his own where he could grow whatever he wanted. "Yes, I think this will be perfect."

She called to Tate and they got back in the car. The next stop was Dan's where they haggled over seed prices. It took so long, Tate wandered to the back with Gypsy. Finally, Dan and Sicily came to an agreement. They could buy everything at a fraction over cost.

"You sure drive a hard bargain, Miss Sicily." Dan wiped his glistening forehead. "I'm giving you my rock-bottom price. But I'm happy to help you. A community garden is going to make such a big difference in our town."

"I think it will too," Corrine agreed, wrapping an arm around Sicily's. "Some people can think up things like this but all I can think about are recipes and cooking."

Sicily patted her hand. "It takes all of us and we can't have one without the other."

Dan tapped Sicily's shoulder. "I have a lot of seeds that I saved from previous gardens that I'll donate."

"That's wonderful, Dan!" Sicily beamed. That's some they wouldn't have to buy.

The farm supply was a sea of men in overalls and plaid shirts. One heard them and stepped forward. "I have a bunch of seeds and you can have them, Miss Sicily."

Then several others came to offer their saved seeds.

"Thank you all," Sicily said, raising her voice to be heard. "You're a big help."

She didn't see the sheriff until he growled at her elbow. "Where's Martha Ann? I told you to have her in my office today."

"Sheriff, I have business to tend to and I'm not the girl's keeper."

"But you know where she is. You're hiding her out somewhere on your place."

"You're mistaken, but I won't hold it against you as I can see it happens a lot." She used her most sarcastic tone, scanning the store for Tate. She relaxed when she saw him talking to the Peevys orphan, George.

"I'll have to arrest you then. Hands behind your back." Bledsoe's voice turned ice cold and his eyes burned with contempt. A cold smile formed. "I hope you won't resist."

"You'll do no such thing as arrest her!" Dan hollered. "I won't stand for it, and neither will these other folks."

The sea of overalls rushed forward, forming a circle around her. Most had their arms crossed over their chests, glowering at Bledsoe as if daring him to put Sicily in jail. She was stunned at this huge outpouring of support.

"Go harass someone else!" Mild-mannered Corrine shook a fist. "She's not breaking any law."

"You ain't telling me what to do in my own town." Sheriff Bledsoe took a step back though as the growing crowd pressed. He found himself trapped against the counter like a rat hunting for a hole to crawl into.

"This ain't your town, Sheriff!" someone in the crowd yelled. "It's ours and you're going to be out of a job come the next election."

Bledsoe waved a bored hand. "We'll see about that."

"Yes, we will!" yelled another. "Wait and see."

"Pipe down or I'll march the lot of you to jail," Bledsoe countered.

"Miss Sicily had left for home a long time before Leroy got run over," Art O'Neil vouched. "I'd say that in a court of law too."

"That's right," said Gertie, one of Sicily's oldest customers who could barely hobble. "I killed Leroy. Handcuff me."

"Go away, old woman," Bledsoe said, giving a push.

Gertie could barely see, hear, or smell. She brought her cane down hard on Bledsoe's foot.

The sheriff yelped, yanking his foot from under the cane.

"Better watch out, Sheriff. Gertie'll wallop you with that cane of hers!" a man shouted.

The crowd chuckled. Gertie's smile showed toothless gums.

The farm supply was bulging at the seams, unable to hold the growing number of men from outside, pushing the sheriff up against the counter. He glanced around helplessly, seeing he'd find no sympathy in their ranks. He raised his hands. "Simmer down. You've made your point. Now let me out of here and you can all go home knowing I won't bother your witchy woman." He cast a frown at Sicily. "At least not today."

At that moment the train arrived, blowing its whistle as it pulled into the station with an ominous rumble. All conversation ceased and the men looked at each other for a long moment.

When the talk began again, Dan drew himself up tall, towering over Bledsoe by two inches. "Glad we could see eye to eye, Sheriff." Then he winked at Sicily and lifted old Gertie up, sitting the wizened woman on the counter where she wouldn't be trampled.

It took a while for the crowd to file out and each one stopped to speak to Sicily. Many thanked her for treating the sick all these years. Others said word had gotten out about the community garden and they'd all help her.

At last, they left the store and stood on the sidewalk. Sicily turned to Corrine. "Go back home and take care of those travelers. I have to speak to a few more people before I'll be ready to leave, and Tate and I will enjoy the walk to our place."

"In that case, I'll run on then." Corrine gave Sicily a hug. "We'll talk soon."

Tate emerged with Gypsy in one arm and the other protectively around George.

As soon as Peevy spied the eight-year-old, he grabbed him, delivering a kick to the boy's rear that sent him sprawling. "Git home. What are you doing sneaking off? I oughta beat you."

George trembled, his eyes wide. "No, please. I promise to be good."

The loathsome piece of manure jerked George up and drew back to hit him. But Sicily's quick grab of his hand prevented the blow to the boy's face. "No more," she said low, her nose mere inches from Peevy's, his putrid breath almost gagging her. "This town is changing and we're not going to stand by and let you abuse this kid anymore."

"What'cha gonna do about it?" Peevy snarled. "George belongs to me. I got papers."

"Slavery has been abolished. Haven't you heard? George is a human with rights."

"He's what I say he is," Peevy snapped.

Anger rose to a fever pitch. She moved even closer so the man wouldn't miss any words. "Well, you heard what happened to Leroy Vaughn, didn't you?" She held his beady eyes captive with her stare until he blinked, then dropped his hand, leaving him with an open mouth. "I think we're done here, Tate. Let's get some fresh air." She marched down the street with the boy while Gypsy raised Cain, clawing to get down to bite the man. Peevy had that effect on everyone.

"We've gotta do something about that," Tate said, his face dark with anger. "He's going to hurt George bad."

"I know. I'm working on it."

Preacher Stover sidled up alongside matching Sicily's stride. The sunlight turned his hair to lighter shades of chestnut. He was probably in his late thirties if she was guessing.

"Miss Sicily, you are a fierce, bold woman." His dark eyes danced with laughter. "You're changing this town little by little."

Sicily shrugged. "Someone had to, and I guess it fell my lot. But it's a work in progress."

"All things are." He winked at Tate, gave Gypsy a pat, and turned into the general store.

She thought about that and decided that life itself was a work in progress and just when you thought it was going well, up popped a bigger problem. Some days you were the pigeon and other days the statue.

Thinking about that, she turned to see Peevy and George getting into his wagon drawn by a pair of flea-bitten horses. As the saying went, it was better to light one candle than curse the darkness.

Chapter Seventeen

THE RED, WHITE, AND blue striped barber pole came into view. Sicily stopped and took a dime from her purse, giving it to Tate. "Go buy you a soda or piece of candy. I need to talk to Art a minute then I'll have to stop by Albert's before we head back."

Tate gazed at her, closing his hand around the dime. "Thank you, ma'am. But I didn't earn this."

She pulled him into a hug and Gypsy tried to wiggle over to her. "Yes, you did. In more ways than one. Now go treat yourself."

"Thank you," he said again, putting Gypsy down. The boy hurried toward the general store with his dog trotting alongside.

Sicily watched them, tears blurring her vision. How she loved them. She blinked hard then went on down to the barbershop. A glance in the window revealed no patrons. Art occupied one of the two chairs with his boots propped on the footrest, reading a newspaper. She breathed a sigh of relief to be able to talk to Art in private.

Art glanced up. "I'm glad you escaped the sheriff's clutches. He was mighty determined to take you in."

"I don't mind and I'm glad it took attention from you, Dan, and the others. We don't need them poking around. What chatter do you hear about the whole mess?"

He folded his newspaper that came from Beaumont each morning by car and set it aside. "Folks are saying all sorts of crazy things but mostly that Leroy got drunk and fell onto the tracks. A few swear Martha Ann somehow did it."

"In her shape?" She snorted. "Have they gotten a good look at her? We've got to shift any suspicion away from her. The girl's been through enough hell."

"I know but most folks don't use the sense God gave 'em. 'Course the ones accusing her loudest are Leroy's friends." He studied her. "She was in town that night. Did you know that?"

Sicily drew in a slow breath, still curious what the girl had been doing in Silsbee.

"Someone saw the poor girl. It's kinda spooky the way she drifts in and out." Art leaned down to wipe some dirt off one worn boot. "Most of the talk has been about folks seeing Leroy's ghost flitting amongst the trees. They claim he's looking for his head. Others say he's dead set on haunting this town and wants revenge."

"You don't say." Sicily held the laughter that rose. "Albert claims to have seen him."

"So have quite a few others. I wouldn't put it past the older boys to throw a sheet over their head and dance around just to scare the old biddies and tongue-waggers."

"Well, it makes as much sense as anything." She glanced down at the black and white checked linoleum floor that was as clean as a whistle. "What exactly is Leroy's bunch saying?"

Even with the man dead, the others still posed a risk to her, Tate, and Martha Ann.

"They get drunk on the regular and vow to seek retribution, claiming someone murdered him. All talk so far and no action."

She winked at Art, laughter in her voice. "Well, you know everyone in Silsbee is a suspect since he wasn't liked. Smarter to just keep out of it and no one will be the wiser."

"Yes, ma'am. I certainly aim to. You do the same."

She laid a hand on his shoulder. "Thank you for being a loyal friend, Art. I've got to stop by Albert's place before I head home." She paused. "Would you mind if folks drop off their seeds here for the garden project? That way they wouldn't have to traipse all the way out to my place."

"Don't mind a bit. I'll get the word out. Glad to help. Tell Albert hello."

Sicily thanked him and left. Albert was sitting in a chair on his front porch with several strings of garlic around his neck and wiping his eyes. "What in the holy hell are you doing, old man?" She took a seat as far from him as she could get and waved away the stench. "You stink."

A hefty stick of wood lay next to his chair. To club the ghosts?

"We got us a haint," he whispered, his eyes round. "I saw it peeking in my window last night and I know it's Leroy. But I was ready and he didn't come in because of the garlic."

"You old fool, that's crazy talk. Get hold of yourself."

"If you lived in town, you wouldn't say that, Miz Sicily. Some say Martha Ann is a ghost too, 'cause Leroy done killed her." He leaned closer. "Have you seen her lately?"

"That's a bunch of malarky. Yes, I've seen her and she's very much alive."

"Well, folks saw her in town the night Leroy died. Ain't no one seen her since. Gertie said she had to be up to something." He shifted in the chair. "Did you bring some remedy for my aching bones?"

"No, I didn't bring any today. I rode to town in Corrine's car and we stopped to talk to some folks camped out down by the river. I think the men are going to help with the community garden. They used to be farmers."

"That's good I reckon. Hope you can trust 'em." He wiped his watering eyes again with a handkerchief. "This garlic is sure hard to live with. Making my eyes water."

"That's a big surprise. Take that off your neck. It doesn't prevent ghosts from getting you. Garlic is to keep vampires away."

He stared at her like she'd spoken in gibberish. "Ain't taking no chances. Do you think those farmers know anything about haints 'n such?"

"Couldn't say." She rose, putting her purse on her arm. "I need to go. Got lots to do."

"Watch out for the haints and keep your mouth shut so they can't get inside you. You know they can just jump in there. Get you some garlic. It ain't got me yet."

"That's because haints avoid Silsbee. Too many crazies here." She rose and put her handbag on her arm.

"Now wait a minute." Albert sneezed then blew his nose. "I almost married me a pretty little thing but it turns out she wasn't real."

"What do you mean?"

He shrugged. "She was a ghost."

"Oh, you poor foolish man. Better watch it or someone will lock you up." She told him bye and left, grateful to be in fresh air.

So, she still didn't know what Martha Ann was doing the night Leroy died and there was only one person could answer that. But if the girl was in town, she might've seen the activity. She collected Tate and Gypsy and the three of them walked home. The travelers were gone from the place they'd parked. They must've gone on to Corrine's.

When they reached home, Martha Ann was sitting on the back steps. She got to her feet. "I hope you don't mind me coming here. The silence was getting to me. Having nightmares."

Tate and Gypsy went on in the house.

"Of course I don't mind you coming." Sicily gave the girl a hug. "We need to talk."

"Yes, ma'am. I have a favor to ask." Martha Ann looked down at her feet. "Are you mad that I came?"

"No. I'm not your keeper and I can't tell you what to do." Sicily opened the kitchen door. "Let's get us some hot tea."

"That sounds good." They went inside and Martha Ann sat at the table. "Since Leroy is dead, there's no reason for me to hide."

Sicily turned from the water pump. "I disagree with you. Leroy's buddies are convinced that maybe you had something to do with his death and have vowed revenge. I don't have to tell you how mean and unpredictable drunk men are. Besides, it's too dangerous with the sheriff wanting to pin the death on someone, but it's up to you if you think it's wise to put yourself in his crosshairs. Several people saw you in town the night Leroy died. Sheriff Bledsoe wants to question you." Sicily sat the kettle on the stove then moved to the girl, smoothing back her wild-looking hair. "Besides, I need to check the break in your arm. Does it hurt?"

"Sometimes if I try to use it."

"It's way too soon for that, silly girl. You'll rebreak it on accident if you're not careful. It probably won't heal for a month, and it's only been two weeks." Sicily checked the sling and found it still snug. Good. "Stop trying to use it."

"But I got a life to get back to now." Martha Ann chewed her bottom lip. "Only I'm not sure where I'll go."

"I've been thinking about that. Corrine has opened up Mabel's big house to folks without a home. Would you like living there and helping her with cooking and things until you can get back on your feet?"

Martha Ann brightened. "Oh yes, ma'am. I'd love that, Mama Sicily."

"Good. It's one less thing to worry about." Sicily glanced up at the sky. The sun was high overhead so it must be noon. "Let's fix some lunch."

"Okay, but first I want to explain what I was doing in town that night. I remembered a necklace my granny gave me a long time ago and I didn't want Leroy finding and selling it. I sneaked back into the house and got it from my special hiding place. Leroy wasn't there. I hurried to get it and leave before he came back."

The answer to the question rolling around in Sicily's head actually made sense and it was something she'd do herself. "I see. But it was a scary thing to do."

Martha Ann nodded, looking down at her hands. "I was worried he'd come back and catch me the whole time." She paused and silence danced between them. "Now for my favor. Will you come into town with me later? I have to take back what Leroy stole from me."

What did that mean? But Sicily knew she'd tell her if she waited.

"Yes, I'll keep you company. If you're not going back to the woods, I'll send Tate to get your things. Then I'll arrange for you to stay with Corrine. She has a house full of migrant workers and one of the wives is pregnant with her first child."

"A baby," the girl whispered, her hand to her mouth. "I'd love to help Miss Corrine with them."

"It's a deal then."

As soon as they finished eating a noon meal, Sicily sent Tate after Martha Ann's meager belongings. While he was gone, Sicily washed then cut the girl's beautiful blonde hair and fixed it in an attractive style.

Tears filled Martha Ann's eyes, her chin quivering. "I used to be pretty once." She glanced up at Sicily. "My granny was kind and good and she used to comb my hair. Once she fixed it in fancy braids and said that's the way they wore it in the old country. But Leroy always told me I was ugly and should be grateful he looked at me." The girl wiped the tears.

"Leroy was a spiteful blackwater snake and you couldn't believe anything he said," Sicily said softly. "He took joy from hurting people. You know that."

"Yes, but after a long while I started to believe his lies."

"Honey, he's gone, and you'll never have to see him again." Sicily laid the comb down and caught Martha Ann's gaze in the mirror. "You're a beautiful woman, and never let anyone tell you differently."

"I'm going to try. But I have one more thing to do first. Tonight, I'm going to burn that house to the ground and it would mean a lot to me for you to be there."

Raw emotion washed over Sicily and lodged in her heart. "Can I ask why?"

"'Cause you are so strong and I can use your strength when I get weak."

Sicily's voice was quiet and emotional. "I'll be honored and even light the match if you need me to. Burn up all those horrible memories and wash your hands of Leroy." She rested her hands lightly on the girl's shoulders. "Then you can start to really live a meaningful life again."

A thought crossed Sicily's mind. Leroy was only renting that house. Burning it down would anger the owner who lived over in the next county. Still, that didn't matter. As run down as Leroy let it get, burning it might be doing the owner a favor. Besides, Leroy was six months behind on rent. Either way, if Martha Ann wanted to wipe the slate clean, that's what Sicily would help her do come hell or high water.

THE MOON WAS FULL AND bright as Sicily got Tate to hitch up the wagon. Their breath fogged in the cold air, and she pulled her coat tighter. She'd never seen a prettier night. Some said it was a beaver's moon, a time of preparation, and it seemed appropriate for the coming activity that would cleanse Martha Ann's soul. Some things were right even when they were wrong.

"I'll come with you in case there's trouble," Tate said, finishing hooking up the harness traces to the whippletree.

"Thank you, I'd like that. We might have use of you if the sheriff tries to stop us. One way or another, that house is going to be ash before we're through."

"I'll put the shotgun under the seat."

Sicily nodded. "Might be best but I'll only use it as a last resort." She glanced up at the sky. "The Native American tribes had a lot of names for the moon, depending on the size or the time of year. I think tonight's beaver, or frost moon is a good sign."

"What's a rustler's moon?" Tate asked. "My father talked about it a lot."

"That's when there's no moon at all so it's safer for criminal shenanigans."

Martha Ann emerged from the house and came down the back steps. Like a caterpillar, she was beginning to emerge into a beautiful butterfly. Each day she had a little more strength to reach for the things that really mattered. Sicily respected that. It took a lot of guts to rise up when you've been beaten down. Love for the girl washed through her.

"Ready, girl?" She reached out a hand.

"Yes, Mama Sicily. I'm anxious to do this." Martha Ann took Sicily's palm and stepped up into the wagon. Thank goodness, she'd worn a coat against the frosty air.

"I think it's best to leave Gypsy at home." Tate helped Sicily up then took his place on the seat. "She'd just bark her fool head off."

"Probably," Sicily agreed and settled Martha Ann between herself and Tate. The boy lifted the reins, setting the wagon in motion.

The night air carried a sweet fragrance that reminded Sicily of the times she went deer hunting with her father, feeling very useful to be given the task of holding the extra ammunition and water canteen. They'd creep through the woods silently and sit under a tree to wait for a big buck. Sometimes hours would pass, with the only visible sign the fog of their breath in the cold night air as they waited and watched. She loved the quiet of the deep night before sunrise when all the world seemed to sleep.

Town was quiet as they turned down the street to the house. Everyone seemed to have found their beds early and a still hush enveloped them. Tate stopped the wagon in front of Martha Ann's former place and set the brake.

"Do you have everything out before you light the match, girl?" Sicily asked.

"There's a quilt of my granny's that I need to get but I can't think of anything else. All my clothes are rags and I don't have anything else. I'm wearing my necklace."

"Okay, I'll go in with you." Sicily climbed down and helped Martha Ann then grabbed the lantern, proceeding into the house.

The rooms were eerily quiet except for the sound of scurrying mice and the lantern cast their looming shadows against the walls. A horrible smell came from the kitchen and the reason soon became apparent. The remains of a dead animal lay on the floor with a dozen mice feasting on the carcass. A woven circle of cord lay nearby.

Martha Ann sobbed and would've knelt if Sicily hadn't stopped her. "My sweet Jezzy. Leroy must've killed her because he was mad at me. I made that cord to put around her neck."

Sicily patted her back. "Honey, maybe you're wrong and that's not her. There's no way of knowing what that animal once was."

While she felt the girl's pain, she also realized that if Leroy had gotten a hold of Martha Ann, she might have met the same fate as this poor animal. A shiver went down Sicily's spine as the walls of this place seemed to radiate the evil of that man.

They hurried to get the quilt and found nothing else of value. Martha Ann pulled a full can of kerosene from the corner which they doused over the floors and walls. Back out on the porch, the girl's hands shook as she struck a match at the door and tossed it inside. The dry wood caught instantly.

"Let's get back to the wagon to watch." Sicily took Martha Ann's hand, and they stood beside the wagon.

Flames engulfed the house in just a few minutes. Martha Ann stared dry-eyed and resolute as she watched with Sicily. One by one, women in nightgowns with a coat thrown over them came from nearby houses and gathered with them, in silent solidarity. This was a message loud and clear to the men in the town. They were done getting hit and beat on and no more.

One of Leroy's buddies sidled up to Sicily. "There's a law against this and you can bet the sheriff will hear about it."

She stared at him, shrugging. "You know, I'd watch out if I were you or else yours might be the next body they find on the train tracks. The women of this town have spoken."

The man's eyes widened, and he quickly backed away as the seven o'clock train whistle blew and the big iron wheels pulled the train up to the station. The timing couldn't have been better. The crowd grew with men now joining them in their hastily donned coveralls with twisted suspenders, their hair sticking every which way. Most wore a solemn expression as reality set in. If they'd brought a bucket for a water brigade, they let them drop to their feet.

Preacher Stover came to stand by Sicily and said loud enough for everyone to hear, "The Lord's work is a beautiful thing. This house needed to go. The Bible says, 'Everything that can withstand the fire must be put through the fire and it shall be cleaned.' This house harbored an evil stench and it's past time to let it go." He lowered his voice where only she could hear. "This town is changing, and you started it, Miss Sicily. I have seeds saved for the community garden."

"Thank you, Reverend. We can use them."

"Also, I plan to work a plow or hoe or shovel. Whatever you need done. You're planting the seeds of a good future for us here and I want to be a part of it."

"Me too," said one bystander.

A few men next to him chimed in, "Count on us too. We stand ready."

The support took Sicily's breath. "Thank you, gentlemen. We start Monday morning."

Within a very short span of time, the house of horror had been reduced to a ball of flame and searing heat, reflecting in the faces of all who watched. No one mentioned a word about filling buckets with water.

The cancer, a blight on humanity, was gone. As with a wildfire after it passed, seeds of renewal were about to be sown. Little green sprouts would replace the dead plants and seeds of hope were taking root. Sicily slipped an arm around Martha Ann, careful of her broken bones. An overwhelming feeling wove through her of all they could accomplish if everyone worked together.

The roof of the old house finally crashed inward sending sparks shooting up to heaven. She imagined it getting rid of the old to make room for the new and hopefully releasing the evil soul of Leroy to whatever path the choices he made took him.

Chapter Eighteen

Amid the crash and tremendous roar of the fire, Sheriff Bledsoe arrived, his car screeching to a halt throwing gravel. His face a black storm, he marched to Sicily and yelled, "Are you to blame for this?"

Martha Ann gripped Sicily's hand tightly and raised her chin. "No, I am. I intend to wipe Leroy's memory from this town, and this is the first step."

"I'm sure with Sicily's help. You didn't plan this on your own. I'll have to arrest both of you." He yanked on her good arm.

The crowd pressed closer. Martha Ann stood there mute, indecision on her face.

Preacher Stover took a step from Sicily's side. "Arrest her and you'll have to arrest all of us. These women only did what we'd been talking about. We all wanted this house and the evil it harbored gone. You're sure making my Sunday sermons easy to write."

People around them chuckled and a deep voice came from the back, "Yeah, Sheriff. You'll have to take us all."

Sicily knew that voice. She strained to see through the smoke and floating ash.

The breeze picked up and scattered the smoke for a brief instant, long enough to make out Jace winding through the onlookers. The unexpected sight rattled her.

He reached her side and took her hand. "I think you're outnumbered, Sheriff. These women have spoken loud and clear. They're demanding change. I've been reading about you in the paper down in Beaumont, and truth of the matter, you really stink to high heaven at your job."

"Who the hell are you?"

"Jace Bonner. I own the Double Diamond ranch outside of Beaumont. Miss Sicily is a longtime acquaintance and I take offense to you picking on her and her friends."

"Go back where you came from," Bledsoe spat. "This ain't none of your affair."

"I beg your pardon, but anyone threatening to throw her and this sweet girl in jail is my business." Jace held Bledsoe's stare without blinking. "I happen to have the governor's phone number and will gladly call him. You see, he's a friend of mine too. He'll send the Texas Rangers if need be."

Bledsoe's beet-red face looked ready to explode. He stepped back and waved his arms. "Everyone go home. The party's over." Then he turned on his heel and marched to his police car.

Sicily released a pent-up breath. "Jace, I certainly didn't expect to see you tonight." She pulled her silent companion closer. "This is my dear friend, Martha Ann."

"A lovely name, Martha Ann. Glad to meet you." He pushed back his hat with a forefinger. "I ran down to bring a plow and a few other things I thought you might need. I can bring them out in the morning if that's suitable."

"How wonderful. Of course, I'm agreeable to taking any-thing you want to offer." She touched his arm and glanced up into the face that she'd loved. The moon's rays illuminated his crooked smile that had once stolen her breath. The silver at his temples only added character and undeniable charm.

"Good. I'm staying at the boardinghouse here in town since Miss Corrine has guests, but I'll be out at your place for break-fast if that's okay."

"I'll have the fatback frying about six-thirty."

"Do you really know the governor?" Martha Ann asked shyly.

Jace laughed. "Know him? Ma'am, I once pulled his skinny rear from a frozen river when we were boys. Kept up with him all my life. Don't agree totally with his politics but he's still a good friend."

"That's nice. Have a good night." Martha Ann moved toward the wagon where Tate sat.

The rest of the crowd began to drift back to their beds.

"That girl's had a hard life." Sicily was proud to stand with her. "She used to live in this house with her sorry wife-beater husband," she explained.

"Oh, I read about the man they found on the train tracks. Was that him?"

"One and the same. He wasn't worth shooting but now the sheriff is trying to pin a murder charge on her and me both. The only thing is, Leroy made a bunch of enemies in this town with his bullying so there's a lot with reason to kill him, if that's what it was. The manner of death is still to be determined."

"How could it be murder without proof? That's reckless of the sheriff."

"Leroy was stinking drunk is my guess. Probably stumbled and fell then passed out."

Jace nodded. "Makes sense. Anytime you need help, I'm only a phone call away."

This from a man who'd stayed away for forty years? How far could she trust him now?

"I appreciate that. Thanks." Her gaze went to the wagon. "I need to go. I still have to get the girl to Corrine's. She's going to stay there to help out."

"That's good. Work helps cure a lot of problems. I need to go too. See you in the morning."

"Jace?"

"Yep."

"Thanks for coming with that plow and other things. We needed it."

"Good." He put a soft kiss on her cheek. "Lady, you're beautiful in the moonlight."

She didn't know what to say to that. Finally, she smiled and patted his arm. "Get you some glasses. I'm old and wrinkled but thank you."

"Mirrors only show what's on the outside. I see in your heart."

What was he trying to do? This was getting awkward.

"Then thank you. Martha Ann and Tate are waiting. I'll set a place for you at breakfast."

They parted and Sicily climbed into the wagon.

"He's nice." Martha Ann snuggled against her side as the wagon rolled forward. "I feel like a child about to open a gift on Christmas morning to find Santa came. Something good is about to happen. I just know it."

"Yes, it is." Sicily patted her hand. "Lots of wonderful, exciting things."

She wanted to ask the girl what she wanted to do with her life but refrained. It was far too soon to even know, and the world was wide open. A person kept in bondage pretty much like Martha Ann needed to simply enjoy freedom for a while. Amazingly, the flames of the fire had freed her to grow and flourish. The way she'd boldly stepped forward as the sheriff was accusing them had shown she'd begun to sprout her wings. Deep satisfaction took root in Sicily.

They arrived at Corrine's and Martha Ann jumped down as the door opened, framed by the silhouette of the benevolent woman. Halfway to her, Martha Ann looked back. "Goodnight, Mama Sicily and Tate. I'll be by in a few days."

Tate waited until the girl reached Corrine and was enveloped in the woman's welcoming arms. She was home.

"We can go now." Sicily patted the young man's hand resting on the seat. "She's safe."

"Yes, ma'am." He shook the reins, and they moved forward. "We did good, didn't we?"

"We sure did."

"Now, can we help George? He needs us. Needs somebody to care about him."

Sicily took in the deep worry in Tate's voice. "Absolutely and the sooner the better. This town is taking shape, and we have support." Her breath fogging in the slight breeze, she glanced up at the millions of twinkling stars. Some days she felt a hundred and then at other times like now, she was as energized as a schoolgirl. "Soon. Let me think on that a bit."

He swiveled on the seat to face her, his gaze filled with hope and love for her too. "I'm ready for whatever you think we should do but we need to hurry. George said Peevy threatened to take a whip to him."

"Yes, then we don't have time to waste." In a lot of ways, Peevy was a whole different animal than Leroy. And a hundred times more dangerous.

They rode along in companionable silence in the darkness, the moon guiding their way. Tate hadn't mentioned going back to live in the woods in a while and she took that as a sign that he was hers for keeps now.

At last Tate spoke again. "I was surprised to see Mr. Bonner tonight but glad he showed up or you could be in jail. The sheriff is trying his darndest to put you there."

"Yes, that was good timing. Surprised me. Nice of him to bring a plow."

"I'll say. It's gonna help a lot."

"Especially since most folks have had to move to town and probably got rid of farm implements and such."

Did Jace have another motive for coming? When she'd looked into his eyes tonight, they seemed very twinkly. She thought she made her feelings clear last time. Well, she'd find out at breakfast she guessed. No use worrying about it now.

They arrived home and Gypsy was giving them what-for at the door for leaving her behind.

"You go on in. I'll take care of the mule," Tate said, pulling the brake.

"Thanks, son. I do appreciate it. The cold has stirred up my poor joints something awful but some chamomile tea will fix that. I have a bit of cocoa I've been hoarding," she added. "There's enough for one cup of chocolate."

His silence puzzled her as he helped her down. Finally, he looked at her. "Don't you want to save that for something special?"

"I have and it's now." She patted his chest and went on inside as he drove to the barn.

At the door, Gypsy almost knocked Sicily down. She picked the little dog up and gave her a big hug before letting her outside then put the hot water on, getting down cups. Soon, she enjoyed her tea in front of the fire with Tate, Gypsy snoozing at their feet. On impulse, Sicily had added a cookie left from their baking session to his plate.

He smiled from ear to ear. "I haven't had hot chocolate since my mama passed."

"Then just enjoy. It's a rare treat and my tin is empty so you won't get it again for a while." Damn this Depression that took and took and took, not giving a blessed thing back.

"Wish we could grow cocoa," Tate said over his cup.

"That would be nice indeed. While we're at it, I'd like a money tree too."

Wishful thinking was the talk of their fireside chat. Impossible dreams and wishes filled their heads before they came back to reality and found their beds.

Sure as his word, Jace arrived the next morning. Sicily had dressed in older clothes since she meant to work outside most of the day. Thoughts of what to plant and where filled her head as she let Jace in.

"A nice morning." She took his jacket. "Just the right nip in the air. You know, it's going to be Thanksgiving and Christmas soon and I haven't a clue what to give Tate."

Jace smiled, removing his hat and hanging it on a hook by the door. "When I was a boy, I wanted something like a fishing pole or a knife."

"Thanks, those are good suggestions. I'll also have to see what I can find to give Martha Ann. Any little something will mean the world to her. Come on in the kitchen. I have coffee made. Hope you like it cut with chicory. Desperate times call for desperate measures." She chuckled. "I'm growing to like the taste of chicory which is fortunate."

"I drink mine that way too. It's not bad." He followed her and sat at the table in her cozy kitchen. She set a cup of coffee in front of him as Tate and Gypsy came through the back door.

"Some of our hens are stingy." Tate set the egg basket on the worn sideboard. "Didn't get much today." He cast Jace a look and nodded.

Sicily glanced at them. "Enough for today but none extra. Actually, hens slow down or stop when there's not enough sunlight. We'll make do with whatever we can get."

Jace lifted his chicory coffee. "Your optimism is one thing I remember about you. No matter how sad or disappointed you were, tomorrow was always going to be brighter."

"No use in being all sad-mouthed. Doesn't help anything." She handed Gypsy a bite of her precious sausage. The times called for sparing usage and the sausage had been payment for some of her remedy. But today seemed the right time to cook some of it.

Jace sipped from his cup, gazing around the room. "You have an interesting place here. It feels like home to me for some reason."

"I'm happy with my life." She mixed up the biscuit dough, noticing the strange way Tate eyed Jace. The boy hadn't been rude, but he did have some resentment that Jace had invaded their world. Mixed in with that she noticed fear that the boy tried to hide as he played with Gypsy.

Tate poured himself some coffee and sat down. "Miss Sicily is about the smartest person I've ever met. She knows lots of stuff."

"I'm sure," Jace agreed. "I see questions in your eyes, Sicily, and Tate's as well."

She took her hands out of the dough and turned. "You can't blame us for wondering why you're here other than to bring the plow which we truly thank you for. Why are you really here?"

Jace cradled his warm cup, a flicker of a smile at the corner of his mouth. "You always were quick to pick up on things." He leaned down to pet Gypsy before he looked up. "I wanted to see you again for one thing." He held up a hand. "As a friend. We've decided to go our separate ways and I know that's best so don't worry on that count. I've been in town several days talking to folks about the situation and I do have something to talk to you about."

Scowling, Tate loudly cleared his throat. "I'm watching after Miss Sicily. We're a team and I won't let anything happen to her."

Clearly upset, he pushed back his chair and went out the door.

"I've touched on a nerve I see." Jace sighed. "I don't know your secret, but everyone has such fierce loyalty to you."

"It happens when you care about people and invite them into your life. Your mother never taught you about that because she never did either." All that woman knew was to spread poison.

"You're right but more's the pity. I really see that now." He got up and went to look out the window. "That's a fine boy out there."

Wistfulness in Jace's voice touched her. She turned to him and started to touch his shoulder but let her hand drop. She took the skillet off the fire. "The finest."

"I wanted kids, really wanted to be a father, and I know not having any was a bitter disappointment to you also." He faced her. "I want to make it clear that if anything happens to you, anything at all, that I'd count it as an honor to take Tate in and give him a home."

Sicily was silent and still. This man had such a big heart. She searched his eyes and found true sincerity. If only they could've made a life together. When she found her voice, she said, "I have worried about what would happen to him. I'm not that young and life is fleeting at best. These bodies are fragile. Bless you for taking that worry. It means a lot and I trust you."

He kissed her forehead. "I worried I'd mess that up and you'd misread my intentions. We do have a special bond that neither time nor space can sever, and my mother knew that."

"You're the second one to mention that to me. Mabel told me the same on her deathbed. She confessed that your mother's strongest fear was that bond."

"You know why, don't you? Because she was powerless to stop it."

"I never knew she was scared of me. I didn't think she was scared of the devil himself."

"She tried to bury it and pretend it wasn't there. Only I saw glimpses."

"Jace, I wish we could've had it all," she said softly.

"Me too." It seemed natural to pull her into a hug and that's what he did.

And it seemed right to give him one back.

He released her and cleared his throat, but his voice was still rough. "While you're fixing breakfast, I'll go talk with the boy and clear the air. Tell him we're just friends."

She nodded, watching him go out the door with Gypsy at his heels. Tears filled her eyes as she finished getting the biscuits in a pan and got the sausage back on the flame. Then she stared out the window at the two men. Whatever Jace said to Tate, it had released his anger and worry. He grinned at Jace and the two shook hands. It was endearing that Tate felt he had to protect her, but yet it was a normal response for a son.

They'd formed a family when she wasn't looking.

She'd thought she'd only been helping him, and he'd eventually move on. A smile curved her lips. He was her boy.

The two men came back in as she was putting eggs on a platter. "Just in time," she said.

"Guess what, Miss Sicily!" Tate's grin stretched wide.

"I give up."

"Mr. Bonner wants me to come stay a week at his ranch."

"That sounds like fun." She slid plates in front of them both.

Tate took a big bite of his biscuit. "It'll have to be after we rescue George."

"Who's George?" Jace asked.

They told him about the poor orphan's plight.

"You know," Jace said, thinking. "When you make your move, find a way to get word to me and I'll come get George and take him to my ranch. No one would ever find him there."

That wasn't a bad idea except getting word clear down to Beaumont might be a problem.

"We also have my hideout in the woods." Tate reached for a second piece of sausage then stopped. "Have you gotten your fill, Miss Sicily?"

"Yes, son. Jace?"

"I'm done. That was larrapin' as they say on the ranch." He wiped his mouth with a napkin. "Well, the offer stands and I'll be happy to help however you need."

After they ate, Tate helped unload the plow, seeds, and other things Jace had brought in his new Model A pickup. The beginning awkwardness had cleared.

He stood with the pickup door open. "Sicily, include George in our deal with Tate. I'll take both boys to raise if anything happens to you."

"Noted and much appreciated. Have a safe trip back."

They parted ways with Jace's promise to see her soon.

Sicily and Tate worked the rest of the day making remedies and storing them. Once the garden got going, it would likely take all of her days for a while. However, Tate was learning the necessary healing plants and amounts to put in each elixir. He'd soon make it by himself. He still studied at night from her books even after she'd gone to sleep. When he was interested in something, he jumped in with both feet.

She started to bed, and he looked up from his book.

"I'm glad we don't have to lay awake listening for gunshots anymore and be worried Leroy will kill us," Tate said. "Miss Sicily, do you think it's a sin to be glad?"

"No, honey. I really don't. Martha Ann lived through years of that with him. She has rights too. It's peaceful now with him gone."

"But not for George. He's over there with mean ol' Mr. Peevy. If Peevy kills George, do you think he'll go to jail?"

"Do you think he might do that?"

"Yeah, I do." Tate sighed. "I wish I could hurry and grow up so I could do more."

She put her hand on his shoulder. "Don't wish your life away, son. And yes, Peevy would go to jail if he's caught and prosecuted." That is if Bledsoe wasn't sheriff. Who really knew?

"But George would still be dead." His voice dripped with sadness.

Sicily thought about that long after she'd climbed in bed. Why didn't people know how to act? Some had no common decency. Were they not taught anything? Might as well be back with the cavemen. How much more trouble would she be in if she stole George?

The problem was, if she didn't do something Tate would. She had to protect him.

Chapter Nineteen

THE SUN SHONE BRIGHTLY on Sicily and Tate Monday morning at the vacant lot with the plow. Everyone seemed eager to get started. Folks from all over town started coming with hoes, rakes, shovels, and garden tools in hand.

They milled around discussing the project and talking about planting. Sicily's heart swelled with happy anticipation and pride. They all had a stake in this like she envisioned.

Corrine arrived with Martha Ann and the two Justice brothers. The two women were immediately engulfed in conversation with friends, so the brothers hurried toward Sicily. Their appearance startled her. Both wore clean clothes that she suspected came from Corrine's locked room. They'd gotten a haircut and bathed. And having food and someone giving them a hand up made such a difference in them. The hopeless look in their eyes was gone and they carried themselves taller with more self-confidence.

Sicily smiled a greeting. "Thank you for helping. My mule can pull the plow but he's pretty old and will have to rest at regular intervals."

"We'll make do," the tallest one assured her. "We're used to crochety mules."

"I'm sorry, but can you refresh my memory with your names?" she asked.

"We get that a lot." The tall one grinned. "I'm Quinten." He pointed to his cheek. "I have this scar on my face from an accident so that might help."

Sicily made a mental note of that.

"And I'm Nick," his brother said, also with a grin that rivaled his brother's. "I'm the youngest, and most handsome."

With the large straw hat Nick wore, he'd be easy to spot.

"I can certainly see that." She smiled back. "Appreciate the reintroduction." She turned to Quinten. "What happened to cut your face? It must've been a deep wound to leave such a scar."

"Yes, ma'am. A few years ago, I fell into a threshing machine. I'm lucky to be here."

She gave his arm a pat. "We're lucky to have you. How are your wives?"

Quinten spoke first. "They wanted to come only Etta wasn't feeling up to it."

"That's a shame. Is there anything I can do?" Sicily asked.

"I don't know, ma'am." Nick ran a hand over his eyes. "I'm worried about her but she doesn't tell me a lot to spare my worry."

"Then I'll try to drop by tomorrow."

"Thank you, ma'am."

"My boy Tate is at the wagon unhitching the mule. If you can help him unload the plow, we can get started. Just tell the rest of the folk what you want them to do. Y'all are the farmers. We'll follow your lead."

"Yes, ma'am. Thank you," Quinten replied. The brothers huddled to discuss the plan.

Corrine and Martha Ann arrived out of breath, carrying a large bucket of water between them. Thank goodness it had a lid or most would've spilled out. They set it down when they reached her.

"This is exciting, isn't it?" Corrine asked, scanning the group.

Sicily gazed across the lot at the crowd. "I never thought I could get this off the ground." She turned to Martha Ann, amazed at the change. Her soft green eyes sparkling, the girl had her hair fixed in a cascade of blonde curls with a side part and didn't look anything remotely similar to the terrified woman with the wild, matted hair. A lot of change for just a few days.

"You look downright beautiful, girl." Sicily kissed her cheek and hugged her.

"Miss Corrine showed me how to wear my hair and she has a room full of clothes that's never been worn so I got to pick what I wanted."

"You're like a breathtaking butterfly that's emerged."

Corrine smiled, touching one of Martha Ann's curls. "She is such a delight. I'm having the time of my life. That old house has finally come alive after years of wasting away in silence. Martha Ann does most of the cooking, cleans and helps the other women. And Quinten and Nick have repaired everything they could find. Nothing squeaks, is about to fall through, or is in need of oil or a nail."

"A sign of grateful hearts that you took them in." Sicily never regretted helping people like that.

"I like playing with the children best," Martha Ann said quietly. "They're fun."

"Good. You deserve some fun in your life. How's your arm?"

"I'm careful with it and try not to use it. Sometimes I can't help it."

"Just a little bit more time before you can do whatever you take a notion.

Corrine leaned in, love filling her eyes like a proud mother. "I'm watching to make sure she minds the doctor's orders. "But that broken arm sure doesn't slow her down any. Even one-handed, she works hard. We brought this water for the volunteers and have sandwiches at the house that we'll get later."

"You seem to have thought of everything. The workers will appreciate it." Sicily went to speak to the Justice brothers who were hitching up the plow to a younger mule of Art's. Old Jessie would get a bit of rest today.

Martha Ann's low cry alerted Sicily. She swung to see Sheriff Bledsoe striding toward them.

"What do you think you're doing?" he bellowed, reaching them.

"Planting. What else does it look like?" Sicily asked calmly. "This will be a community garden for everyone's use."

"Did you get the city's permission?"

Corrine scowled, drawing up straight. "This lot doesn't belong to the city so it's none of your business. Mabel owned it and she left this lot to me. I don't need permission to plant on my own land. Why are you trying to tear down the good people are doing? Everyone is starving and what we grow here will feed many mouths. Anything else?"

"This is going to lead to nothing but trouble," he snapped, his eyes cutting to Sicily.

"Well, Sheriff, that's where you and me disagree." She arched an eyebrow and raised her voice a little. "I think people who are well fed are much less likely to steal to get something to eat or turn to crime to support their families, don't you?"

He opened his mouth to speak but closed it, squinting at Martha Ann. "Do I know you?"

"I believe you do, Sheriff. I was married to your rotten cousin."

"Martha Ann?"

"That's me." She swung to Corrine. "I think I left something in the car."

Bledsoe's mouth hung open as she moved away. Finally, he found his tongue. "I don't want to have to come back when there's trouble here. And there will be."

"Well, if someone causes mischief in the pumpkin patch, you're the first one we'll call." Several people working nearby laughed then went right on with their job. Sicily leaned toward the troublesome man. "You know, Sheriff, you don't look so good. Maybe you've caught something. Better go lie down."

The lawman spun around and returned to his car.

Corrine giggled. "I'd like to buy that man for what he's actually worth and sell him for what he thinks he is. He's determined to get you, Sicily."

"I'm not hiding. Let's get to work."

About noon, Albert came hobbling down the street on his long walking stick and stopped. "You're finally doing it."

Sicily wanted to smack his arm. "Told you I would. Where's your garlic necklace?"

"Had to take the blasted thing off." He rubbed his neck. "Got where I couldn't stand it."

"I'm glad you got some sense at last. Are the ghosts gone?"

"I ain't seen 'em in a few days." He cackled. "Maybe my good looks scared 'em off."

Sicily shook her head. There was nothing she could say. "Grab a shovel and you can still contribute."

"'Fraid I'd have to be carted off with a heart attack." He motioned to the sheriff's car. "I see he's watching."

"Good. Maybe he'll learn something. He's been sitting there all morning. Bet he's about to pee his pants by now."

"Nah, probably has a jug he's going in. He told me once he kept one in the car."

"That explains it. I've got too much to do to give him any thought. Maybe you'd best hobble back home while you still can."

He leaned on his stick with a pitiful expression on his face. "I don't reckon you brought any of that remedy?"

"Not today, Albert. I'll send Tate by tomorrow with some. How's that?"

"It's fine I guess." He straightened. "I wish I could talk to ghosts. I'd send them over to scare Bledsoe."

Sicily laughed. "Now, that I'd like to see. Go home, Albert, and stop your wishful thinking."

"Guess I might as well." With a wave, he left for home.

By the end of the day, the men had plowed every inch of the lot and the women went behind them planting seeds. The sheriff had parked his car nearby and watched everything but Sicily paid him no mind and went on about her business.

They were about to leave when little George hurried by to speak to Tate. The two talked for only a bit before George went on.

Sicily hurried to thank the Justice brothers for their work. "You men really didn't mess around. That part is all done. Thank you."

Quinten wiped sweat from his forehead with a shirt sleeve. "Yes, ma'am. It felt good working with the soil again. There's rich dirt here."

"I've never had much trouble growing anything."

Nick brought the plow over and put it in the wagon. "It's a sight for sore eyes to see folks working together. Everyone seems excited to be a part of this."

Sicily nodded. "I thought they would grasp any bit of hope in this god-awful Depression gripping the country. Helping each other is the only sure way to get through it."

"Do you think we will, ma'am? Sometimes I fear this will stay for good," Quinten said.

"Don't lose hope." She rested a hand on his broad back. "One day this might be like a bad dream."

"From your mouth to God's ear." Nick glanced up at the sky. "Are those clouds on the horizon?"

"I sure pray they are. Wouldn't it be something to get rain on this freshly planted field?" Sicily sniffed the air. She couldn't tell yet, but rain seemed favorable.

Clouds steadily began to gather as everyone packed up and left.

Slowly meandering home in the wagon, Sicily brought up the subject of Peevy's orphan kid. "I noticed George came to speak to you, Tate."

"Things are bad, Miss Sicily. He had tears in his eyes. Said he's thinking of hopping the freight train when it comes by. The only problem is Mr. Peevy chains him up at night and locks the barn door too. He asked me for help."

"Tate, climbing aboard a moving train can get him killed! Talk him out of it and we'll find a better way."

He shook the reins and hollered at Jessie to get going again when he stopped. "I think I'll poke around a bit tonight after they go to bed."

"Not without me. It wouldn't hurt to see the lock."

Tate gazed at her with worried eyes. "I don't know if we can get close enough. Mr. Peevy has a big dog with scary teeth, George says, and it roams free at night on their place."

"Then, we'll have to be careful. An easier plan might come to me. Let me think on it."

"It might be better if we catch George in town and hide him then," Tate said low as if he was mostly talking to himself.

"That's what I was about to say." The homeplace came into view and she drank in the sight. Lord, she was tired and Bledsoe watching her every move had stretched her nerves thin. She was looking forward to shutting out the world with all its problems for a while.

Hours later, the rain came that night, putting off their plans to check out Peevy's barn. The sound of water meeting the earth was pure music to her ears and she breathed in the smell. The deluge pounded the roof for a good half hour, giving the town garden a good drenching without washing the seeds away. Sicily lay there snuggled in her bed under the covers, listening to God's bounty, thankful smiles in her heart.

But soon, her mind whirled and she was making plans for the next day, including some pondering of what to do for George. She didn't arrive at a solution before sleep came.

EARLY MORNING FOUND SICILY at Corrine's door with a bag filled with various herbs and things. "I told Nick yesterday that I'd stop by and see Etta," she told the woman. "He mentioned that she wasn't doing well."

The sun's golden rays kissed Corrine's fashionable waves and eyes alight with joy. "Come on in. I'm glad you came. We're all worried about her. She's in the kitchen."

Sicily followed her through the house with its spacious rooms down a hall to a sunny room.

Martha Ann sat on the floor playing with the children. "Good morning, Mama Sicily. We're playing dolls."

"How fun. If I didn't have a million things waiting on me, I'd sit down with you." Sicily turned her attention to the two women at the table. The oldest she remembered was Josie, Quinten's wife and her extremely pale companion had to be Etta. "Morning, ladies."

"Remember Sicily, the lady who was with me at the river?" Corrine asked.

"Of course." Josie smiled and motioned to a chair. "Have a seat and help us shell peas. The men traded a bit of work for these from a farmer down the road."

Sicily took a seat. "Etta, Nick told me you're not doing too well. Are you in pain or something ailing you?"

Though she was shocked at Etta's thin frame and sunken eyes, she kept silent. Enough people were probably telling her to eat and drink fluids. Corrine was for sure.

Etta pushed back strands of silky brown hair and smiled. "Nick is such a dear but he's prone to exaggeration. He didn't need to bother you."

"He didn't. I stopped on my way to town is all." Praying the Lord would forgive her for lying, she reached into her bag for a jar of chamomile leaves then one of rose hips she'd cut off her bushes at the end of their growing season. "These make nice, refreshing teas that are very relaxing. I think you might enjoy them."

"We used to have a lot of rose hips," Etta said. "Until the dirt piled up covering the bushes. It'll be wonderful to have some again, won't it, Josie?"

"Oh my goodness, yes. I've missed that. It'll be like home again." A wistful look came into Josie's eyes. "If only we could see it as it once was again. But that's crazy thinking."

"Doesn't hurt anything to yearn for better times." Sicily also pulled out some greens from her garden and handed them to Corrine. "These will add a lot of vitamins and minerals to a diet."

"Yes, they will." Corrine took them to the sink. "The problem is Miss Etta doesn't have much of an appetite."

"I'm just not hungry," Etta said.

Sicily chatted with the women a bit while the women shelled peas, but Etta didn't volunteer any particular complaints. However, Sicily suspected her condition was due to a poor diet and eating whatever they could scrounge up. "Etta, please try to eat more greens and drink lots of fluids. They'll give you strength."

"Yes, ma'am, but I throw up everything I eat."

"Then make a tea from the rose hips and drink it. Another good tea is mint. That'll settle your stomach." Sicily pulled out a jar of honey from a beehive she'd found in the woods. "This is good to sweeten teas and things and there's a lot of nourishment in it."

"I like honey. Thank you, ma'am."

Seeing there was nothing more she could do, she soon left.

At the house, Tate was chomping at the bit to go over to the Peevy place so she went with him only to find it was a wasted trip. They never caught a glimpse of George or the Peevys. Then they returned the following night and stayed out of sight in the tree line, but the huge dog kept them from getting closer. They didn't dare alert the sour-faced couple in the house. Nothing would stop Peevy from shooting at them.

"What do you suppose the man has done to George?" Tate whispered.

"There's no telling but it is strange that we haven't seen him."

"I'm worried."

She was too, but she didn't put her fears into words. Unable to get any closer, they returned home.

Two days after that, a knock came on the door, sending Gypsy into a conniption fit. Sicily opened it to find Nick Justice twisting a floppy hat.

"Good morning. Come in." She motioned for him to enter.

"This isn't a social call, ma'am. It's my wife Etta. She's in pain." He lowered his voice. "And there was blood on the sheets this morning." He leaned to pick the dog up, rubbing her ears.

"How much blood?" Sicily asked.

"Just a few spots."

"The sight of blood gets us in a tizzy but sometimes it isn't anything to get alarmed about right off. I'll go see what I can do for her pain." She smiled. "Then we'll know if it's a problem we need to worry about.

"Bless you, ma'am."

Sicily glanced out to see a Model T in front. "Let me get my things."

She quickly explained the situation to Tate and gathered some jars of various medicines.

He lifted his bag from a nail and put it over his head. "I'm going to the woods, so I'll see you later."

"Be careful," she warned him.

"I will."

On the drive to Corrine's Nick asked her about the remedies she made. "How long have you been doing this?"

"My father was a healer, so I've done it most of my life. I took a job as a schoolteacher in Beaumont for five years then came back and have been here ever since."

"You're a remarkable woman," Nick said, turning into Corrine's, killing the engine. "You remind me of my dear mother who's gone to Glory."

"I consider that a compliment, Mr. Justice." He opened her car door, and she got out.

"I'm glad you could come," Corrine said, stepping out on the porch. "I've done all I know how."

"I'll see what I can do." Sicily followed Corrine up the stairs to a bedroom wondering how much more these vagabonds could take. And how much more would be stripped from them like bark from a willow tree.

This Depression was stealing people's humanity. When would it end? And at what price?

Chapter Twenty

Etta's sister-in-law, Josie, was sitting on the end of the bed and rose when Sicily entered. She was older than Etta by probably five years and although thin as well had a more healthy glow. "Help has arrived, dear. Miss Sicily will know what to do."

Sicily contained a gasp at the sight of Etta's deathly pale face. Her deep blue eyes stood out against the gray of her skin. Something was dreadfully wrong. She couldn't be more than eighteen, if that.

Now it was even more clear this young woman was in serious trouble.

Corrine moved quietly about the room, putting up laundry in the drawers.

"The doctor?" Etta asked weakly. She had to be out of her head.

Sicily lifted the girl's limp hand and managed a warm smile. "They call me the healer, but I guess I'm the only doctor in these parts. Like I was telling you yesterday when I called, I mostly make potions, elixirs, and the like. The woods are full of healing plants and other things. Tell me where you're hurting."

"Across my stomach and back too."

"Does it come and go?"

"Yes. That's why I didn't pay any mind at first but then I had blood this morning and Nick said he was going after you." Etta paused and wiped her eyes. "It's too early for my baby. I have another month. Maybe more if I figured wrong."

Josie murmured that she had to check on the kids downstairs and left.

Corrine stood by the head of the bed. "I'll stay in case you need anything."

"Thanks, Corrine." Sicily directed her attention to Etta. "Nick is such a nice young man and I'm sure a good husband. He's beside himself with worry and I can see how much he loves you."

Etta tried to smile but it was more a grimace. "He can't wait to hold his child."

"Then we're going to have to see that he gets the chance. Do you mind if I check you?"

"I don't mind, ma'am."

Everything in the room was silent while Sicily examined her then drew the covers back up. She put her ear to the woman's stomach, listening through a silver cone-shaped device. Soon, she raised. "The good news is, you're not in labor and your baby is not in trouble. The heartbeat is strong." She put the silver cone into her bag. "Sometimes there is a little bleeding late in the pregnancy for reasons we have yet to know. I want you to stay in bed and drink more fluids. You're very dehydrated."

Corrine seemed to struggle to put on a brave face and patted Etta's shoulder. "I'll see that she drinks more. Poor nutrition might be to blame, don't you think?"

"Most definitely. She needs lots of greens because they're loaded with vitamins and minerals. I have more in my garden that I'll send over."

"Good news, isn't it, Etta?" Corrine asked, adjusting a quilt on top.

Sicily nodded and caught Etta's gaze. "But stay in bed and on your left side as much as possible. If not, you might jeopardize both your lives. Drink lots of water and that will help. Dehydration will bring on an early delivery before the baby is ready. There is lots of growing the last month and it'll give the baby more of a chance."

"Yes, ma'am. I do want my baby strong and healthy."

"And you, too. That's sound advice, Etta." Corrine grabbed a pillow. "Let's get you on your left side now."

Etta rolled into position and Corrine put the pillow against the girl's back. "What about helping with the cooking and house? I need to do my part," Etta protested.

"No, ma'am," Corrine said firmly. "We'll take care of that."

Sicily lifted a little bottle from her bag. "This is lavender oil. I'm going to massage it onto your back, feet, and legs. Then I'll leave it here so someone can keep doing that."

"I love lavender, ma'am," Etta said. "Thank you for coming. I'm not as scared now. You have a way of calming me."

"That's my goal. I care about you and your baby, Etta. Remember that."

The door opened and Nick entered. "Is it okay for me to come in?"

"You're right on time," Corrine said with a smile and told him everything Sicily had said.

Nick ran a hand through his brown hair. "We'll just have to do what we can to see this through." He kissed Etta and sat down next to the bed, rubbing her back. Sicily handed him the lavender oil and he proceeded to massage it on his wife's arms and legs.

Sicily motioned for Corrine to move toward the door where they stepped out into the hall and had a private conversation. "It's going to be a miracle if Etta keeps this baby. She's in very poor health."

Concern deepened the lines on the woman's face. "I'll do everything you recommend but getting her to eat is hard. She says she's not hungry and I can't force her. Maybe after your frankness she'll improve."

"I hope so. I don't think she can go through childbirth in her condition. She's just too weak."

Corrine nodded. "Let's just pray this baby holds off until we can make Etta better."

"Send Nick for me any time of the day or night." Sicily put her bag that was much lighter now on her shoulder. "I need to be going. Tate is going through something and will need me."

"He's such a nice young man and I love the way he cares for you."

Sicily's gaze met her friend's. "Corrine, I have a favor to ask."

"I'll be happy to help." Corrine laid a warm hand on her arm. "You're almost like a sister to me. I never had one, you know."

"Nor I," she answered. "I feel the same about you. I couldn't love a sister more than I do you."

"Now what is it?"

"That young orphan at Peevy's place. I believe he's eight or nine. Tate and I are going to attempt a rescue, but I don't know where exactly to hide him."

"Bring him to me," Corrine answered without batting an eye. "I've seen the way Peevy treats him, and the sheriff ought to do something. But that will never happen. Just bring him here. We'll give him a bath, put clean clothes on him, and cut his hair. George can pretend to be one of Quinten's kids."

Sicily kept her laughter low. "Hide George in plain sight. Yes, that's perfect. Bledsoe and Peevy will never even see him."

"When will this rescue happen?"

"I can't say. We have to find the right opportunity but if not today, very soon."

"I stand at the ready so bring him when you get him."

The two women hugged, and Sicily put on her cap and gloves. She went out not bothering Nick. He needed to stay with his wife. She walked the mile home, enjoying the fresh air that still bore the scent of yesterday's rain.

Tate was in front of the house with Gypsy girl when she arrived. The little dog ran for her with excited yips, her tail wagging forty to nothing. Sicily scooped her up and gave the dog hugs. The animal's short fur had collected the damp, earthy smell of the woods that Sicily loved.

"The sheriff was here looking for you," Tate said with a frown.

"What did he want?"

The boy pushed back his knit cap and put a hand on his hip. "It seems George is missing and Peevy insists you had something to do with it. I told him Peevy was all wet, but he didn't believe me."

"That's his problem. Will they blame me for every kid that goes missing?"

Tate snorted. "Probably." A moment passed then he asked, "Where do you suppose George went? I told him to come here if he managed to get away but there's no one in the barn or the plant shed."

Oh Lord, the train! If the kid managed to get on, they'd never see him again. And if he failed to make the jump—he was a lot better off than his present situation. And that was sad but true.

She put an arm around the boy's waist. "Tate honey, maybe he'll show up. He might be waiting for darkness to make his presence known."

"Maybe. We'll be ready if that's the case."

Tate's voice shook a little. "I just worry about him, you know? I know how it feels to be all alone and scared and George is a lot younger than I was."

Sicily hugged Gypsy tighter. What could she say to that? The boy was too smart to offer meaningless words. "Let's hitch up ol' Jessie and ride into town to look at our garden after the rain. Maybe George will find us there. I think we'd best leave Gypsy home this time."

An hour later, Sicily gathered some jars of remedies and they went into Silsbee, passing Corrine's big house, the first of many perched at the edge of town as though looking for a chance to make a run for a more favorable community. As they passed what used to be Leroy's house, folks were there digging in the ash for anything they could sell for a bushel of apples or corn. It hurt Sicily's heart to see that kind of desperation. They had to get this garden growing and fast.

They stopped at Albert's and Sicily took the remedy to his porch where he sat watching the folks walk past. He was probably keeping an eye out for a pretty girl he could propose to.

"How you doing, Albert?" She handed him the jar of remedy.

"A lot better now that I got this."

"Well, I told you yesterday I would bring it by, so I wanted to keep my word. There's not much else of value in this world right now other than a man's word."

"Ain't that the God's honest truth?"

"Anything happening in town?"

"Peevy's orphan done ran away and he and the sheriff are look-ing high and low for you." Albert unscrewed the lid on the jar and reached for a spoon next to his chair. Wiping the utensil on his shirt, he took a spoonful of the remedy and smacked his lips. "That's good. Where did you put the boy?"

"George? I don't have him, Albert. I know nothing about his whereabouts. Why does everyone assume I do?"

"'Cause you usually do. Wonder where the boy disappeared to if he didn't come to you."

"Maybe someone else in town is hiding him."

Albert scoffed. "Ain't nobody here with your kind of guts. But I reckon getting a backbone might be rubbing off. I think Dan at the farm supply is one." Albert waved to Tate sitting in the wagon. "Why didn't the boy get out?"

"We only stopped for a minute. We're on our way to check the garden plot."

"Well, you might as well stay for a chat," he grumbled.

"Another time. Besides, I can't be gone from home long. Nick Justice's wife is in a bad way, and I fear she might lose her baby. Poor thing."

"Nick Justice? Who in tarnation is that?"

"He and his brother were traveling and stopped to rest at the creek. Corrine persuaded them to bring their wives and kids and stay at her house for a while. They were exhausted. Nick and Quinten plowed the lot for us yesterday."

"Oh yeah. I didn't exactly catch their names."

Sicily rose and patted his knee. "I need to run. Take care, Albert, and keep your ear to the ground."

He laughed. "Like an Indian. Go hide, Miz Sicily, where the sheriff can't find you."

"I'm not about to do that. It's not how I live my life."

"Well, if he arrests you, I'll bring you a saw in a cake."

"You do that, Albert." Sicily waved and got back in the wagon with the sound of Albert's cackling following behind.

They went on to the garden lot. The rain had left the ground very soft but everything looked in good shape and made her heart sing.

"Grow, little vegetables," she said low. She walked off to look at the corner and Tate stood next to the wagon.

A flash of something came from the corner of her eye. Tate was lifting a tarp in the back. George. There he was and Tate was tucking the boy under a tarp.

She hurried back. They needed to get out of town as fast as possible.

Sheriff Bledsoe took the corner at a high rate of speed and came to a screeching halt beside the wagon. He jumped out with his gun drawn and Sicily's heart plummeted to her stomach. He must've spotted George. She wanted to scream with the injustice of it all.

Chapter Twenty-One

THE SIGHT OF THE deadly weapon pointed at her set Sicily's heart hammering. Bledsoe must've spotted George.

"Sheriff, do you think the gun is called for?" Sicily asked, fighting to stay calm. She could outwit this man. Even a ten-year-old stood a chance. She gave him a wide smile and chuckled. "I'm not a dangerous criminal. Put that away before you hurt yourself."

Bledsoe blinked as though trying to process her words. "Peevy claims you stole his orphan boy George. I came by your place, but your boy said you were gone."

Just stay calm, she told herself. If he'd seen George, he would've marched to the back of the wagon.

"Well, here I am. Just a moment and we'll sort this out." She swung to wide-eyed Tate tapping his foot nervously. "Go ahead and take the delivery on over to Corrine's place. She's waiting for it. That girl staying there is awful sick. I'll meet you there once I'm done here."

"Sure thing, Miss Sicily." Tate nodded at Bledsoe. "Sheriff."

"Tate." Bledsoe seemed to suddenly remember the pointed gun and stuck it back in his holster.

"Now, Sheriff, what's this about Peevy?" she asked as the wagon passed and turned at the corner.

"The orphan boy he and the missus took in out of the goodness of their hearts is missing and he claims you have him."

"That's preposterous. Where would he get such a crazy notion?"

"Because that's what you do when you think people are mistreating someone. You take 'em and—"

Sicily stepped closer. "And what, Sheriff? Give them a better life? Clean them up and make them feel human again instead of like some rabid animal?" She took another step that brought her within a foot, proving he didn't intimidate her. "What exactly is it that you're accusing me of?"

"Meddling. You're a meddler, Miss Sicily, and you stick your nose into things that ain't none of your business."

She drew herself up straight and took a deep breath. "Martha Ann would likely be dead in the ground right now if I'd turned a blind eye and you know it. I did not take Peevy's orphan. There, does that satisfy you? I don't know where he is. Maybe he hopped a freight train with the hobos and is long gone." She shrugged. "Or maybe Peevy killed him and fed the boy to his hogs. Have you ever thought about that?"

"Watch it, Miss Sicily." Bledsoe shook a warning finger. "We have laws against making false accusations."

"I think we're done here—unless you want to search me. I could be hiding that boy underneath my skirt."

He stared at her clothes as if trying to see any bulges where there shouldn't be. He gave her a frown and hooked his thumbs in his belt. "I guess that's all for now but if I find you're hiding that boy, I'll lock you up and throw away the key. I'm fed up with you women of this town doing whatever blasted thing you want."

Preacher Stover came walking by and stopped. "Sheriff, I hope you're not harassing Miss Sicily on such a beautiful day."

"My business with her is concluded," Bledsoe snapped. "And mind your own ball of wax."

"Yes, sir. I was just looking at this garden that the good Lord blessed with rain. Miss Sicily, you knew exactly the best time to plant. Didn't she, Sheriff?"

"If you say so."

"This garden is just like the passage in the Bible where Jesus multiplied the five loaves of bread and two fish and fed five thousand people. Miss Sicily is going to feed all the poor and hungry in this town if you'll let her be. 'Course, I wouldn't want to be you if you persist in making her life hard."

Bledsoe scowled. "That sounds like a warning, Preacher."

"No, sir. Simply an observation."

"I don't have time for this double-talk." Bledsoe spun around and got in his car, spinning out on the muddy street.

Stover laughed. "That man needs to learn how to control his temper. Did you get the best of him again, Miss Sicily?"

"Seems so. It doesn't take much."

But at least George got away and that was most important.

"Can I assume it's over the orphan boy at Peevy's disappearing?"

"They're accusing me of taking him. They think I'm hiding him."

"I ain't asking but if you did, I say God bless you. That boy was mistreated in the worst way."

"Tate talked to him from time to time and the boy said he was going to try to hop the train when it came through. If so, he must've made it on safely."

Stover's eyes darkened. "That's dangerous business for a little eight-year-old."

"I agree. Preacher, it's always good to see you but I have something I need to do. A young girl in the family way that is staying with Corrine is in very poor shape and might lose her baby."

"Then I won't keep you. Good day, Miss Sicily." He tipped his hat to her and walked on.

She hurried in the opposite direction that would take her to Corrine's. The soft breeze ruffled the tendril of hair at her temple and made her glad to be alive. She tilted her face to the sky and gave thanks for keeping George from being detected. He was safe for now at least.

Thoughts of Mable ran through her head. The woman's death had paved the way for helping so many folks. That big empty house had come alive, the rooms filled with a multitude of voices both young and old. Corrine was doing important work.

Indeed, the entire town was changing with more people doing good deeds. She couldn't take the credit. No, the catalyst was Martha Ann. That started it all. Now, Silsbee had returned from the dead and was thriving again. Folks were much nicer to each other. It would only keep growing from here.

Change was in the wind and hope in each person's voice. They just had to be shown that if they all banded together, they could make real change.

Children playing outside greeted Sicily when she arrived at Corrine's. Quinten's boy and girl scampered after each other, playing tag. They were clean and fed and happy. The clothes had to be from the locked room Corrine had found. Both had their hair combed.

Tate must've seen her and came out of the house. "Everything's good with George. He wolfed down some food like he hadn't eaten in a long while and is taking a bath. Miss Corrine brought him different clothes to put on to hide his bruises then she's gonna cut his hair. I don't think Peevy or anyone else will recognize him."

"His life depends on it. Thanks for understanding what I said. You did real good." She put an arm around his waist.

"The sheriff coming up and pointing his gun scared me," Tate admitted. "I thought he might arrest you. Or shoot you. I don't know how you could act like it was an everyday thing to have a gun pointed at you."

"Remaining calm is the only way out of a situation like that. Had I panicked, he might've pulled the trigger. And I believe I might've made him feel a bit foolish pulling his gun on an old woman." She snorted. "Like I was some kind of desperado. Good Lord!"

They dodged the playing kids.

Tate laughed. "You do remind me of an outlaw. Maybe Pretty Boy Floyd or John Dillinger."

"Bledsoe's nothing but a blowhard. Let's go in to see George so we can go home. Hopefully, before Bledsoe sees us and realizes we made a fool of him again."

"Yeah, you sure did." Tate chuckled. "You were ordering him around and he didn't know how to stop you."

Martha Ann opened the door before they knocked and immediately hugged her. "How happy I am to see you. Come in."

"I think you grow more radiant each day, child. Tate and I want to see little George for a moment if that's okay." The fragrance of wood polish assailed Sicily and she glanced around at the beautiful light cypress wood floors and staircase that made the house so special. Mabel's husband had hauled it in from Louisiana and Mabel had kept it polished to a high sheen. Folks preferred cypress due to it repelling insects.

"Miss Corrine is cutting his hair." Martha Ann wound her arm through Sicily's. "We're trying to decide on a new name for the boy to go with his new looks."

"Of course, we have to change it." Sicily went with Martha Ann through the house to the back screened-in porch. "I've always been partial to Randolph but that wouldn't do for a little boy."

They stepped through to the porch. Corrine looked up. "We could shorten it to Randy."

"How about Grant?" Martha Ann asked. "No one on earth would associate Grant with George."

"No, they wouldn't," Sicily agreed.

"I kinda like that. Well either one would be good." The generous woman trimmed the sides of the boy's hair. "How is he looking?"

Sicily wouldn't have recognized the child. Tears filled her eyes. Gone were the ragged clothes and hungry eyes. "You've worked wonders, Corrine. But I knew you would."

Josie came out. "I just love my adopted boy. I heard you talking about names. Why don't we let George decide?"

"That's a good idea." Corrine snipped some more. "But let's wait until I put these finishing touches on."

While she did that, Sicily turned to Josie. "How is Etta doing?"

"Not much better, I'm afraid, Miss Sicily." Josie released a sigh. "Nick hasn't left her side. He's fearing this won't end well even though he's trying to stay positive. It's hard."

"Yes, it is." Sicily noticed Quinten raking out the flower beds, working alone. The slope of his shoulders revealed his sadness. "When you had your farm in Oklahoma, did you each have your own land or share some?" Sicily asked.

"We lived together." A far-off look came into Josie's eyes. "It was family land the boys inherited from their father. Losing that farm broke their spirits."

"I'm sure. It broke a lot of folks." The door softly closed as Martha Ann went back into the house. Sicily sat down in a chair. "Do you need anything from me, Corrine?"

"No, ma'am. I can take it from here until Etta's time comes. I've never been present during a childbirth and know absolutely nothing." She was silent a moment as she worked, then she removed the sheet from around George and dusted the hair off him. "Well, what do you think?"

The boy stood, feeling his neck.

Josie handed him a mirror she'd brought from the house. "What do you think, George?"

He began to sob. "My mama would like it. I miss her. She always told me I was handsome like my pa."

"That's because you are," Sicily said softly. "You're not going to be locked up anymore or forced to do a man's job. You can play like the child you are."

Corrine wiped a tear. "All that is true."

"But what if Mr. Peevy comes and takes me away?"

"I won't let him. I won't let anyone take you," Corrine said firmly.

"Or me," Josie added. "You're safe now."

"I think I'd like to be Grant now, ma'am." George struggled to hold back tears, trying to be a man. "Grant Justice like your name, Miss Josie," he whispered hoarsely.

"That settles it then." Corrine picked up the sheet and swept up the hair. "I like it. If the sheriff comes asking questions, remember you're Grant Justice."

"Yes, ma'am." He wiped his nose on his sleeve and sniffled. "A long time ago I used to belong to Russell Becket. He was my pa, I guess. But one day he took a gun to his head." Tears trickled down his cheeks. "Then they took me away to the orphanage. Told me I wasn't a Becket anymore."

"Oh, you poor child." The sting of tears lurked behind Sicily's eyes, and she put her arm around him. His life had been bad for most of his short life.

Josie wiped her eyes and knelt in front of the eight-year-old. "That's gonna change now. You'll be with us and very loved." She rose. "But get one thing clear—we do not own you. No one owns another. We'll feed, clothe, and love you. Quinten and me want to give you the best life we can."

Sicily read the truth in the young mother's eyes. George was going to be wanted and loved, the things he needed most. And it seemed Josie had gotten taller as well. It was true what they said about having a purpose. Fulfilling a need tended to lift folks up and make them better people. And that turned into a wave that rippled out to everyone around them.

Who knew what the boy's future held, but Sicily had a feeling he was going to do important work.

Maybe this community garden would give folks hope and replace the haunted, hungry look in their eyes.

How she wished Etta had some of Josie's strength. The sun disappeared behind a cloud and Sicily shivered, pulling her coat tighter. Foreboding raced through her that her wool coat and gloves could not block. Some battles were just too big for certain women. She'd seen the look of defeat in Etta's eyes that said she was weary to the bone of living. Unless a miracle happened, this was not going to end well, and Etta already knew it too.

Please, God, let the baby be stronger than its mother.

Chapter Twenty-Two

Sicily and Tate rose early the next morning in mid-December and bundled up for a walk in the winter woods with Gypsy. Their breath fogged in the humid air that occasionally carried bits of tiny sleet. The weather had turned decidedly colder, and the land seemed a little more alive than usual. A gust of wind kicked up a fuss as a shower of golden leaves fell around them, some of the last still left on the tree. The dog went crazy chasing and trying to bite them.

"That dog has more pep than twenty." Sicily laughed at the sweet pup as she ran after Tate. Gypsy did love that boy and Sicily did too.

She stopped for a moment and filled her lungs with the earthy fragrance of pine and the damp muskiness of the leaves and roots. Today, she didn't come especially to gather. She needed this to soothe the worries twisting and turning inside her.

This brought back memories of her people's cabin in the Appalachian Mountains. By now, they'd be buried under several feet of snow. But here in the Piney Woods of East Texas, they didn't get much snow. Although, sometimes they got a dumping of the white stuff that turned the woods into a winter wonderland.

This was one of those mornings when her world seemed about perfect. They found a cluster of mushrooms and willow bark down by a little creek.

Tate gleefully pounced on them and put them in his sack then glanced over at her. "Miss Sicily, I wish this day would never end and it would go on forever. We saved George and Martha Ann. Who are we going to save next? I guess there's nobody left."

"Count your blessings, boy. This is only a lull before the next wave crashes down. There are always people needing help. Like Etta Justice. Don't forget we still have to make the garden grow and feed the townsfolk."

"But there's nothing else to do there 'cept water, hoe the weeds, and make sure the plants don't freeze. I have to get those willow branches ready to drape the sheets and tarps over. The growing is up to God. Miss Sicily, do you think God sees what we're doing?"

"Absolutely. He sees all things. I'm a firm believer in His power."

"Me too. I think God will be very happy with what we're trying to do with the garden."

"I expect so."

"My mama used to read the Bible by the light of the fire, especially when my pa got sick. She'd cry and pray a lot."

"I can understand that. Do you know the story of Christmas and how Jesus was born in a manger?"

Tate nodded. "It's one of my favorites. Christmas will be here soon. Do you put up a tree?"

"I used to, then it got to be too much for an old woman. Maybe you can pick us out a pretty one this year. We'll string popcorn and I have some tinsel I saved from way back. When I was a schoolteacher, my students had such fun making decorations."

A wistful look came in Tate's eyes. "I wish you'd been my teacher. The ones in the orphanage yelled a lot and hit us with a ruler. I don't think they liked kids."

Sicily could only imagine, and her heart went out to him and others like him. "Don't dwell on it, son. Just think about happier times when you were living in the woods."

"And learning from your books. That makes me happy."

They walked back to the house in silence as Sicily pondered these bits about his life. His upbringing in the orphanage instilled in him a deep sense of justice and righting wrongs. In a few more years, he was going to make a fine man and a caring husband for some lucky woman.

When the house came into full view, Gypsy ran barking her head off. When she and Tate arrived, she saw the reason. Sheriff Bledsoe was waiting next to his car. The little dog's hackles rose which said she meant business and would bite him if he didn't leave. The man must've known that the way he backed up against the car with the door open in case he needed to jump inside. Sicily almost laughed but the anger on his face stopped her.

"Sheriff, what are you doing here? I haven't broken any laws."

He removed the handcuffs from his belt. "I'm here to arrest you. Peevy says you stole George and I'm inclined to believe him. I'm taking you in."

"This is ridiculous. If you think we're lying, just take a look around."

Tate moved in front of her and took a protective stance. "We don't have George. How many times do we gotta say it? Leave us alone."

"Do you think I'm stupid? There's a million places for you to hide someone, especially one little boy." Bledsoe moved closer, the handcuffs dangling from his hand.

Gypsy darted in and bit his leg then ran out of reach.

"Ow!" Bledsoe clutched his ankle and snarled, "I'm going to kill that damn dog."

Glaring, Tate hurried to pick Gypsy up. "You'll have to kill me too."

For the boy to talk back to the sheriff meant he was mighty upset. Bledsoe was fast losing the respect of everyone, young and old, in and around Silsbee.

Sicily held up a hand. "Stop. This is getting out of hand. I'll go with you, but you aren't putting those handcuffs on me." She turned to Tate. "Take care of things here. I will be back as soon as we sort this out."

The boy nodded but looked sick as though he was about to throw up.

"I'll be fine. You'll see," she assured him. Then she went on to the car and climbed in.

The drive into town was silent for the most part. Her thoughts were on Etta. If Sicily failed to keep her freedom, it could spell disaster for the poor girl. Corrine would do her best, but she already admitted she knew nothing about birthing a baby.

She spared Bledsoe a glance. "This is utterly ridiculous, and you know it."

"I do know two things. You have something to do with everything that goes on here including Leroy's death and you helped that orphan boy escape. I haven't figured it all out yet, but I will." Bledsoe braked for a dog that ran out onto the road. "Stupid dog," he muttered darkly.

She didn't say anything else the rest of the way. At the jail, she silently got out of the car and marched inside. The one-room jail had been built of rock with cells on the right side and a desk on the left. A potbelly stove stood between them at the back, and the smell of burning wood gave the place a homey feeling—except it wasn't home. Not even close.

Her mouth set in a tight line, Sicily perched stiffly on a chair in front of Bledsoe's desk. "You have no proof I did what you're accusing me of, and you know this is illegal."

Bledsoe pointed his finger at her. "All I care about is regaining control of this town. You've stolen that and got folks laughing at me. I'm gonna show you who's boss here. I know you had something to do with Leroy getting on the train tracks and furthermore, I know you took Peevy's orphan. Get up and empty your pockets. You're going in a cell."

Sicily swallowed hard and glanced at the iron cages lined up in a row on the right. Keep calm, she told herself. He's bluffing. "You're locking me up?"

"Yep." He lifted a ring of keys on his desk.

Panic rose. She had too many things to do and Etta to look after. She just couldn't. "What's the charge and where's the proof?" The words came out louder than she intended but she had to make it clear to Bledsoe he was making a mistake. He couldn't just lock her up because he didn't like her. "I have responsibilities."

"So do I. Now empty your pockets and don't take all day." He bit his words out like they were something that tasted bad. Anger had turned his face scarlet. She hoped he wasn't having an apoplexy.

After she turned her pockets inside out to show she had nothing, he took her arm and led her to a cell. The key made a sharp, metallic clang then the heavy iron grated on the floor. "Make yourself comfortable."

"I demand to see the judge."

"All in good time." He yanked on his hat, coat, and gloves and went out.

The silence usually didn't bother her, but this kind wormed into a body's soul like a black oily snake. She sat down and began to hum softly to pierce the gloom.

The only windows were in front by the door and didn't allow much light through the dirt. She tried to decide what time it was. Must be nearing noon, best she could figure. Icy panic choked in her throat and she had to keep pushing it away. Then as she sat there, a big rat scurried across the floor. That wasn't exactly comforting but it was one of God's creatures.

About an hour later, Bledsoe returned dragging Martha Ann by her arm. The girl was sobbing but stopped when she saw Sicily behind bars.

Bledsoe patted her pockets then opened Sicily's cell and shoved Martha Ann inside. "You two can keep each other company."

"For how long? We both have things to do." Sicily wrapped an arm around Martha Ann and glared at their jailer. "I want to speak to the judge."

"In good time," Bledsoe snarled, spit flying from his mouth. "You're both charged with murder and kidnapping. Think about that."

"And the proof?" Sicily demanded. "This is low even for you."

"A matter of opinion. I have people who swore they saw you in both instances. They also swear they saw a group of people carrying something in the murky night right before Leroy was found. You were both there and you, Sicily, were probably the ringleader if I were to guess. You both hated him." He slammed the cell door with force and turned the key in the lock. "Who can swear you were at home that night? No one." He stomped to his desk and sat down.

The futility of the situation sank in. A group of people carrying something he'd said. She couldn't dispute that. Even though she was far away at home, she knew it to be true. And someone had to take the fall.

Sicily led Martha Ann to the cot against the stone wall that reeked of urine, vomit, and who knew what. She yanked the mattress off and threw it on the floor. They sat down on the bare wooden slats. "It'll all come out in the wash. You're innocent, Martha Ann. Remember that."

Martha Ann huddled next to Sicily. "I'm glad I ain't in here by myself," she whispered. "This is scary. I hear things scurrying about."

"That's Bledsoe's plan. Get us scared enough we'll confess. Murder. Kidnapping." She released a derisive snort. "Leroy wasn't murdered. He drank himself into a stupor and fell on the tracks. Everyone knows it. There was no foul play and I'll tell that to the judge if I ever get to talk to him."

"Me too. But I'm glad Leroy is gone. I won't lie about that."

"I know, honey." Sicily patted her hand. "A good many people are glad."

Bledsoe had barely propped his feet on the desk and leaned back when the door opened.

Albert stepped inside with his long walking stick. "I gotta speak to Miz Sicily. An urgent business matter." Without waiting for a reply, he went straight to the cell. "I can't believe this. Who's gonna make my remedy now, Miz Sicily?"

"I have some already made up. Tate can give it to you. But I don't plan to be here long."

"Good. We need you out and I'm speaking for a whole slew of folks." He rubbed the back of his neck. "I'll go make you a cake." He gave her an exaggerated wink and chuckled.

The cake with the saw in it. She remembered. "You do that, Albert."

"That's really nice of you, Albert." Martha Ann stood and went to the bars, reaching through to touch him.

"I'll be back." Albert cleared his throat and spoke loudly. "When word gets around, everyone in town will be marching in here fit to be tied."

"They better not!" Bledsoe yelled.

"Well they will." Albert turned, his face red. "You cain't just lock up an old woman with no call to do it. You're crazy, Bledsoe."

The sheriff waved his arm. "Get out of here, you old coot, or I'll lock you up too."

Giving him a black glare, Albert teetered out on his spindly legs, muttering dire predictions about the ghosts getting Bledsoe.

He no sooner left than the door opened again and Tate came in. Ignoring the sheriff like he wasn't there, the boy came straight to the cell. "Miss Sicily, I think it's time I called Jace. He'll come and straighten this out."

"Let's wait a bit. Bledsoe might let us go after he thinks he scared us enough."

Tate looked down. "I stopped at Miss Corrine's and Miss Etta has worsened. What do you want me to tell her?"

Oh dear, just as she feared. "Tell Corrine to keep the fluids going and try to get Etta to eat. Nick might have better success with that. Have you seen him?"

"Yes, ma'am. He's looking bad. His eyes are all sunk in."

"Nothing we can do about that. Is everything all right at home?"

"It's good." Tate reached in to touch her arm. "I mainly wanted to see if you're okay. I needed to hear your voice."

"I'm fine, Tate. I'll be home soon."

Giving her a nod, he turned and walked toward the door.

"Wait!" Bledsoe's feet hit the floor. "You can't just waltz in here like you own the place, boy. From now on, you ask me proper-like if you can see the prisoners. Got that?"

"Yes, sir. But you got folks plenty riled up."

"Ain't no skin off my nose. I'll run things as I see fit. I'm boss here."

Making Bledsoe mad wasn't going to help the situation. He was set on making a point. Tate shrugged and walked out.

Sicily pulled Martha Ann back to the cot. "We may as well make the best of it. Would you like to hear about my grandmother? She lived near Cumberland Gap in the Appalachian Mountains and she had some cousins that belonged to the blue skin people."

"What? Did they actually have blue skin?"

"Yep, they did. And they were hunted like animals. My grandmother was a healer like me, but she was also a seer. That's a psychic person who knows what's going to happen before it does."

"I'd like to have known her."

"I was just a girl the last time I saw her. I can still see her standing on her porch, waving as my parents and I left. While I was there, she told me that I was going to have a very rewarding life but to watch out for someone with a gun who would be an enemy."

"Do you think she meant Bledsoe?" Martha Ann whispered.

Sicily shrugged. "Who's to really know? Fortunetelling isn't my area. But Granny predicted a lot of things that came true. I just can't live my life knowing, worrying about what's going to come. I'd rather not know. What would be the joy of living if you knew the future?"

Martha Ann laid her head on Sicily's shoulder. "I don't wanna know the bad stuff."

"Exactly. You'd just fret about it before, then double when it actually happened. No thank you."

The piercing whistle of the train sounded as it pulled into the station a few blocks away. A cold shiver went through Sicily as though someone walked over her grave.

An old saying ran through her head. *Do not fear the battle, and do not flee from it; where there is no struggle, there is no virtue.*

Chapter Twenty-Three

TWILIGHT HAD FADED INTO night by the time Bledsoe brought them some food, such as it was—one piece of cornbread and a bowl of beans to share. He said nothing when he left it. Nor did she. He lit the lamps on an uncertain day filled with turmoil.

Bledsoe came to the cell and barked, "Don't go anywhere." Then he laughed like he'd made a joke of some kind.

"Hold on a minute." Sicily hurried to the bars. "You can't leave us without any water or a place to relieve ourselves."

He pointed to a bucket in their cell. "There's your toilet. You'll be fine 'til morning. I'll bring water then."

He closed the door and locked it, leaving them alone. With only one naked bulb hanging from the ceiling, Sicily could barely see. Panic that she'd kept at bay crept in. She took in her dismal surroundings. One rickety washstand stood in the corner with a metal washbowl on it and next to that was the "bucket."

"What are we gonna do, Miss Sicily?" Martha Ann clutched her arm, eyes wide in a pale face.

Sicily forced a smile and put an arm around the girl. "This is no different from when you were hiding in the woods. Now is it? We're going to be fine and tomorrow we'll get out of here." She glanced around, taking stock in their cell. Besides the cot that Noah probably brought over on the ark, it was pretty bare. Bledsoe had left them no blanket to share but they had their coats. It looked like the potbelly stove was still going, at least until it burned up the wood. She sighed. There was nothing much to be done except suffer through it and pray tomorrow would be the end.

"We'll manage. We have to," she said, hugging Martha Ann.

"I'm not sleeping on that sorry excuse for a mattress," the girl stated. "It's got bugs."

"I know. We'll make do with the bare wood." She chuckled. "I hear it's pretty soft when a body's tired enough. We'll pretend it's the softest feather bed we've ever slept on."

Martha Ann straightened tall. "Yes, we will." She yawned, covering her mouth. "Everything will look better in the morning. I'm glad you're here with me."

Sicily sat down on the wooden slats and Martha Ann curled up beside her.

"Tell me more about your granny." The girl rested her head on Sicily's shoulder.

"Well, she smoked a pipe like a lot of mountain women and was married to a very kind man who wore a hat like a riverboat captain. Grandpa liked to tease me. Called me Little Britches. Oh

Lord, how he loved to dance, and I still recall how tenderly he held Granny, waltzing all over the yard. How they would laugh."

The two women spent the night telling stories about their kin and laughing even though they didn't feel much like it. At last, daylight crept through the front window and optimism replaced the worry. Sicily would find a way to get out. She had to.

People gathered outside and tapped on the window. Even though they couldn't see her, Martha Ann waved. "I'm glad they came. Do you think the sheriff will change his mind?"

"I guess we'll have to see." But the crowd of folks heartened Sicily too. Not that long ago, they didn't have the courage to speak. Now, they were standing up to Bledsoe.

As soon as Bledsoe arrived and unlocked the door, they all rushed in along with the frigid air, carrying blankets, pillows, hot biscuits, coffee, and all manner of things.

Albert thrust an oblong cake through the bars that didn't quite cover the tip of a saw. "Hide this."

Sicily took it and looked around for a place to put it. The washstand. She quickly put it in the metal washbowl.

"What in God's name are you all doing?" Bledsoe bellowed. "This ain't a sewing circle."

Dan Williams from the farm supply stepped forward with plates and silverware. "We don't appreciate you arresting Miss Sicily and Martha Ann on such flimsy charges. You don't have a shred of proof. As long as you have them locked up, we're going to bring the comforts of home to them."

Albert shook his fist. "Yeah, and they're hungry too. You don't even got the decency to feed 'em! It's plumb shameful the way you treat good, upstanding citizens yet you let Leroy and his bunch get drunk and terrorize man and beast."

Beast? Sicily chuckled.

Everyone started yelling at once. Bledsoe pointed his gun to the ceiling and fired, releasing a shower of plaster. "Shut up! Everyone out! This ain't the social hour."

Old Gertie brandished her cane at him. "You're being a real horse's patootie!" Then she asked sweetly, her toothless gums showing, "Can you tell us when the social hour is so we can come back?"

"There is no social hour!" he yelled, his face red and spittle flying. "This is a jail! Not a party palace!"

"What kind of place are you running?" Gertie slammed her cane down on the floor before turning for the door.

Sicily couldn't help but laugh then quickly sobered. All of this was pushing Bledsoe over the edge and it was anyone's guess what he'd get in his head to do next. He clung to his authority as though it were a shield and he seemed bound and determined to show these folks who was boss. He was fast losing self-control and that terrified her.

Everyone stomped their feet and began to chant, "Let them go! Let them go! Let them go!"

Bledsoe fired another shot. "Get out! Get out now. The next shot will be in one of you."

Finally, Dan herded everyone out the door after which Bledsoe locked it.

He stalked over to the cell frowning at all the comforts folks had brought. "None of that is allowed in here."

Sicily stared and put grit in her voice. "You put us in here with nothing. Us women have needs. It was freezing in here last night and we didn't have a single thing to keep us warm. You can't have things both ways. If you're going to hold us, then treat us like humans." Martha Ann's arm slipped around her for a moment, bringing a measure of comfort.

Martha Ann suddenly stretched an arm through the bars. "Care for a biscuit? They're still warm and pretty tasty. We'll share."

Bledsoe blinked in surprise and paused, eyeing the biscuit. "Well, I suppose I could take one. I didn't get breakfast this morning." He took it from her. "Thanks."

When he finished that one, Martha Ann handed him another. Then he wiped his mouth. "I guess you can keep what they brought. But nothing more. This is it."

It was interesting how food could change a person's mood.

"Do you think I might speak to the judge today?" Sicily asked. "I have a patient in serious trouble and close to dying."

"Out of the question." He tried to put some bark in his answer but almost choked on biscuit crumbs, so the words lacked volume.

"Do you want a woman's death on your conscience?" Sicily pressed. "And possibly her baby too. It's already a bad situation."

Bledsoe ignored her and whirled around. Without a word, he went out, slamming the door on her request.

"Let's see what else they brought us." Martha Ann sorted through the boxes and poured coffee for them both into chipped cups that advertised horse feed and manure.

Sicily sipped slowly on hers. "This is real nice of everyone."

"You're a hero, Mama Sicily," Martha Ann said softly. "You got rid of Leroy and had the idea for a garden to feed everyone. You care about them and you're always kind." The girl draped a quilt around her and kissed her cheek. "You're my hero too."

For some strange reason, tears threatened. She wasn't one to cry but Martha Ann touched something deep inside. She was no hero. Just a regular person with things to give.

She sniffled and smiled. "That's nice to know. But I haven't done anything heroic."

"Suit yourself." Martha Ann sat on the cold wooden slats with her coffee and a colorful quilt wrapped around her shoulders. "This ain't so bad now."

"It's certainly improved." It still smelled of urine and vomit, soot lined the walls, and large spider webs hung in the corners. Plus, it was colder than a well digger's bottom. But sunshine spilled through the window, and they had the support of the townsfolk, brightening Sicily's outlook.

Bledsoe returned then, stomping inside with a bucket of water and bleach which he slid into their cell. "Make yourselves useful and clean this place up."

"You're a real prince," Martha Ann murmured, shooting him a dark glare.

After they ate the meager offering that tasted heavenly from folks with nothing extra to give, they set about making the cell more homey. Someone in the group had pitched in some curtains so they strung them up across the bars. Next, they scrubbed the floor with the bleach and water. Everything smelled much fresher. They couldn't do anything about the thin sweat-and-urine-soaked mattress so they rolled it up and stuffed it in a corner. By the time they finished, it seemed livable—at least for a short while, until the smell returned.

Sicily wondered how Etta was doing not that it did any good since she couldn't go to the girl's bedside. She feared for both their lives but her ability to help was at a standstill at the moment.

Two hours passed before Bledsoe returned. He'd rounded up about a dozen more women in town. He froze when he entered with the new group. "What in God's name? If I wanted curtains and gewgaws in here, I'd put up the blasted things!"

"Can you blame us for wanting tastes of home?" Sicily asked pointedly. "We're trying to make the best of this."

"Hell!" He removed his hat and threw it on the desk then grabbed the ring of keys. "You ladies will have to share. I brought you some company."

"Are you crazy! I ain't done nothing!" one woman yelled.

"You've lost your mind!" another hollered. "We got rights."

Amid the loud complaining and dire threats, Bledsoe divided them all between the two cells and slammed the doors.

"I have to be home by 2:30," said a prim woman named Freda who owned a dress shop. "I have a customer coming to pick up a wedding dress and another needing alterations."

Abigail clutched the bars in desperation, her face pasty white. "I'm getting a phobia locked up in here. You have to let me out or I'll go mad."

"You'll be fine," Bledsoe snarled. "Sit down and shut up." He began to pace.

Cold and heartless described their jailer. Sicily went to the bars. "Women have to have their tea. When will you bring us some? And what are you gonna do about the ones having their monthlies? Huh? Have you thought about that? And what if the rats bite us?"

The grumbling only got louder, forcing him to put his hands over his ears and keep pacing. The trapped chaos was getting to him. The women were inside hollering and the men outside with their yelling.

Soon a line of men formed from the door to his desk. Art O'Neil was first. "I'm here to confess. I killed Leroy."

Bledsoe pointed to the door. "Out."

But they kept coming. One by one, men from town each confessed to either being the murderer or stealing George.

"We all done it," Albert crowed. "Ever' last one of us. You have to let the women go."

Old Gertie wobbled up and stuck out her wrists, teetering on her spindly legs as her cane clattered to the floor like a gunshot. "Slap the cuffs on, copper. I did it. I killed Leroy."

"Out!" Bledsoe shouted. "Out of my jail!"

"Let these women go!" Dan and Albert both yelled. "They belong at home."

"Don't tell me my job," Bledsoe responded. "I'm the sheriff. Me." He jabbed a finger in his chest. "And I'm the law."

"For now. But that's about to change," Dan barked sharply.

No one had probably ever confronted Bledsoe like this before. The look of authority he wore about him, like some righteous mantle faded. He took a step back.

Sicily had never heard the mild-mannered man raise his voice. She shook her head. This was making things worse. They had to do something before this turned very ugly.

Preacher Stover came in the door letting in more cold air. The jail was never going to warm up at the rate they were going.

Stover was carrying his Bible, and his customary smile was gone. "Miss Sicily, things are in a fine pickle and it's going to take someone higher up in the law ranks to fix it." He glanced at Bledsoe. "That man has dug in his heels worse than a contrary mule and gripping his authority with both hands. Seems the more folks gripe about it, the more determined he gets."

Sicily followed his gaze. "I couldn't agree more. He refuses to let me speak to the judge. Keeps saying all in good time. I know the judge wouldn't stand for this."

"No, ma'am. He sure wouldn't." Stover talked to Martha Ann and a few of the other women before turning back to Sicily. "Is there anything I can get you short of the key to unlock these cells?"

"No, thank you." She waved to the mountain of items piled in a heap. "I think we have about everything."

He put his hand on hers as she gripped the bars. "I'll go now but I'll be back."

Tate came rushing in bypassing all the men crowding Bledsoe and went straight to Sicily's cell. "It's bad. Real bad. Miss Etta is dying, and Miss Corrine doesn't know what to do. There's so much blood and it won't stop. Blood everywhere."

"Take a deep breath, son." Sicily reached through the bars to squeeze his shoulder. "Go make the call to Jace. Tell him to hurry. We need him." There was no time to waste.

But would he be there for her this time unlike years ago? Maybe all those sweet words he said at her breakfast table were nothing but hot air.

Wild-eyed, Tate hurried to the door and was almost knocked down when someone flung it open.

Nick Justice rushed inside and pulled up in front of Bledsoe. "My wife is dying! If you have any compassion, release Miss Sicily at once! We gotta save her."

Chapter Twenty-Four

S HERIFF BLEDSOE SET HIS mouth in a tight line as he glared at Nick. "I won't let Sicily out so forget it."

Tears streamed down Nick's cheeks. He slammed his fist down on the desk then pointed his finger in Bledsoe's face. "Then her blood, and maybe that of my child's will be on your hands!"

"Go to the doctor in Woodville." Bledsoe stuck his face into Nick's and hollered, "Get it through your head, dumbard! Sicily Rossi is not a doctor! And she's staying put."

"She's all I have. If my wife dies, I'll be back, and I won't be alone."

"You can't threaten me!" Bledsoe shouted. "I run this town. And furthermore—"

Before he finished, Nick spun on his heel and raced out the door. A heavy black cloud descended over Sicily. She gripped the bars, willing them to open.

What was Bledsoe trying to prove? That he was boss? And all while a young woman's life and that of her child hung in the balance.

Martha Ann wrung her hands. "What are we gonna do? She needs you."

Sicily sadly shook her head. "There's nothing to do until Bledsoe lets us out."

Jace was only twenty miles away. It shouldn't take him long. An hour at the most. But maybe Tate hadn't been able to get him on the phone.

The clamor of the other ladies yelling and crying was almost more than she could bear. A frightened woman sobbed into a sopping wet handkerchief. "What have I done? I haven't broken any laws. I have children to feed and a husband that loves me. Why am I here?" She glanced up at Sicily with red swollen eyes.

Sicily sat next to her and gave her a comforting shoulder to lean on. "It'll be fine. Do you have anyone watching your children?"

"My boy will fetch my sister down the street. He's smart."

"We'll hopefully be out soon." But was that just wishful thinking? Sicily didn't know at this point. Bledsoe had lost his mind.

All that afternoon, a steady stream of people walked in bearing food and confession. Some swore twice to committing the crimes. Sicily was heartened by their need to help get her and the other women released. Time ticked by and Jace hadn't arrived.

Was he going to fold like he'd done years ago?

Although she tried not to, she couldn't help looking each time the door opened. And each time she was met with disappointment.

What was happening at Corrine's? And with Tate? The boy was more distraught than she'd ever seen him. Time seemed to stand still, and her self-control hung by a thread.

She glanced toward the soiled mattress they'd rolled up in the corner. The women had eaten the cake and hid the saw Albert had brought inside the rolls of that mattress.

As the train came through town at noon, she heard Jace's voice outside. He stepped through the door. "Sheriff, you're done here. Open those cells."

Relief such as she'd never known flooded over Sicily in waves and the women all in the cells went suddenly silent. She could've heard a pin drop.

"Now you listen here, you cain't tell me what—" Bledsoe's mouth hung open as three Texas Rangers appeared behind Jace's tall, commanding figure.

How had she ever thought him weak? With his mother in the ground, he'd finally become his own man.

One took the keys from Bledsoe's desk and opened the cells. "You ladies go on home," he said.

Sicily rushed from her prison. Freedom at last. Now to get to Etta. Maybe someone outside would give her a ride.

Jace broke from the group of men. "Wait, Sicily, I'll take you."

"I have to get to a young woman at Corrine's. She's dying." Before she could say more, Nick entered looking haggard, his red-rimmed eyes large spots in his face. And she knew.

"She's gone, Miss Sicily. My Etta is gone," he sobbed. "It's too late to save her."

A powerful rage raced through her. She pulled from Jace's hold and marched to Bledsoe. Without a word, she delivered a stinging slap to the man's face, amazed at the satisfaction running through her. "You're nothing but a murderer. A good for nothing low down murderer."

"Don't blame me. I didn't touch her," he snarled, her handprint clear on his cheek.

"I'm trying hard not to break your face. You didn't need to touch my Etta." Nick's fists clenched at his sides. "You killed her all the same by keeping Miss Sicily locked up. I hope these rangers arrest you." He thrust his nose to Bledsoe's. "If they don't, I'll kill you."

Bledsoe's gaze shot to the famed law officers. "You can't let him talk to me this way. You heard his threat." He took a breath and moved closer to them. "You know how it is for us lawmen trying to keep the peace. Folks don't appreciate it, especially when things don't go their way. What are you going to do about this hayseed's threat?"

One young ranger shook his head. "I didn't hear anything, did you fellas?" he asked his companions.

"Sounded like a bunch of wind to me." A ranger with a handlebar mustache tore the sheriff's badge from Bledsoe's shirt and another took his pistol. "Outside, Bledsoe. We're taking a ride." Two of them grabbed Bledsoe's arms and strong-armed him toward the door.

"Where are you taking me? I got rights." Bledsoe glanced at Sicily. "Tell them I didn't hurt you."

"Don't you understand?" Steel laced Jace's voice. "You're done here. You're over."

"I'm the sheriff."

"Not anymore." This time it was an older ranger. "You're fired. Here's what's going to happen. You're going to get in our car and we're driving you out of the state. We'll leave you afoot in Louisiana with the alligators."

"But I have personal belongings."

"Nope. You don't get to take anything."

"You can't do this!" Bledsoe yelled, struggling against the rangers' hold.

"We can and we are," answered the young ranger. "You've abused your power and worn out your welcome. Now come on."

Bledsoe turned to Sicily. "You can't let them do this. I didn't hurt you. Tell them."

"Can't help you," she answered coldly. "You had a chance to do the right thing and passed it up."

"I have a wife. I won't leave her." Bledsoe clutched the young ranger's shirt. "You can't do this."

"I'm sure she'll be glad to be rid of you. From all accounts you weren't a model husband."

Sicily watched the ongoing argument. She'd seen Bledsoe's wife and more often than not, the woman had sported a black eye.

"Come on," Jace urged her, a hand on the small of her back. "Let's go. Nick, how did you get here?"

"I drove my brother's car," the distraught husband said, rubbing a hand over his eyes. "You go ahead, and I'll be along."

"Martha Ann? Come on, child." Sicily clutched her arm, and they went out together. "Corrine and Josie will need us."

They climbed in the one-seater car and Jace broke the speed limit. "I tried to get here earlier," he said. "Tate explained the situation, so I knew how dire it was. But I had to round up the rangers that were free to come with me. It wouldn't have done me any good to come alone since I have no authority. I just prayed we'd get here in time." Jace took the corner very fast. "I'm sorry I came too late, Sicily."

She covered his hand with hers. "The important thing is that you did come. Some things are meant to be and there's nothing anyone can do to change that. I saw Etta right before all this and knew she was too weak."

Huddled beside her, Martha Ann sobbed. "Poor Etta. What's Nick gonna do?"

"I don't know." She hadn't heard anything about the baby and didn't know if it lived or died with its mama. She guessed she'd have to find out when they got there.

If the child lived, maybe it would help Nick heal. She'd seen that and there were plenty of hands to help with the little thing's care. But how sad the child would grow up without a mother.

Chapter Twenty-Five

S ICILY TURNED HER FACE to the beautiful sunshine, letting it warm her face. She didn't know if she'd ever get that putrid smell of the jail out of her head. Maybe in time. Jace pulled his auto up to Corrine's and killed the motor.

Tate threw open the door of the house. He came running and threw his arms around Sicily, sobbing. "I can't believe Miss Etta's gone."

"I'm sorry I wasn't here." She patted his back, murmuring soothing words.

He lifted his angry, tear-stained face. "It's all the sheriff's fault. If he hadn't kept you from helping her, she might've lived."

"We don't know that for sure. When it's your time, you'll leave this world."

Finally, Tate pulled away and they went inside. Jace made himself comfortable in the sitting room. Sicily hadn't decided if she wanted to sit. She could see there was work to be done.

Corrine entered with a wrapped bundle. "Want to see something beautiful?" she asked.

"The child lived?" The news brought a smile. After a horrible tragedy, a small life would give them hope.

"Yes, and she's quite a looker." She handed the baby girl to Sicily. "I don't know if I did everything right, but I tried my best. Lord knows I did. Common sense said to keep her warm, so I put the oven on and warmed blankets to line a basket with. It kept her toasty. At least I knew that much."

"You did exactly right." Sicily stared at the infant, taking in the dark hair and tiny features. Her bow-like mouth opened like she was going to speak. "I think she looks a lot like her mama."

Martha Ann crowded in. "Oh, how sweet. What did Nick think of her?"

"That man took one look and left. He hasn't held his daughter or shown a speck of interest," Corrine answered sadly.

Sicily had seen that before. Grief sometimes took such a hold on the husband that he couldn't look at his child. "Give him some time. He has a lot to sort through but in time he'll come around."

Jace rose from his chair. "I think I'll take a stroll outside."

"We'll have some coffee shortly," Corrine said.

Sicily handed the baby to Martha Ann and went to Jace. "I'm glad you're here. I just wish things had turned out better."

"Me too." He squeezed her fingers. "I couldn't bear to think of you locked up."

"I survived." She touched his jaw that had a day's dark growth. "If you see Nick out there, talk to him. He's hurting."

"That's what I plan to do." He kissed her cheek. "You always care more about others than you do for you. I think that's what attracted me all those years ago."

She didn't know what to say so she just nodded. "Try to get Nick to come in for coffee."

"I will."

Her admiring gaze followed his tall form to the door. Part of her still loved him and always would. If not for him, she'd be locked up with no hope in sight. He cared about her that much she knew. They were bound by the past, and a deep friendship cemented that.

Once he'd disappeared outside, she turned to Corrine. "Now, I'm ready to help."

"I can sure use your practicality. We have to prepare Etta for burial. I'm not sure if Josie can help you. She's taking this really hard since the two were like sisters." A sob rose before Corrine stuffed it back down. "It was horrible. There was so much blood and it kept soaking all the towels and everything else I could grab. I feel like I've fought a war and lost."

Silently, Sicily put her arms around the woman, her friend, with a huge heart. They held each other and cried for Etta who would never know her daughter. Finally, they dried their tears and steeled themselves, preparing to tackle the funeral preparations.

Martha Ann rose from her chair with the precious bundle. "I'll help, Mama Sicily."

"Thank you." Sicily glanced around. "Where's Tate? Do you know where he went?"

Corrine nodded. "He's keeping the little kids occupied since Josie is unable right now."

"He's a wonder." She might've known the tenderhearted boy was making himself useful. He'll be good with the children.

For the next several hours, Sicily cleaned Etta's body and put her in a freshly washed dress that Josie brought her. Then she fixed the girl's hair and Jace helped arrange her in a simple wooden coffin that Quinten bought in town. He'd had to wake up the carpenter, but the man hadn't minded.

By the time she finished setting the bedroom to rights and cleaning until there were no traces left of the horrible tragedy, the clock was chiming midnight, and she was exhausted. She learned Nick had never come inside and her heart felt raw and used up. Jace drove her and Tate home for which she was very grateful. Walking that late at night wasn't safe.

He kissed her cheek softly at the door. "You're worn out. Get some sleep."

"Sounds good to me." She forced a smile and brushed his cheek with her fingertips. "You're a good man, Jace Bonner. When will you go back?"

"I'll remain for a few days. The ranch is fine to leave with my foreman during these cold months." He was silent a moment then he added, "I heard Miss Corrine say the funeral was set for day after tomorrow."

"There's no use to drag our feet. Few here even knew Etta." And Sicily had always seen that healing doesn't begin until they put the deceased in the ground. "You're welcome to take breakfast with us tomorrow."

With a nod of thanks, he went back to his car. She parted the curtain and watched him drive away. What would her life be like if she'd chosen to fight his mother for him? She'd never know. The only thing she was sure of was that her life was deeply satisfying and rich. Knowing that, she locked up the house and went to bed.

JACE CAME TO BREAKFAST and talked about Etta's death. "Nick's going to bury her in the Silsbee cemetery under a wide cottonwood tree He's still stuck in grief's hold and refuses to hold the baby. I talked to him at length, and he's convinced that the baby is to blame. If Etta hadn't gotten in the family way, she'd still be alive. I told him that child had nothing to do with Etta's death."

"No, she didn't but I understand him blaming the child. In a loss like this, it's easy to blame the innocent babe." She brought the plates of eggs and fatback to the table and sat down. "Tate, want to bless this food?"

The boy finished dumping eggs into Gypsy's bowl and hurried to the table.

"Yes, ma'am." He offered a short few words over the meal. "Amen."

"It's good to have you where you belong, Sicily." Jace buttered a biscuit and took a bite. "You haven't lost your touch. These are still the lightest biscuits in four counties."

She laughed. "Only four?" she teased.

His eyes twinkled. "Let me rephrase that. How about all of Texas?"

"Yeah, they're really good," Tate said, his mouth full.

They ate in silence then Jace shooed her out of the kitchen. "Go take a walk. Tate and I are gonna take care of the dishes. Besides, this is a chance to talk him into coming to spend some time with me at the ranch."

Tate's face lit up. "Can I, Miss Sicily?"

"If you want to. The choice is yours. I'm done telling you what to do." She glanced down at Gypsy jumping around in excitement at talk of a walk. The dog knew the word walk and many others as well. Such a smart little thing.

And that's how the day got started. Sicily took the dog for a walk in the woods and by the time she returned, Jace had gone back to Corrine's. She and Tate were sitting on a new porch swing Tate had made, soaking up the sunshine that sure felt mighty good on her bones.

Tate picked up Gypsy. "I've decided to go stay with Jace for a few days after Christmas. He has some good horses to ride. We won't be too busy here until spring. What d'ya think?"

"Honey, I told you this morning it's up to you. You've been making decisions on your own for quite a while. I think you'll love being around a man for a change and those horses sound fun." She patted his hand. "And like you pointed out, it's slow here right now."

"Okay." He looked relieved to have told her.

Not wanting to hurt her feelings she guessed although he should've known what her answer would be.

A wagon halted in front of the house and Albert took thirty minutes to climb down. She'd begun to think the poor man was going to break something. She knew by the excitement on his face he had some town news.

Gypsy started barking her head off then wagged her tail at recognition.

Albert petted the excited pup and no more than sat down before he began. "Thought I'd best come and give you the lowdown on things. The rangers appointed a temporary sheriff and guess who it is?"

"Who? You?" she asked. The Texas Rangers sure moved fast.

"Nope. I'm too busy trying to find a wife. This morning, they appointed Dan and he accepted." Albert wiped his mouth. "Just temporary until an election next May."

"He'll be good." She put an arm around Tate sitting beside her.

"Anything is for the better," the boy added. "Mr. Williams is nice."

"And guess what else," Albert prodded about to bust a gut with a tidbit of news.

Sicily stopped the swing. "Don't keep us in suspense, spill it!"

"Well, lots of folks noticed the Peevys boarding the train this morning." Albert leaned forward. "Seems they didn't think they'd get a fair shake from Dan."

Tate was all ears. "Just to visit someplace?" he asked.

"Nope. They moved, lock, stock, and barrel. Loaded up everything. Left their farm to rot."

Curiosity got the best of Sicily. "Where did they move? Tell the whole story, Albert."

"Give me a blasted minute, woman. They moved to California." He leaned back in his chair, satisfied.

Sicily digested that. "Well, well. That surprises me but California folks might not be any more receptive to their kind than we were."

Albert laughed. "They have tar and feathers all over this country."

"That's for sure. They were lucky to have escaped here. I guess they saw the handwriting on the wall," she said. "Good riddance. We don't need their kind."

It was nice when the trash took themselves out.

Little George—Grant Justice now—was safe.

Chapter Twenty-Six

Once Albert left, Sicily spent time over at Corrine's helping get things in order for visitors and the funeral the following day. Tate went along but stayed outside with Quinten and Nick when they arrived.

"My heart's breaking for Nick," Corrine said, keeping her voice low. "He barely eats, and I know he's not sleeping. He wanders through the house with vacant eyes looking like he's ready to join Etta in that coffin. He still hasn't given the baby one glance."

"I hate to say this but it's typical, especially given the way Bledsoe kept me locked up and unable to help. For Nick, watching his wife die and be helpless to do anything will scar him for a long time."

Sicily took some folded laundry upstairs. With three children and five adults, they had to wash twice a week.

She passed the bedroom that was Martha Ann's and the baby's and saw the girl changing the little one's diaper. The babe was so tiny they had to make diapers out of wash cloths. She sure could've used another month in Etta's womb. Sicily knew the frailty of this newborn's life, and no one could take another tragedy.

She said a quiet prayer then stepped into the room. "How's it going?"

Martha Ann glanced up with a smile. "Everything's fine and dandy now that I changed her. I'm about to give her a bottle and put her down. Do you need anything?"

"No, honey." She watched the loving attention the girl gave the child, swallowing a big lump in her throat. Martha Ann had taken on much of the infant's care. She adored this sweet baby. It was a shame she didn't have one of her own. "Holler if you need me."

Sicily went back down and fixed a cup of tea for herself. She was sitting at the kitchen table when Nick entered the back door. "Come have some coffee or just sit with me a minute." Sicily motioned to an empty chair.

He nodded and sat down. "I'm glad you're alone."

"I agree. We need to talk. There's coffee on the stove."

"I think I'll pass on that. My stomach's not in the best shape since Etta…" His words trailed and he couldn't finish.

"I understand." She patted his hand. "I want you to know I feel real bad. I don't know if I could've saved her, but I sure would've tried my best. Please don't blame me."

"I don't." He raised his sorrowful eyes. "The fault is with that rotten sheriff. He had no right to hold you. None at all." He glanced away and spoke low, "I just have all this rage inside, clawing and trying to get out."

"It's perfectly normal and will take some time. But you have a daughter to care for now and she needs you," Sicily said softly.

"I'm sorry but I can't." He stood and paced the length of the kitchen. "It hurts too bad to look at her. She reminds me of all our lost dreams. Everything is lost. Gone. We had plans to get a farm back in Oklahoma again, raise a family, and live a happy life. But those dreams have been torn away and I might as well be dead too."

"Please don't say that. You can't see it now, but you have so much to live for. Your daughter." Sicily ran a finger around the rim of the teacup. "That child needs a name. Do you think you can give her that much? Did Etta have a middle name?"

"I can't do this right now." He raked his hand through his hair, pacing some more. "I know I should, but I have no words, no names in my head. They're all gone. Everything's gone."

"Can you please think about it? We need to record her birth in town."

"I'll try. I can't even think of Etta's mother's name at the moment." He turned on his heel and went outside.

Although the north wind had a bite to it, he didn't have a coat on, but she doubted he even felt the wind. Her heart ached and she wanted to cry for him, but that wouldn't fix anything.

They'd bury Etta tomorrow and Christmas would come two weeks after that. No one felt like celebrating, but Quinten's and

Josie's children were looking forward to it, so they'd force a smile and do what needed doing. They needed a Christmas tree. She'd talk to Jace. Tromping around in the woods was great for healing grief.

She went in search of Jace and found him sitting on the floor of all things, playing I Spy with the three children. She stood in the door watching him for a long moment. He'd never shown this side of himself before, and it truly amazed her. The children's new addition, Grant, also surprised her. He was laughing and playing like he'd always been a part of the Justice family.

Jace glanced up and saw her. "Join us, Sicily?"

She laughed. "Sorry. My knees won't let me do that. If I got down there, I couldn't get up."

"We'll help you, Miss Sicily," said Libby, or so she thought that was Quinten Justice's oldest daughter.

"No thanks. I'll pass." Sicily went in search of Tate and found him still with Quinten and Nick. They weren't doing much talking, just standing there together. She pulled Tate aside. "Corrine says the children need a Christmas tree. Why don't you see if you can get Nick to go with you to the woods? It might soothe some of his grief."

Tate nodded. "I was trying to think of something we could do. I think giving Nick something to do will help. And you know how healing the woods can be."

"Yes, I know. Just see if he'll go with you."

Satisfied she'd done what she could, Sicily went back inside to see what else needed tending to before the funeral tomorrow. They'd need to cook some food for mourners who might stop by. She helped with the food and before she knew it, the men had returned with a tall tree. With the baby sleeping, Martha Ann helped Corrine make a place for the tree in the big parlor.

Tate was mysteriously absent.

"He said he had to see about the dog," Quinten said with a gleam in his eye. "So, he went on home." He glanced around the chaos. "I don't think he's used to all of this."

"I think you're right." Sicily followed his gaze to the tree, her eyes misting. It was beautiful. It had been years since she'd put one up, content to leave them in the woods.

The children danced around, holding hands. "Let's decorate it," Libby said. "Grant and my brother Tye want to help too."

Sicily laughed at Quinten's three. Children loved a tree.

Corrine got everything down from the attic and they set to work. Sicily excused herself and left for home. The walk was pleasant, and she got the surprise of her life when she stepped inside her house.

There in all its glory was a perfectly formed pine tree with red holly perching on each branch. Gypsy appeared from underneath it with silver tinsel hanging from her nose and whined for Sicily to pick her up.

"Oh, Tate." Tears filled her eyes as she lifted Gypsy girl up, touching the soft pine needles. "It's the most beautiful thing I've ever seen."

"You like it?" Tate asked.

"I love it. Thank you." She wiped away a tear, putting an arm around him. "I didn't think I needed one and haven't put one up in years, but this is really special."

"I think so too." He kissed her cheek. "I think it's prettiest without a lot of decorations on it. Just the red berries and tinsel. And I found an old bird nest I put on a branch. See it?"

"Yes, I do. I always love bird nests. You know, you're awfully wise for a fourteen-year-old." She gave him a squeeze and set Gypsy down.

That night, Jace joined them, and they had tea in front of the fire, looking at the Christmas tree. It almost seemed natural to have Jace there, like he was part of their family. A brother she never had.

Jace stretched his long legs out in front of him and she noticed Tate did the same. The boy needed a male influence and Sicily was glad he was going to the ranch for a few days after Christmas.

THE SUN DAWNED BRIGHT the next morning for which Sicily was grateful. Etta's funeral would be sad enough, but clouds and gloom would make it worse.

Preacher Stover delivered a beautiful service that was more a celebration of Etta's life than something overly sad. Martha Ann stayed home with the baby since it was so tiny. Corrine, Tate, and Sicily sat together behind the family.

Stover set the tone. "We're here to honor a beautiful life cut short. Etta Justice, beloved wife of Nick, was deeply loved by all who knew her. Nick said she never spoke ill of anyone. Etta had a pleasant disposition and enjoyed children. As a testament of her love for her husband, she left a sweet baby girl behind."

The service continued with beautiful music then afterward, the mourners filed over to Corrine's for a tasty meal. Once everyone had been fed, Sicily missed Nick and found him upstairs in a rocker holding the baby. She paused in the door and watched him touch the little face of his daughter.

"I guess it's you and me now, baby girl. I'm sorry I turned my back on you, but you see, it was too hard. You look so much like your beautiful mama who's gone to heaven. I didn't think I could bear to look at you." Tears ran down his face and his voice trembled. "I don't know much about being a father, so I hope you have a lot of patience while I figure it out. Just know one thing." He tucked the blanket tighter around the small form. "I love you and I always will."

He glanced up and spied Sicily in the doorway. Wiping his eyes, he motioned her inside. "You wanted a name to record in town."

Sicily went in and sat in a nearby chair. "Yes, we need a name so we can make her birth official."

"Etta and I talked about naming any girls we would have after our mothers. Rose was her mama's name and Cali was mine. I'll name her Cali Rose."

"That's beautiful, Nick. I love Cali Rose Justice." Tears filled her eyes, and she had trouble swallowing. "Your little one is going to have a wonderful life."

"If I have anything to do with it, she will." Nick ran a tender knuckle across the baby's cheek. "I want to apologize for turning my back on Cali Rose, but I was hurting too bad and filled with all this horrible anger."

"It's normal and there's nothing to feel sorry for." She patted his knee. "That will ease over time."

"I imagine it will, ma'am."

A brilliant shaft of sunlight burst through the window and lit up the baby's sweet face. Sicily suspected it was Etta caressing her child and blessing her new name.

She offered a silent prayer of thanks then got to her feet and left the room.

It was the perfect end to the day. She'd always remember Etta but would take comfort in the joy and the one spectacular moment of a mother's undying love.

Martha Ann met her outside in the hall and led her to a private alcove in the back of the house where they sat. "I wanted to talk to you away from the others for a moment, Mama Sicily," she said softly, wiping the tears.

"I take it you heard what Nick said."

"Yes, I did and I'm glad he gave Cali Rose a name." Martha Ann smiled through tears. "I don't know where I'd be or any of us for that matter without your care. I know I'd probably be dead."

"Maybe. But you aren't. I guess we'll never know, child." Sicily tenderly tucked a strand of hair behind Martha Ann's ear. "What's going to happen to you? What do you want to do with your life now?"

"I might get married, only this time I'm going to make sure he treats me right." The girl bit her lip. "The preacher has come calling and says he wants to marry me."

"That's wonderful."

"I don't know though." Her voice dropped to a whisper. "I'm attracted to Nick."

"Has he indicated a leaning toward marriage again?"

"No, and it's way too soon. For him and me both. We have to heal. I just know that I don't want any man who beats his wife and I'm gonna make it clear right off to anyone who asks me that I'll never take that again. Not for one second."

"Good for you. No woman deserves to be hit and knocked around."

"I won't put up with that, Mama Sicily." Martha Ann smoothed Sicily's palm. "I want babies and a house. Flowers and a garden. I want all the things that have been denied me."

"Those are excellent to work toward," she agreed.

"I'm finding my wings, but I don't know how to fly yet. Sometimes my heart seizes up in my chest with fear and I'm afraid I'll fall."

"Give it time and you'll soon be soaring. You have a good head on your shoulders and friends who'll stand beside you no matter what."

"I know." Martha Ann was silent a moment. "I remember how it felt when I held a baby bird in my hand and it opened its hungry beak. That's the way I feel right now."

"You don't have to figure it out all at once," Sicily reminded her.

"I'm glad I can take my time." Martha Ann glanced up. "I just wanted you to know that I'm looking at my options and not rushing into anything."

"That's wise. You're an intelligent woman and I'm so proud of you."

Relief washed over Sicily that Martha Ann was taking time to choose her life going forward. She was going to be all right. Like the seasons that passed one into the next, a person needed to savor the growth. Green shoots had to poke through the ground first then reach for the sunlight and rain in order to grow strong roots and stand tall. When storms battered the plant, it wouldn't fall over and die.

Martha Ann and Tate were growing strong roots. A big smile formed. Pride threatened to burst from her chest.

Chapter Twenty-Seven

Two weeks after laying Etta to rest, Sicily and Tate were finishing up the supper dishes and making plans for the following day which would be Christmas. A knock sounded on the door and as usual Gypsy commenced barking like crazy. Sicily dried her hands and opened it to see Sheriff Dan Williams clutching his hat in his hands. "Come in, Dan."

"Miss Sicily, I can't. I came to fetch you. There's a woman in town needing help."

"Can you tell me what's wrong with her? I ask so I can bring the right medicines and potions."

"Just gather a little of whatever is handy," he answered.

"What is it, Miss Sicily?" Tate asked.

"Apparently someone's sick in town. Go get your coat. You can come too." Sicily hurried to the kitchen and filled her burlap bag with plenty of everything then slipped into her coat.

She got into Dan's Model A and Tate jumped into the rumble seat. They set off for town through the growing darkness. Sicily's head was whirling. Maybe someone got burned or fell and knocked themselves out. What could this be about?

Sheriff Dan turned down the paved main street and everything was all lit up. For a town that rolled up its sidewalks at dusk, especially during the Depression, this was very unusual.

"What's going on?" She sat up straighter, twisting her head to see everything.

"A celebration." Dan waved to a group on the sidewalk and parked. He held the door for her, and she got out.

The townsfolk gathered around, all talking at once.

Then Sicily saw a banner stretched across the front of a building. *Merry Christmas! Thank you, Sicily Rossi.*

"What on earth! Why is my name up there? You tricked me."

"You're a hero," Dan said, taking her arm. "You were instrumental in ridding us of bad seeds and not only that, coming up with the idea of a community garden. Don't blame us for wanting to show our appreciation."

"And getting rid of Bledsoe," Albert hollered.

"But I didn't do anything and certainly not by myself. It was all of us working together to make things happen," Sicily protested. "Give this honor to someone else. Not me."

"Hush," Dan said. "If not for your courage and strength, we'd still be mired in trouble."

"I'm serious." She gripped his arm. "I can't accept this."

"Is everyone ready?" Dan asked the crowd loudly.

At a resounding yes, he motioned to someone in the darkness and a big Christmas tree in the square was lit up in twinkling lights. Then a small band began to play Christmas songs, and people paired off in couples, dancing in the street.

Tate grinned at her. "You might as well hush because it's done."

"Did you know about this?" she asked.

"I was sworn to secrecy. I happen to agree with them. You're a hero." He pointed to a new arrival and waved. "There's Jace. I'm glad he stayed longer in town."

Jace hurried to them. "Sicily, I'm finally going to get the dance I've waited most of my life for. Let's show these whippersnappers how to do it."

Tate danced by with a pretty young girl who lived by the train tracks. Both were talking and laughing. And Martha Ann was in the preacher's arms, smiling to beat everything.

Up above, the full, big, beautiful moon shone down on it all.

The night seemed magical. She couldn't have said what song the band played, and it didn't matter. She gazed up at the handsome features of the man she'd once loved and knew she'd always remember this night in the Piney Woods of Texas with all her friends.

"Are you cold?" Jace asked.

"No, not a bit. Would you like to go look at the town garden? I have a hankering to see it by moonlight."

"Then we shall." He put his arm around her, and they took the short walk.

The rows lay perfectly straight in the moon's rays. She suddenly stopped. It looked like... But it couldn't be yet. Sicily stooped to touch a green young shoot protruding from the ground. "Jace, look."

"Your miracle. This vision was yours and it's coming to pass. Soon, these greens will be big enough to eat. You'll feed a lot of hungry mouths." He was silent a moment then said, "Mary, Mary, quite contrary. How does your garden grow?"

"With silver bells and cockle shells, and pretty maids all in a row, kind sir." She laughed. "I hadn't thought of that nursery rhyme in years."

"Me either."

"Now that you've seen your handiwork, are you ready to return to the celebration?" he asked, offering his arm. "I have a hankering to dance some more."

"I know it's too soon after Etta's funeral, but I think we all needed this. The townsfolk had to see that it's true Bledsoe is gone. This should convince them." She chuckled. "Do you think the alligators have gotten our former sheriff yet?"

He feigned a look of shock. "Sicily Rossi! I never knew you had a streak of meanness!"

"Only when it's deserved." She took his arm. "I've been around Albert too long. It's rubbing off."

They slowly returned to the music and laughter.

"There's no way to know but I'd put some money on a bet," he whispered in her ear. "As the young people would say, would you like to cut a rug?"

"That sounds interesting, but I didn't bring any scissors."

"You just made a joke, Sicily. Are you trying to be hip and make me an old fogey?"

"You're really on a roll with the expressions. Did you learn all these from the cows on your ranch?"

"I don't speak cow language, dear friend. It's much too complicated."

Sicily loved how they could tease and joke like they were siblings. The awkwardness was gone, and each knew where they stood.

Martha Ann interrupted them and took Jace off to dance. Sicily stood there in the shadows watching the people she loved who had been with her in the trenches when times were really bad and in the jail when everything looked grim.

They were her tribe, her patients and friends, and she was happy to take care of them and let them care for her in return. It gave her joy to walk this path with them. This Depression made life difficult, but it couldn't last forever and while it lingered on, she'd feed and nourish their bodies as well as their minds.

When her time on earth was done and her work finished, she was confident others would be ready to take up the mantle and carry on.

Tate came over to stand with her, as tall and sturdy as an oak. He softly kissed her cheek. "You've done good here, Miss Sicily. They're gonna be all right."

"You think so?"

"Shoot yeah. Folks talk a lot about going in search of a promised land but it's right here. It's inside all of us. Everyone has the power to make their life a little better and help themselves as well as others. They just have to look."

She stared at him a long moment. "I think you've discovered the secret. And here I thought you were just a handsome face with a love of books."

"I learned it from you. You teach things that aren't found in books."

Sicily hooked her arm through his. "Someday you're going to be doing important work."

They watched as old Gertie hobbled up to Albert and kissed him full on the lips. She and Tate laughed.

"I think Albert finally found someone to marry," she predicted.

Epilogue

Silsbee 1960

TATE ROSSI RETURNED FROM the woods and unloaded his burlap bag, a copy of the one Miss Sicily made for him all those years ago when he was only fourteen. He hung some nice mushroom specimens up to dry and admired the buttonbush plant he'd collected. From it, he'd take the bark and make medicines. Research was a large part of his life. He'd become a detective of sorts.

A gentle breeze drifted through the house he'd built in the Piney Woods ten years ago for his bride. They both decided to renovate and add on to Miss Sicily's cabin and had loved the results of combining the past with the present.

Sounds coming from the kitchen told him Allison was making lunch. As soon as he met her, he knew this blonde-haired knockout was the one for him—beautiful, kind, and very smart. It helped that she wanted the same kind of simple life he did. She'd graduated from Texas A&M University with a veterinary degree and set up her practice in Silsbee. Folks said she was the best around for fixing up animals.

His beautiful Allison entered and strands of silky blonde hair brushed his cheek as she pressed close to look at the results of his walk. "Oh, those are excellent. It's good to see buttonbush. That'll make some of the older folks in town happy."

He kissed her, breathing in her soft fragrance. "I'm glad you didn't come with me, or I'd never have seen these."

Her green eyes twinkled. "Are you saying I distract you?"

Tate tweaked her nose. "You know very well you do. Is lunch ready?"

"It is and we'll need to get a move on, or we'll be in the middle of the meal when the reporter comes. Who did you say this one is with?"

"The Washington Post." He gave her a wide grin and shrugged innocently. "They think I'm smart. Not sure how they got that idea."

"Because you are smart, Mr. Rossi." She nibbled on his neck. "Come on. We have to eat."

"I'll call the kids down from the treehouse." He ran a finger-tip across her soft cheek. He loved this woman who completed his life and gave it meaning.

Their ten-year-old daughter Maddie had vague recollections of Miss Sicily who'd been up in years by the time she was born. But the woman who'd meant so much to Tate never got to see their six-year-old son, Dakota. She would've loved his kids' curious minds.

Tate pushed the memories aside and went to the table. He might have a million things running through his head, but he always made a point of being present for Allison and the kids.

AT THE APPOINTED TIME, their doorbell rang, and Tate greeted Ed Barclay. "Thank you for coming," he said. "I'm curious why you want to speak to me though. Why come all the way from Washington to this little town?"

"Easy. Your work here as a renowned botanist brought me. But also, the important history of this place." Barclay smiled wide. "We have much to discuss. I smell a good story."

The man removed his fedora and Tate hung it on a hall tree. He looked ready to work with his white shirt sleeves rolled up to the elbow. Tate noticed they were about the same age, still sporting a full head of dark hair with a smattering of gray creeping in at the temples. He should know the man. Maybe he'd seen him long ago.

Once the pleasantries were over, Barclay opened a notebook. "I've long been intrigued about Sicily Rossi and her work in Silsbee. She put this town on the map and folks still talk about her kindness and how she had compassion for everyone."

"You'll need three or four of those notebooks to record it all." Tate laughed. "She was quite a woman, and I knew that from the moment I first met her. It was the middle of the Depression and folks were starving. She got the idea of putting in a community garden in town and those who helped care for it reaped the rewards."

"That was really ingenious. It sure helped my parents Robert and Lavinia. Maybe you remember them. They moved away when I was fairly young."

Tate searched his memory, but came up empty. "Sorry, but I don't recollect any Barclays." It did explain why he'd be interested in Miss Sicily.

Barclay scribbled in his notebook then glanced up. "Where did you get the seeds?"

"That's the thing. Everyone contributed and no one went hungry. Enough food was available to feed them all. If you helped, you reaped the rewards."

"Fantastic." He scribbled something else. "You were fourteen I think when you first came."

Tate nodded. "I'd been hiding out in the woods for a year after escaping an orphan train. I didn't want to get caught again so I lived on berries and plants, staying away from town. Occasionally I'd find a rabbit in my trap, and cook that. Then Miss Sicily found me and brought me here." Unexpected emotion welled up and a thickness filled his throat. "We became a family, she and I, and I got a wonderful education. When I married, we kept her house, fixed it up, and built a big new addition." He gave the reporter a flicker of a smile. "These woods still speak to me."

"It's a beautiful home." The reporter leaned forward with an intent stare. "I want to know about the death of the man named Leroy Vaughn. Some say he was murdered. Others claim he got drunk and staggered onto the train tracks and either fell or lay down. I've always wondered what truly happened. My father never knew. Then the story came across my desk again about a month ago and I had to come see what I could dig up." Barclay grinned. "As the older generations would say it put a bee in my bonnet."

Tate rose and stood at the window that looked out to his wife's office. Someone was bringing a horse for Allison to doctor. He thought about Barclay's remark about Leroy and part of him wanted to keep the secret. Let sleeping dogs lie.

"Why do you want to know?" he asked a bit sharply, turning away from the window. "And why would it interest anyone in Washington?"

"It's just something that's haunted me since I learned of it. We were living here at the time and the stories they told about Miss Sicily were astounding. She was a bold woman with a head full of knowledge, my father would say." Barclay leaned back and crossed his legs, giving Tate a friendly appraisal. "Everyone loves a good mystery."

"Understand one thing. You may not remember, but Leroy was a mean drunk. He used to beat his wife, Martha Ann, to a bloody pulp and if ever anyone needed killing it was him. But this could hurt her. She still lives here as do a lot of other folk. And I can't make this any plainer." He pointed his finger. "If you mess with Miss Sicily, the whole town will come after you. I never want anyone to cast any shadow of a doubt over her compassion and love for these people."

"Listen, I respect that. I'm not here to ruffle any feathers or do an exposé. My father said Leroy's cousin, the sheriff, would turn a blind eye. He terrorized this town from all accounts."

"To put it mildly." Tate sat back down. "I'll tell you what happened about that night when the train came through and ran over Leroy. But I don't want this in the papers."

"Deal. You're calling the shots, Rossi." He laid down his stubby pencil.

"Miss Sicily never talked about that episode. However, on her death bed, she wanted to clear the air and state for the record that it was accidental. Leroy was out of control. She didn't have a plan, but when she left for town, she slipped a vial filled with a mushroom concoction in her pocket. She neared the saloon by the railroad tracks and a painted barmaid ran up to her. She warned that Leroy was planning to kill Sicily, me, and Martha Ann before dawn." Tate paused, remembering that night and wishing a thousand times he'd been with her. He shook himself to clear his head.

"Leroy's death was a group effort of six concerned friends who'd had enough," Tate went on. "She handed the vial to the preacher and went home. The potion wasn't enough to kill Leroy, just knock him out. One of them slipped the contents of that vial into Leroy's beer and not much later, he collapsed outside of the bar. The six men carried him to the train tracks and while they tried to figure out what to do with him, they dropped him. Before they could pick him back up, the train rolled down the tracks and ran over poor Leroy." Tate fell silent. "Like I said, this better not wind up in the article."

"Wow, what a story. No, I won't mention it. But thank you for finally giving me the facts. It's bugged me for a while. And Sheriff Bledsoe?"

"About six months following the rangers taking him over to Louisiana and leaving him afoot, Bledsoe's wife received an official letter advising her that someone had shot and killed her husband for stealing a car."

"Justice was served. That probably made Miss Sicily happy."

"Just that she didn't have to worry about him ever coming back for revenge but she took no joy in his death. She wasn't like that. She just quietly picked up with her life and went on." Tate lapsed into silence while Barclay scribbled.

After a minute, Tate asked, "Are your parents still living?"

"Sadly, no. I miss them every day." Barclay shot him a wry smile, glancing at his watch. "But let's move on. What happened to Martha Ann? She had such traumatic experiences."

"She still lives here and brings a lot of joy with her sunny smile. After much contemplation, she married again—to Nick Justice whose wife died in childbirth, leaving a baby girl. Martha Ann finally got a baby like she'd always wanted and a kind husband who cherished her. Cali Rose bloomed under her care plus she and Nick had three more kids together. She went to work for the bank and has become the president's right-hand assistant. Their daughter, Cali Rose, is married now to the preacher's son and very happy."

"Wow, that's a switch from being married to a lowlife like Leroy Vaughn. I'm glad she ended up with a happy life." Barclay licked his stubby pencil and jotted more in his notebook.

"Nick Justice was the exact opposite of Leroy. Martha Ann really came into her own after all that and is a vital part of this community." A noise outside drew Tate's attention to the window where the kids were chasing each other with a water hose. He turned back to Barclay. "Martha Ann and I are making sure Miss Sicily's community garden keeps going. That was a large part of her legacy. Still is."

"That and the remedies she concocted from plants, roots, and bark she collected from the woods. Scientists have taken note and are making some beneficial medicines using nature's remedies." Barclay drew something in his notebook. His voice was quiet. "I'd like to have known her. She was an extraordinarily forward-thinking woman."

"I could talk all day about her and the contributions she made to society as a whole." Tate's mind whirled with memories. "The orphan George was one. She rescued him from a horrible man named Peevy and changed his name to Grant Justice to avoid detection. He's a lawyer now who's made quite a reputation for helping kids, especially orphans."

"I'm glad to hear it. I catch bits of news about him and his work in Austin," Barclay admitted. "My dad said the best thing to happen to this town was electing Dan Williams for sheriff. He and Sicily Rossi made a formidable team from all accounts."

Tate nodded. "They got us through the Depression for sure. Towns all across Texas started these community gardens, copying Miss Sicily's vision of helping folks and that bled over into the Victory Gardens that everyone had during WWII."

"You don't say. That's really something. What happened to Jace Bonner? Miss Sicily's lost love."

"I used to spend a lot of time with Jace at his ranch. He treated me like a grandson and when he died, he willed the ranch to me. I quickly learned I wasn't a cattleman and sold it."

Barclay shut his notebook and got to his feet. "Thank you for doing this. My article for the paper will be heartwarming. But I won't mention anyone's involvement in doing away with Leroy Vaughn. That'll be our secret."

Tate walked him to the door. "You'll send me a copy?"

"I will be happy to do that."

Long after Barclay's car roared to life and faded in the distance, Tate sat, letting the memories flood his head. Miss Sicily started him on the road to manhood and instilled in him a love for learning that never left.

He could still hear her say, "It's better to light one candle than curse the darkness."

"Amen to that," he whispered softly. One candle could lead to a dozen, then a thousand or more, changing the world.

Allison entered and came up behind where he sat on the sofa. She folded her arms around his neck. "A man brought his horse in, and I'd like to discuss the gelding's symptoms if you have the time. It's a most unusual case, and I can use your knowledge of vegetation."

Tate smiled. "I always have time for you, my love. Always."

Two weeks later, he opened a letter from Barclay containing the front page of the Washington Post newspaper. The headline in big bold letters said, *Sicily Rossi, A Brave Pioneer Who Wrote Her Name in History.*

The article was all about her community garden during the Depression that kept so many folks from starving. And there was no mention at all of Leroy Vaughn.

Thank You for reading this.
If you enjoyed the story, I
hope you'll consider
leaving a review.

Acknowledgements

Many people helped in the creation of this story. Dee Burks, thank you for designing this awesome cover and Zooming with me on most Fridays to critique and lend support. You always have the best suggestions about things I hadn't thought of. To Jan Sikes my very talented sister, you have a tremendous sixth sense of what knowing what a story needs and you inspire me to write the very best I know how. You push me to think of new, different stories and implement ideas when I'm unsure of the path. I can always count on you to offer love, advice, and lend a shoulder when I'm down. We all need someone who won't hesitate to leap into the trenches with me and both of you are mine. I just hope I give enough in return because this is a two-way street. As always, I thank Bruce Edwards, Charles Curfman, and so many others who help along the way. You make my stories so much better. And deepest thanks to my brother Irvin and his wife Connie who read everything I write.

Special thanks to Jodi Thomas for giving my stories the extra spark they need.

A Quick Note:

This story may remind you a little of Fried Green Tomatoes that came out many years ago. I loved that story with it's rich characters and unique plot. I've never forgotten the Whistle Stop Cafe with Mrs. Threadgoode, Idgie, Ruth, and the others. Wildwood Healer appeared in my mind with all the force of a bulldozer and wouldn't let me rest until I got it written. Miss Sicily was quite insistent on keeping me writing. Although the subject matter is a bit dark, I have lots of humor to offset that and at times would have to stop writing and just laugh a while. Books should be like a party and I certainly felt I was smack in the middle of one throughout Wildwood Healer. I hope they make you laugh too.

Sometimes I look back and wonder how I managed to write almost fifty books and short stories. It doesn't seem possible. Each one has been special to me and I left a piece of my heart in them. Becoming a New York Times Bestselling author was beyond my wildest dreams and yet it happened. I've won many awards through the years that were validation. Most of my career was spent in the Wild West, hunkering down with cowboys and there was nothing wrong with that. I loved those. I'm proud to be a mother, grandmother, and now a great grandmother. I'm glad to have them to carry on the family name. I have many passions and one is genealogy. I enjoy tracing my roots and seeing where I come from. Another passion is rock collecting. I'm a dyed-in-the-wool rockhound. And of course my books. Each one is an old friend and I can't bear to part with them. I hope you have plenty of passion in your life. I'm off to tell another story. You can find me

on my website, Facebook, Twitter, Amazon, Goodreads, and Instagram. Sincere thanks for reading this book.

www.ingramcontent.com/pod-product-compliance
Lightning Source LLC
Chambersburg PA
CBHW021412010826
48972CB00014B/1774